DEATH AL FRESCO

Previously published Worldwide Mystery titles by
LESLIE KARST

A MEASURE OF MURDER

DEATH AL FRESCO

LESLIE KARST

W🌐RLDWIDE

TORONTO • NEW YORK • LONDON
AMSTERDAM • PARIS • SYDNEY • HAMBURG
STOCKHOLM • ATHENS • TOKYO • MILAN
MADRID • WARSAW • BUDAPEST • AUCKLAND

To Robin, whose patience and support
allowed me to make my deadline.

WORLDWIDE™

ISBN-13: 978-1-335-29986-4

Death al Fresco

First published in 2018 by Crooked Lane Books,
an imprint of The Quick Brown Fox & Company LLC.
This edition published in 2020.

Recycling programs
for this product may
not exist in your area.

PUBLISHER'S NOTE: The recipes contained in this book are intended to be followed exactly as written. The publisher makes no promises, representations or warranties regarding these recipes. It is the user's responsibility to know their own specific health or allergy needs and adapt the use of these recipes accordingly. The publisher is not responsible for any adverse reaction to food prepared in accordance with the recipes contained in this book.

This edition published by arrangement with Harlequin Books S.A.

For questions and comments about the quality of this book, please contact us at CustomerService@Harlequin.com.

Harlequin Enterprises ULC
22 Adelaide St. West, 40th Floor
Toronto, Ontario M5H 4E3, Canada
www.ReaderService.com

Printed in U.S.A.

DEATH AL FRESCO

ONE

ERIC WAS LATE. Not at all surprising, but it irritated me nonetheless. Normally I would have simply shaken off his tardiness and leaned back on my bench to enjoy the colorful scene playing out around me on the wharf: young fishermen with white plastic buckets of bait at their side, elderly Italian men arguing over their game of bocce, Russian tourists in Giants baseball caps leaning over the railing to snap photos of the noisy sea lions lazing below.

But Eric was my go-to sounding board when I had to get something off my chest, and right now I was itching to tell him the news I'd just gotten from my dad. Even more important, I was hungry, and the aroma wafting up from the two takeout boxes beside me on the bench was making my mouth water something fierce.

Checking the time once more—it was already a quarter past twelve—I dropped my phone back into my bag with a shake of my head and returned to watching the pudgy teenager one bench down who'd been trying for the past five minutes to untangle a hopelessly knotted fishing line. He continued to pick at the line with his blunt fingers, mumbling to himself all the while, and then slammed the rod down on the wooden bench. With an oath, the young man pulled a jackknife from the pocket of his canvas shorts, cut the line, and dropped the tangled mess at his feet.

That made two of us who were annoyed.

Perhaps a little prodding was in order. I retrieved my phone, typed a "where ARE u?!" message, and then, as soon as I'd sent the text, spied Eric's black Lexus cruising by. The car disappeared as he passed the So-lari's building, and then another several minutes elapsed with no sign of the guy. I was about to walk over and see what the hell had happened to him when my cell buzzed.

"Here and ready to eat!" I read on the screen and looked up to see Eric's slight form sauntering around the corner. Ignoring my sour expression, he avoided a stray bocce ball that had bounced out of the court and crossed to my bench.

"Hey, Sally." Eric shoved the boxes aside and took a seat. "How's it going?"

"I'd be better if you'd been on time. Now we'll have to inhale our lunch if we don't want to be late for class."

Eric patted me on the knee—the sort of patroniz-ing gesture he knew I hated almost as much as having to rush through a meal—and handed me the top box and one of the paper napkins I'd tucked underneath. "Guess we'd better get to it, then," he said, opening the other container and extracting the enormous crab sandwich within.

Part of me wanted to shove the gooey sandwich in his face, but I resisted the urge. He was, after all, just being Eric. And it was good to have periodic reminders of why we'd broken up several years back—sometimes the charming side of Eric could make me temporarily forget this other bratty side. Much better to have him as a best buddy, whose faults I could simply ignore when I chose. Like right now.

I unfolded the white cardboard box and spread its sides over my lap. "So, to answer your question," I said, "it's not going all that great. My dad dropped a huge bombshell on me this morning. Just when I think I've finally extricated myself from Solari's, he announces he's taken on that big ol' sister-cities dinner next month."

"The one for that Italian mayor who's visiting? I read about it yesterday in the paper."

"Uh-huh." I lifted my sandwich from the box. "It's a very big deal. She's the mayor of Sestri Levante, the town in Liguria where the original Sixty Families came from."

"The Sixty Families?"

"You know, the Italian fishermen who settled in Santa Cruz back in the day? Like my great-granddad Ciro. And it sounds like all sixty families, plus every single one of their friends and relations, are coming to the dinner. Dad says they're expecting well over a hundred people."

I took an angry bite of my sandwich, causing several chunks of crab to squirt out the sides. From previous experience, I knew to lean forward so they'd fall onto the box rather than down the front of my pale blue, button-down shirt.

"Wow." Eric had wisely tucked a napkin into his T-shirt and was using a second to wipe mayonnaise from his mouth. "Where're they all going to sit? No way can Solari's fit that many."

"He has this plan to set up a big tent out here for the event. But that's not the point." I popped one of the fallen crab morsels into my mouth before going on. "The point is, he's guilted *me* into coming back to

Solari's to help out with all the planning and with the dinner itself."

"Sucker," Eric said with a grin, removing his horn-rimmed glasses to clean a speck of mayonnaise off the lens.

"Yep. But it's not like I had much of a choice. Dad started doing this whole guilt thing about how it's our 'heritage,' what an honor it is for Solari's to be chosen to host it, how great it's going to be for business." I stared glumly at the young fisherman, who had now restrung his line and was casting some live bait—an anchovy, by the looks of it—out to sea.

"Well, he's right, you know," Eric said. "The publicity should be enormous. It said in the paper that tons of city officials are going to be there, as well as a bunch of business owners and other big mucky-mucks. Hey, I wonder if the DA's office will be invited. It'd be nice to get my ticket comped—"

"You're still missing the point," I interrupted. "Don't you see? This is Dad's way of sucking me back into Solari's yet again. He just can't seem to let me go. And Javier's going to be livid. Now that he's actually gotten some confidence in my abilities as a line cook, he's depending on me at Gauguin. Especially after that great review we got the other day in the paper, which is sure to bump up business the next two weeks. What's he going to say when he finds out I'm going to be AWOL for a huge chunk of that time?"

Gauguin was the restaurant I'd inherited from my aunt after her grisly murder the previous spring. It had taken months to convince its head chef to start teaching me to work the hot line—something my dad had never allowed me do at Solari's—and only recently had

I finally gained Javier's trust as both owner and cook. Trust that could quickly be lost if he saw me as favoring my dad's restaurant over Gauguin.

"I'm sure you'll be able to work it out. Javier's a reasonable guy." Eric stuffed the last of his sandwich into his mouth and smashed the cardboard box flat. "C'mon," he said, standing up. "You can eat the rest of yours on the way. We wouldn't want to be late for class."

Like you've ever worried about that, I thought as I followed him to his car.

AFTER SWINGING BY my house to pick up Buster, we headed back down to the water, me spending the entire return trip elbowing the dog's hairy muzzle out of the way so I could finish my sandwich in peace. Buster had been my aunt's dog, and I was still getting used to the change in lifestyle that came with adopting a rambunctious pooch. But it was impossible to ignore his pleading brown eyes, so I saved the last bite and passed it to him in the back seat.

"You do realize you'll never get him to stop begging if you always cave like that," Eric said.

"I know, but it means so much to him. Even if it's just a piece of dry bread, I swear he acts like it's filet mignon."

"Uh-huh." Eric found a spot in the parking lot across from Its Beach—a lucky thing on a warm Saturday in late September—and the three of us climbed out of the car. But as soon as Eric popped the trunk, we realized we had a problem. How the heck were we going to transport all our gear down to the beach? Not only did we have easels, paint boxes, pads of paper, and jars of water, but we also had an eager dog straining at the leash to get down to his playmates and romp in the surf.

This afternoon was the second meeting of the painting class we'd enrolled in. Or rather, that I had signed up for and then convinced Eric to take along with me. About a month earlier I'd bought a book about Paul Gauguin, having decided to educate myself about the painter after whom my new restaurant had been named. The more I read the story of the free spirit who'd left France for a life in Tahiti and the more I gazed at the eye-popping canvases he'd created while there, the more I'd become inspired to try my hand at some painting myself.

When I mentioned this to my pal Allison, she'd told me about a friend who needed a few more students to fill out an art course he was teaching. It was a plein air class—outdoor painting—consisting of five Saturday afternoon sessions at various spots along the coast. *Perfect!* I thought. But it would be a lot more fun if I could get someone to take it with me.

Eric was the first one I asked, since I knew he'd dabbled in watercolors in college. And besides, I figured he owed me after having convinced me to join his chorus the previous summer and where *that* had gotten me. When you sign up to sing the Mozart *Requiem*, even though it is a mass for the dead, you don't expect the experience to include investigating the murder of one of the tenors.

I was still surprised, however, by how readily Eric had agreed to take the class with me. Was he reading more into my invitation than I'd intended? It did seem as if he'd been wanting to spend more time with me of late. But I'd shrugged this notion off. We'd been broken up for several years, and he had to realize how much better we worked as best pals than as a romantic couple.

In any case, here we were with a stack of art supplies, an overexcited dog, and only five minutes till the start of class.

"Why don't you take Buster and your easel," Eric said, "and I can carry one load with you over to the stairs. Then you can wait for me there while I go back for the rest of the stuff."

"Very chivalrous," I said as the dog ran circles around me and barked his impatience. "And given the circumstances," I added, grabbing hold of the car to steady myself as I freed Buster's leash from about my legs, "I'll take you up on it, this one time."

Once down on the beach, we headed to the far end, below the lighthouse, where a dozen other art students were already congregated. Its Beach is dog friendly, so as soon as I'd dumped my gear onto the sand, I unhooked Buster's leash. He immediately took off after a Jack Russell terrier with a tennis ball in its tiny mouth, and the two of them commenced a game of chase. *Good.* He'd get some vigorous exercise and then hopefully settle down and sleep after we got home.

It was warm on the sand, so I shrugged out of my outer shirt down to a yellow tank top. For the past several days we'd been experiencing what folks around here call the Diablo winds, blowing in offshore from the coastal range. Most people hate these hot, dry winds, and for good reason, since September is also fire season in Northern California. But I've always found them a welcome change from the dreaded marine layer that can shroud Santa Cruz in fog for most of the summer.

The teacher, Omar, clapped his hands for attention

and we all gathered in a circle. "Okay," he said, "last week we concentrated on site selection and composition as well as the blocking in of the darker masses and shadows. Today we finally get to the fun stuff—applying the colors!" With a shake of his bleached-blond dreadlocks, Omar pumped his fist like a running back who'd just scored a touchdown.

"As I talked about last time," he went on, "it doesn't matter a whole lot what colors you use for your underpainting since it's mostly going to be covered up later on. But I like to use the blue palette for the cool shadows and yellow ochre for the warm areas, especially for landscapes." Omar held up the painting he'd started the previous Saturday as a demo, pointing first to the muddy purple areas blocked out in rough brushstrokes for the cypress trees and sandstone cliffs, then to the golden highlights where the light hit the rock.

Once he'd given a short lecture about mixing and applying our colors, Omar directed us to set up our easels, and we all did our best to find the exact same spot we'd been in the previous week. As we began mixing colors and dabbing them on our paintings, the instructor circulated among us, providing advice and commentary where needed.

After checking on Buster's location—he and a plump brown-and-white corgi were now investigating a pile of kelp that had washed up onto the beach—I clipped my work-in-progress to my easel and opened my box of paints.

Our class was working with gouache, a water-based paint similar to watercolors but more opaque, which makes it way more forgiving to work with, because you can paint over your mistakes. I had chosen the view looking west, toward the natural bridge at the far end of the beach, for my composition. As I was squeezing some green paint onto my palette—an aluminum pie tin with a plastic snap-on top—Omar came up behind me to watch.

"Think before you apply that color," he said in a quiet voice.

"Huh?" I capped the tube and turned to face him. "It's for the green vegetation," I said, pointing to the ice plant draped over the sandstone cliffs.

"Yes, but remember," he said, "gouache remains active even after it dries, so the undercoat will have a tendency to blend with any color you lay on top of it, especially if you use a wet brush. You've blocked in your cliffs with a dark blue, so what do you mix with blue to get green?"

"Uh...yellow," I answered.

"Right. So rather than applying green from the tube here, perhaps you should experiment with some yellows and reds to achieve the deep green you're looking for."

"Good idea. Thanks." I leaned down to extract the yellow ochre from my box, and as I stood back up, I saw that Buster and his friend were now knee-deep in the kelp, digging furiously at the center of the pile.

Oh, no. Any second now, he was going to roll over and go for a full-on scent bath in the stinky mess. "Buster, no! Leave it!" I hollered, knowing damn well that even if he could hear me from halfway across the beach, the dog would feign deafness.

Setting my brush and palette carefully on top of my paint box, I darted over the sand toward the two dogs, continuing to shout. "No! *Leave* it!"

Even once I got to the edge of the kelp, where I *knew*

he could hear me, Buster wouldn't budge. He and the corgi continued to paw at the seaweed, now shoving their muzzles deep into the dense, brown mass.

Cursing the stubborn dog, I stepped gingerly onto the pile. Rubbery bladders popped under my feet and I was immediately swarmed by thousands of tiny flies. "Buster, you are *so* going into a time-out," I said as I grabbed hold of the dog's collar. "What the hell is so interesting down there, anyway? Not that I even want to know."

I yanked his nose out of the kelp and was about to turn away when a glint of silver caught my eye. Was that jewelry? Holding my breath, I bent down to get a better look at the piece of metal reflecting the light of the afternoon sun.

It was a wristwatch. A pretty expensive one, too, by the looks of it. I reached down to take hold of the watch, but it was entangled in the mat of kelp. Pulling harder, I finally succeeded and the watch came free from the seaweed.

And with it, the arm to which it was still attached.

TWO

RELEASING THE WATCH with a yelp, I jumped back, dragging Buster with me. *What if I'm standing on...the rest?*

My cry startled the owner of the corgi, who had arrived at the kelp pile to collar his own dog. "What?" he said, jumping back, his wide eyes a mirror of mine.

"There's a...a..." I pointed at the ghoulish sight poking out from the tangle of seaweed. The forearm was pale and had the rubbery look of a giant doll that had washed up onto the beach. Until you noticed how its wrinkled skin was starting to peel away from the hand to reveal yellow fat deposits below.

"Ohmygod." The man's hand went to his mouth and his eyes got even wider. He stared at the appendage for a moment and then knelt down. I thought he was going to be sick, but instead he began to frantically pull the kelp from around the arm, tossing it aside in great heaps.

"Wait," I said, as the form of a man's body began to appear. "I think it might be best if we didn't touch anything until the—" But then I stopped.

He had uncovered a head with silky white hair and a stubbled gray beard. The left temple bore a large abrasion, the blue-black tinge of its ragged skin a marked contrast to the pale color around it. Only part of the man's face was visible, the rest buried in the wet sand, but I recognized him. It was Gino, an old Italian fisherman from my *nonna*'s generation. One of Solari's regulars.

"Hold on." I reached out to prevent the dog owner

from disturbing the body any further. "I know who he is. We really need to call the cops."

"I already did," said a woman from behind me. I turned toward the voice and saw that a crowd had gathered to gawk at the bloated corpse lying on the beach, most of the plein air painting class included.

Eric came up to my side. "Oh, lord," he said. "Not again."

"What's that supposed to mean?" I turned to face him. "I actually know the guy. He hangs out at Solari's all the time. Or, well…used to."

"Sorry." Eric laid a hand on my shoulder. "It's just that I couldn't help thinking that bodies seem to be following you around of late. Or you, them."

"I could say the same thing about you, too, buster. Buster, *no!*" This last bit was directed at the dog, who had crept forward once more and was sniffing at Gino's arm. I stepped forward to grab his collar and pulled him all the way off the pile of kelp.

At the sound of sirens, the crowd turned to watch two police cruisers pull over along West Cliff Drive above us. The officers climbed out of the cars and made their slow way down the stairs, assessing the scene before they stepped onto the beach.

"It won't matter if I take off, will it?" I asked Eric. "I've had enough of policemen of late. And it's not like I can tell them anything that the rest of you can't."

Eric shook his head. "I think you'd better wait. You're the only one who can ID the body. And you did find it. Him."

"No thanks to you, Buster," I said, reeling in the dog once more. "It's all your fault."

The police officers both knew Eric, since he was a local district attorney. He filled them in on the situation and then introduced me to the two men. After telling them how I'd found the body and what little I knew about Gino—that he came into Solari's most afternoons for a couple of beers and that he'd been a fisherman most of his life—I walked with Eric and Buster back to where we'd left our easels. By now a full-on crime scene had been set up, with officers cordoning off the area of the beach around the pile of kelp.

A few students had stuck around and had gone back to working on their paintings, but most had picked up and left. I guess the sight of a decomposing corpse isn't all that conducive to artistic endeavors.

"I'm gonna take off, too," I told Omar, who nodded his understanding. "See you next Saturday. We're meeting out on the wharf, right?"

"Right," he said. "By the old fishing boat that's on display."

"The *Marcella*. I know it well."

Eric and I packed up our paints, easels, and other supplies and carried them across the sand, letting Buster run free ahead of us. When we got to the base of the stairs, I set down my gear. "Did you notice that big ol' scrape on Gino's temple?" I asked as I leashed the dog.

"Yeah, it was hard to miss."

"I wonder if that's what killed him, or if he drowned."

"Well, the autopsy will show if there's seawater in his lungs. That wouldn't provide a definite answer, but at least it would mean he was still breathing when he fell into the ocean."

Neither possibility presented a pretty scenario.

WE DROVE BACK to my place to drop off Buster and my art supplies and then Eric took me out to the end of the wharf, where I'd left my car. But instead of heading straight home, I pushed open the heavy wooden door to Solari's and made my way across the dining room.

Glancing into the bar area, I thought about Gino. He'd been such a fixture there, hunched over every afternoon in his faded blue fisherman's cap, sipping from a bottle of beer and trading stories with the bartender, Carlo. And now I'd never be able to imagine the old man the same way again. Forevermore I'd picture him as I found him lying on the beach, his body bleached and swollen by the water.

What a horrible way to go.

With a shake of the head, I shifted my focus to the dining room. The restaurant had closed at two, but about a dozen people were still finishing up their lunches, scraping clean plates of tiramisu and cannoli and sipping espresso.

Cathy, the new head waitress, was over in the corner, helping Giulia clear the water and iced tea glasses, bread plates, and unused silverware scattered about the vacated tables. From the looks of the mess, it must have been a busy lunch. Not surprising, given the balmy weather we'd been experiencing the past few days.

"Is my dad still here?" I asked Cathy.

"Yeah, he's in back somewhere," she said, hefting a stack of white plates stained a Bolognese red.

I found him in the kitchen, wiping down the six-burner range. "Hi, hon," he said, looking up from the sauce-spattered surface. "How was class?"

"It ended early. There was a body washed up on the beach."

"You're kidding." Dad stopped his cleaning to stare

at me, as did the line cook, Emilio, who had just come into the kitchen from the walk-in refrigerator.

"Nope, not kidding." I met my dad's gaze and tried to control the shaking that had started to overtake my body. "And I know this is really weird, but believe it or not, I'm the one who found him."

"Oh, *bambina*." Dropping his side towel on the stove, he crossed the floor to hold me in his arms. "This is really too much." He released his embrace and took me by the shoulders. "You okay?"

"Yeah, I guess so," I lied. The shaking had now subsided, but it had been replaced with a vague sense of dread. Eric was right: it *was* creepy how dead people seemed to be following me around.

I leaned back on the counter next to the range, my palms splayed out on its butcher block surface. "That's not all, though," I said. "I recognized the guy. It was Gino, that old fisherman who comes into the Solari's bar every afternoon."

"Gino? How could…?" Dad frowned and thought a moment. "That is so strange."

"You're telling me."

"You know," Dad said, "he hasn't been in for a few days, come to think of it. I guess this explains why."

"When was the last time you saw him?"

"It was dinner several nights back."

"Dinner?" I stood back up. "He never comes in for dinner."

"Yeah, I know. That's why I remember it. He hadn't been in that afternoon, and then he came in during the dinner shift and actually sat in the dining room and ordered a meal. Elena was so surprised that she came back into the kitchen to tell me. And get this." Dad got a conspiratorial gleam in his eye. "He came in with a woman. A *young* woman."

"Really? How young?"

"I only got a quick look at her through the pick-up window, but I'd say maybe in her late twenties or early thirties. A real looker, too."

"What night was this?"

He retrieved his side towel and folded it into a neat square. "I dunno... Monday, maybe?"

And today was Saturday. "Do you know who waited on him?"

"Elena didn't say. Wait." Dad turned toward me with a frown. "Don't tell me you're—"

I held up my hands to stop him. "Don't worry. The last thing I want to do is get involved in this."

I LEFT MY dad to his cleanup and headed back out to the dining room. Other than the four-top next to the picture window, all the customers had now finished lunch and were examining their bills and pulling credit cards from their wallets. The remaining table didn't appear to be in much of a hurry, however, as one of the women was flagging down Giulia for coffee refills as I emerged from the kitchen.

Her accent sounded French—"a leetul mohr cohfee?"— and I could well understand why tourists like them would want to linger a while longer. The panorama from the tables along that side of the restaurant is magnificent: stand-up paddleboarders and fishermen in tiny skiffs floating on the sparkling Monterey Bay, with cypress tree-lined cliffs and stately Victorian homes along West Cliff Drive as their backdrop.

I crossed to the hostess stand, where Cathy was

studying the old-school leather-bound book Solari's still uses for reservations. "Only eight tables tonight," she said as I walked up. "It's gonna be slow."

"No worries. We're bound to get a lot of walk-ins. It's teeming with tourists out there today, many of whom will certainly get a craving for cioppino and lasagna right about dinner time."

"You're probably right. I guess I'm still not quite used to how much foot traffic there is out here on the wharf."

"So," I said as Cathy closed the book, "I wanted to ask you about a customer who was here for dinner earlier this week." Yes, I had just told my dad I had no desire to get involved in Gino's death, but I was curious why he'd so dramatically changed his routine and come in for dinner—with a young woman, no less. "An old Italian guy, with a light blue fisherman's cap. Gino is his name. He hangs out in the bar most afternoons for a couple beers, so you might know him from that. I gather he was with a much younger woman the night he was here for dinner."

"Sure, I remember him. I thought the age difference was interesting," Cathy said with a giggle. "But I just figured, 'Hey power to ya, guy!'"

"Do you remember who waited on them?"

"I did. They sat at table four. Why do you ask about him?"

"Well, he actually…uh…" I cleared my throat and glanced around at the few remaining customers.

"What?" Cathy asked in a whisper, leaning across the podium.

I took a step closer to the waitress. "His body was found washed up on Its Beach today," I said, keeping my voice low enough that only she could hear. I didn't mention that I was the one who'd found him. Better to keep the memory of that pale, rubbery skin as far away as possible. "And according to my dad, he never came back after that night."

"Really?"

"Yeah. So I was wondering if maybe he said anything odd during dinner, or maybe you noticed something unusual about him."

She shook her head. "No, nothing that I can think of. They stayed till almost closing, talking away the whole time." Cathy frowned as she thought a moment. "He was pretty animated, now that I think about it. And I remember they both had the baked halibut, because he went on and on to me and his, uh…companion about this thirty-pound halibut he caught a few years back. He was bragging about how long he had to fight it before he was finally able to reel it in."

I smiled. "Humility was never Gino's strong suit. Especially in front of a member of the opposite sex."

I thanked Cathy and headed out the front door. The obvious answer was that he'd simply been wooed out of his normal routine by the prospect of dinner with a beautiful young woman. *But why*, I wondered as I unlocked the door to my yellow '57 Thunderbird, *would she have wanted to have dinner with an old geezer like Gino?*

Oh, well. I wasn't going to fret about that. Thank goodness it wasn't my problem, because I had enough on my plate right now with that damn sister-cities dinner my dad had suckered me into helping out with. And now I had the unpleasant chore of breaking the bad news to Javier.

THREE

SATURDAYS ARE ALWAYS popping at Gauguin, and tonight was even crazier than usual. We'd had a glowing
write-up in last Wednesday's food section of the local
paper, which had called us "a radiant pearl, standing
out in an ocean of seemingly interchangeable trendy
restaurants that now dominate our culinary culture."
Describing Gauguin's French-Polynesian menu, the re-
viewer had stated, "It is impossible to pick a favorite,
as the offerings—from the Sesame-Ginger Cucumber
Salad, to the Tahitian Sea Bass, to the Seared Pork
Chops with Apricot Brandy Sauce—are uniformly
delectable, with exquisite presentation."

And Javier had been positively unbearable all week
after being dubbed "a rising star in the constellation
of talented chefs who now inhabit the Monterey Bay."
Right now he was holding court at the Wolf range as
he splashed brandy into the pans for three orders of
the aforementioned seared pork chops, telling Brian,
Kris, and me about the time Michael Pollan had come
to Gauguin several years back and about the special
meal he'd prepared for the acclaimed food journalist.

But Javier's excitement was understandable, and I
was caught up in all the fervor as well. Notwithstanding its overblown language, a review like this could
generate serious traffic for Gauguin in the weeks or

even months ahead—and make all the difference to our continued success.

Once the rush was over, Javier relinquished the hot line to Brian and me and headed out to the front of the house to schmooze with the customers. Brian was our new line cook, and he and I had gotten off to a rocky start; suspecting him of murder wasn't the best way to commence an employer-employee relationship. But the cook had graciously forgiven me and now only occasionally ribbed me about believing him capable of pushing someone out a second-story window.

Whisking cubes of butter into a saucepan of beurre blanc, I watched Javier through the pick-up window as he made his way around the dining room, stopping at each table to ask about the meal and smiling at the series of compliments this query generated. At one table in particular—occupied by a woman dining alone—I noticed that the chef lingered an extra amount of time, leaning over to say something and then laughing at her response.

"Who's the woman?" I asked when he pushed through the swinging door back into the kitchen.

"What woman?" Javier asked, avoiding my eye.

"The gal at table seven. The one you were having that intimate moment with just now."

He started up the stairs to the office. "Oh, her. She's just a customer who's been in a few times before." Was he blushing?

A few minutes later I followed him upstairs. There were only five tickets left, which Brian and Kris could handle fine without me. Javier was at the oak desk, studying something on his laptop screen.

"Sorry about that," I said as I sat down in the pale

green wing chair across from him. "I didn't mean to embarrass you down there."

He responded with a dismissive wave of the hand and swiveled the computer to face me. "What do you think of replacing the salamander with this?" he asked, tapping the screen. Our wall-mounted broiler was on the fritz, and we'd decided that rather than repairing the ten-year-old unit, we'd go ahead and buy a brand-new model.

"How soon can they get it to us?" I asked. Having to use the regular oven to brown our gratins and make the toast points for our *pâté en croûte* was a real pain. Since it was directly under the range top, whoever was on *garde manger* would end up obstructing the line cooks every time he or she opened and closed the oven to check on the appetizers. "If it's in stock and they can FedEx it, and if you like the model and the price, I say go for it."

"I'll check." Javier turned the laptop back toward him and typed for a moment. "Yeah," he said, "they do have it, and it can be here the day after tomorrow."

"Good." I sat back to wait as he entered the order, studying the Gauguin print on the wall. It was of two Tahitian women, one holding a slice of watermelon, the other a spray of pink blossoms. Now that I'd read the painter's biography and learned more about his fixation on young women—girls, really—the print made me slightly uncomfortable. But the craftsmanship and beauty of the piece was undeniable.

Getting up from my chair, I went to stand before the print and examined the brushstrokes up close. So simple, yet they conveyed so much feeling. And the bold use of color—vibrant yellow, red, blue, and green—you could definitely see the influence in Gauguin's work of his friend and sometime painting partner van Gogh. *If only I could learn to paint like that...*

Javier closed the laptop. "Done," he said.

I returned to the wing chair. "There's something I wanted to talk to you about. It's about Solari's."

"Uh-huh?"

"So my dad's agreed to host this big dinner next month in honor of the mayor of Sestri Levante, the town in Italy that's the sister city of Santa Cruz."

"Sister city?" he asked.

"Yeah, it's this thing towns do to promote peace, love, and understanding, and all that between countries. The cities send people back and forth to learn about each other's communities and cultures with the idea that it helps improve diplomatic relations around the world."

"Seems like maybe it would be good to do that with places in the same country, too. You know, have Santa Cruz become a sister city with a town in, I dunno... Alabama, so they could learn about each other's different cultures."

I laughed. "Not a bad idea, that. Anyway, so Sestri Levante, one of our sister cities—actually, it's Sestri Levante and Riva Trigoso combined—is the area where most of the original Italians who settled in Santa Cruz came from. What they call the original Sixty Families, the Genovese fishermen and..." I trailed off as I remembered the Italian fisherman I'd seen washed up on the beach that afternoon. Swallowing, I fought back the acrid taste rising in my throat.

"What?" Javier asked.

"I... I found one of those fishermen—well, more

like a son or grandson of one of them—dead on the beach today."

"*Dios mio.*" He leaned back in his chair with a quick intake of breath, as if trying to get as far away from me as possible. Or so I imagined, anyway. "You knew him?"

I nodded. "Not well, but he was a Solari's regular."

"I'm so sorry." Javier continued to eye me for…what? Signs of sprouting black wings, like an angel of death? I knew the Michoacán native wasn't all that religious, but he could be superstitious at times. And given my frequent association with dead bodies of late, it would certainly make sense for this to be one such instance.

"It's okay," I said. "I'm trying not to think about it too much, actually. So let's get back to that dinner my dad's hosting in a few weeks. The thing is, he's roped me into helping with the planning and preparation, 'cause it's going to be a real big shindig."

"Huh?"

"Sorry. A big bash, celebration." Javier had been in the States for years now and spoke fluent English, but there was a lot of slang he didn't have down yet. "Which means I might be gone from Gauguin more than I'd like, especially during the week right before the dinner."

"When is it?" The chef didn't look happy. His fine features were pinched into a scowl as he leaned toward me, hands gripping the desktop.

"The second weekend in October, so two weeks from tonight."

"Great," he said.

"I know. Lousy timing, what with that review just coming out. And the last thing I want to be doing right now is working at Solari's again, but my dad didn't re-

ally give me much choice. I swear I'll make it work,
though."

"If you say so."

THE DISCOVERY OF Gino's body was the front-page story
in Sunday's paper. One of the gawkers crowding around
the pile of kelp the day before had clearly been an in-
trepid reporter who'd heard the call from dispatch over
the police scanner and immediately raced down to the
scene. Not only that, but once the journalist had gotten wind of Gino's identity—had he heard *me* say his
name?—he'd obviously headed out to the wharf to do
some investigation regarding the Italian fisherman. And
he'd hit the jackpot.

"Gino Barbieri, an eighty-year-old bachelor with no
known family, was apparently last seen dining Monday night at Solari's on the Municipal Wharf," the story
read. "According to a witness, he was noticeably intoxicated as he left the restaurant. The police have as yet
declined to state whether they are treating the death as
a homicide, but given the large abrasion on the fisherman's head, it seems possible."

And, as if that weren't bad enough, underneath the
lead story about Gino was a sidebar—set off in its own
little box—about me:

"The body was sniffed out by the dog belonging to
Sally Solari," this secondary, below-the-fold piece read,
"whose family runs the iconic Italian seafood eatery of
the same name, where Gino Barbieri was last seen dining. A former lawyer, Sally Solari is now the proprietor
of Gauguin, the restaurant started by her aunt, Violetta
Solari, whose brutal murder last April the niece helped
solve. And only two months ago, Ms. Solari was in-

volved in the investigation of yet another death—that of talented local singer Kyle Copman. One therefore has to ask: Do we now have our very own Jessica Fletcher here in Santa Cruz? And will she take on the Case of the Fisherman in the Kelp?"

No, no, nooooo... I smacked the newspaper down on the red Formica kitchen table, startling Buster, who had assumed his usual position underneath as he waited for dropped toast crumbs and his daily after-breakfast plate licking.

I'd never hear the end of this. And although some folks say any publicity is good publicity, I was pretty sure neither my dad nor Javier would be all that happy about Solari's and Gauguin being so closely identified with the string of deaths recounted in the story.

Well, I was going to find out in just a few minutes how my dad felt, since I'd promised to meet him at Solari's that morning to discuss the menu for the sister-cities dinner.

After bribing Buster with a dog biscuit as I left the house, I backed my T-Bird out of the garage and then, setting the parking brake, climbed out again to swing the wooden garage doors shut. It was not yet ten in the morning, but I could tell we were in for another warm day. The Diablo winds were still coursing down from the hills and the air felt as if it were charged with an electrical current.

Adding to the heat were the remnants of the hot flash that had descended upon me while reading that newspaper article. At least the drive down to the wharf should cool me off.

I cruised down Bay Street with the T-Bird's ragtop down, my shoulder-length hair flying about in the wind. My phone buzzed a few times in my pocket, but I ignored it. Punching up KPIG radio on the tuner, I heard Robert Earl Keen's nasal twang come through the car's tinny speakers. Maybe listening to the Texan sing about his famed five-pound bass would take my mind off that damn article.

It didn't work for long. No sooner had I dropped my handbag on the metal desk in the Solari's office than Dad followed me into the tiny room, brandishing today's rolled-up newspaper like a truncheon. "Did you see this?" he bellowed.

"It'd be hard to miss," I said. "I got four texts just driving down here, and I bet every one of them has a snarky reference to Jessica Fletcher." I tapped open the first message. "Told you so," I said, displaying the screen for my dad. "I knew Eric wouldn't miss the chance."

I patted the folding chair sitting in front of a storage shelf jammed with office supplies and cardboard boxes. "C'mon. Let's talk about the big dinner. There's nothing we can do about those articles."

Lying in bed that morning, I'd allowed myself to get progressively more angry at my father for roping me into coming back to work at Solari's. I couldn't help feeling that the sister-cities dinner was merely an excuse, or that maybe he'd even agreed to take it on solely as a way to bring me back into the fold of the family restaurant.

But now with that article in today's paper, I didn't have it in me to give him a hard time about the dinner. Not right now, anyway.

Dad sat heavily on the folding chair and I pulled a yellow legal pad from the desk—a vestige of my former life as associate attorney with the law firm of Saroyan, Davies & Lang. "First off, how many courses were you thinking of serving?"

"Okay." Dad slapped his hands on his thighs and then leaned back in the chair, nearly bonking his head on a carton of plastic straws protruding from the shelf. "I think we should have a few antipasti for while people are milling around beforehand, and then some pasta, a couple different mains and sides, and then the dessert—or maybe two. What do you think?"

So he really did want my opinion. Well, that was something. "How much are you charging per person?"

"That'll depend on what we decide to serve. I told the sister-city folks I'd let them know the cost by this Thursday. But some of the dinners will be comped, of course."

"Of course." That was the way it always worked with events like this. "You have any kind of theme in mind?"

"Italian," Dad said, and then laughed.

"Duh. But are you thinking, like, to try to recreate a menu from the Sestri Levante area? Or going for a more Italian-American type thing?"

"I think we should do something traditional to *our* culture, not try to recreate theirs. That's what I would want if I visited someplace." He tapped a finger on his leg, contemplating the faded cycling poster of "Super Mario" Cipollini above the desk. "I was thinking, what if we did a menu based on what the Sixty Families would have eaten way back when? You know, as a sort of homage to the original Italians who settled Santa Cruz."

"Like Nonna's Sunday gravy?" I asked.

"Sure, we could do that. But also the old dishes like *stoccafisso* and Garibaldi cake."

I wrinkled my nose. "You sure they'd want to eat salt cod and fried polenta? What about that stuffed veal pocket Nonna used to make for special occasions? Do you have the recipe?"

"No, but she probably remembers it. And I could fake it if she doesn't. But we'd have to check on the price of veal breast. It's not the cheap cut it used to be back when Nonna made it."

I jotted a note to look up the price and ask Nonna about her recipe. "And there's also that pasta you make sometimes when the bolete mushrooms come into season, which is now, right? You know, the tagliarini with porcini, brown butter, and sage? It's amazing."

Dad smiled. "Yeah, that's a terrific idea. If I can round up enough fresh porcini."

"I'll talk to Javier," I said, making another note. "He has contacts with the Santa Cruz Fungus Federation."

"We could also do a chicken cacciatore," Dad said, "which is a good autumn dish, and everybody likes that. And maybe stuffed cabbage for a vegetarian plate. We could use the same stuffing as for the veal breast."

"Good plan. What about dessert?"

"That I've already decided. I want to serve panettone, which is what we had for the holidays every year when Letta and I were young. And I can bake them in advance and freeze them, so it'll make it easier the day of the dinner. We could serve it with gelato."

I knew well these eggy cakes, studded with pine nuts, raisins, and other dried fruit. The store-bought variety tended to be dry and horrible, but Nonna's home-baked version was always tender and moist, and I, too, had looked forward to them every year. Of late, however, she'd stopped making the panettone, so it had been a while since I'd eaten the yummy cake.

We discussed some ideas for sides—roasted broccoli and cauliflower, creamy polenta, baby spinach salad, maybe something with artichokes—and I played secretary and wrote everything down on my legal pad.

"Okay, good," I said when I'd finished making my notes. "That's a start, at least. After I talk to Javier about the boletes and check on the price for veal breast, I'll get back to you. So, you need anything else right now? 'Cause I'd love to go home and just chill for a while before Sunday dinner."

"No." Dad stood and stretched his neck. "I'll need to do some food-costing before we finalize the menu, and we need to get the tables and chairs rented."

"And the tent, too," I reminded him.

"Right. We can talk about all that this afternoon."

"Sounds good. See you later at Nonna's."

I had almost three hours till our weekly meal at my grandmother's house and planned to spend most of it flaked out on the couch watching the Giants baseball game, which—since they were playing the Mets in New York—had just started.

My car was across the street from the restaurant, but before climbing inside I leaned over the wharf railing to enjoy the view. Several fat sea lions were swimming about below, taking turns trying to jump up onto the lower pilings and failing in their efforts with dramatic splashes. Across the water, the stretch of sand fronting the Cocoanut Grove ballroom was starting to fill up with beachgoers, and I was surprised to catch snatches of delighted screams from the Giant Dipper roller coaster. *Must be the offshore wind*, I reasoned. Normally you couldn't hear many sounds from the Boardwalk all the way out on the wharf.

Extracting my ring of keys from the depths of my bag, I opened the car door and folded my tall frame into the T-Bird's bucket seat. I checked the rearview mirror as I started the engine and noticed two men with fishing poles who'd just climbed out of a big truck looking my way. They were no doubt checking out the car; I was used to guys ogling its creamy yellow paint job and retro-futuristic fins.

I backed out of my spot carefully so as to not hit their ginormous truck—which was sticking well out into the roadway—and then smiled and waved as I jammed the stick into first and let out the clutch. But although the men continued to stare, neither smiled back.

And then, after I'd pulled about a car's length ahead, I heard one of them yell after me, "You guys killed Gino!"

FOUR

"Who were the men?" my dad asked that afternoon when I told him about the incident. We were at Nonna's house, but I'd waited till she left the kitchen to go answer the phone before bringing up the subject. "Did you recognize them?"

"I don't know which one yelled at me, but I'm pretty sure one of the guys was Stefano's kid, Bobby. Didn't he used to crew on Gino's boat sometimes? That would explain his attitude." Stefano's family owns what used to be one of the bait shops out on the wharf but is now more of a T-shirt and gift store that sells a little bait and tackle on the side. His son was about five years younger than me and had always struck me as a bit of a bully. "I didn't recognize his friend, though."

"What the hell is that supposed to mean, anyway: 'you guys killed Gino'?" Dad grabbed a wooden spoon from the counter and poked impatiently at the pot of braised meat in red sauce—the Sunday gravy—simmering on the burner. "That we, what? Fed him dinner and then shoved him over the side of the wharf?"

"I doubt they meant anything like that," I said. "They must have just heard about that article in the paper this morning and think we're to blame for letting him get drunk and then leave the restaurant."

Dad swore under his breath as he continued to jab at the meat.

Her phone call over, my grandmother returned from the hallway and took the spoon from his hand. "You gon' break all the pieces up," she said. "Here." Nonna handed him a platter piled with rolled-up prosciutto and salami, marinated vegetables, and sliced provolone and mozzarella cheese. "If you want to help, you can take this out to the dining room. We ready to eat now."

I could tell Dad wanted to talk more about what the guys on the wharf had shouted at me, but we held off while Nonna was present. No need to upset her. Though, had she been with me to hear the mudslinging, chances are the feisty eighty-seven-year-old would have come up with a colorful response.

It wasn't until we were leaving after our meal that we got a chance to discuss what Bobby—or his friend—had shouted. "You think it's possible what the paper said?" I asked my dad as he followed me across the street to my car. "That Gino really was drunk when he left the restaurant?"

"How would I know? I was in the kitchen the whole time."

Dad fiddled with the keys in the pocket of his brown slacks. "We couldn't be held liable if he did drown because he was drunk, though, could we?" he asked. "You know, if we sold him the beer?"

"No, huh-uh." I'd stopped practicing law several years back, but this was one thing I knew without having to look up, since it was so important for restaurant owners. "California got rid of that law a long time ago. You're only liable for damages if you sell alcohol to an obviously intoxicated minor who then goes out and gets injured or hurts someone else."

Dad nodded. "That's what I thought. So it doesn't

really matter then, even if he did drink a bunch at Solari's and then go out and fall off the wharf."

"But it *would* matter for our reputation. Gino may have become almost a joke to a lot of folks over the past few years, but he was one of the last of the old guard. People who didn't even know him are going to get all sentimental now that he's gone, and if they think we were the cause of his death, well…"

"Oh, lord," Dad said, rubbing the bridge of his nose. "You're right." He dropped his arm and let out a long breath. "Look, there's something I guess I need to tell you. I know Gino always came in for just a beer or two in the afternoons, but I have actually seen him at Solari's when he's had too much to drink."

"Oh, no."

"Not often, only a couple times. And they were both in the last month or so." Dad put his hands back in his pockets and returned to jingling his car keys. "And Carlo swears he's never served him more than two beers and neither have I. So he must have been drinking before he came into the bar."

"When was the last time this happened?" I asked.

"That's the thing." He rocked back on his heels and cleared his throat. "It was the day before he came in for dinner—so probably the day before…"

"…he died," I filled in.

Dad nodded. "I was tending bar that afternoon and there were a couple girls in there, barely drinking age—I had to card them—and they struck up a conversation with Gino. But after a while he started getting really annoying. Coming on way too strong, you know?"

"Yeah, Dad. I'm a woman. I know."

He ignored the sarcasm in my response. "So anyway,

I asked him to cool it and leave them alone, at which point he got all belligerent. He came around to my side of the bar and grabbed hold of me, and when I tried to push him away he threw a punch—though he missed pretty bad. I ended up having to eighty-six him, and I can tell you he was not happy about that."

I stared at my dad. "This is *not* good. Especially with the timing. He was kicked out for being drunk and belligerent and then someone sees him lurching out of Solari's the very next night?"

"I know. It's why I asked you about what the law was."

"But like I said, it's not just about the law. It's about our reputation. *And* about doing the right thing, like not serving liquor to a drunk old man." It was my turn to rub my brow. "Oh, God. And now, with that sister-cities dinner coming up?"

Opening the T-Bird's creaky front door, I rummaged through my bag for my car keys. "I guess I better talk to Cathy again to see if he really was acting intoxicated the night she waited on him. And who knows, maybe we can even find the bill for their dinner to prove we didn't get him drunk."

But then I thought of the antiquated Solari's cash register, which didn't record the table numbers, and our paper guest check system—a stack of carbon copies impaled on a nail sticking from a chunk of two-by-four my dad had painted red about twenty years earlier. It could be quite the undertaking to locate that receipt now, almost a week later.

"Good luck with that," Dad said, reading my thoughts.

NEVERTHELESS, THE NEXT day during the lunch shift I did ask Cathy about the receipt and whether she remembered what drinks Gino had ordered the previous Monday night.

The waitress frowned as she thought a moment. "He had a beer, or maybe two, is my memory. And I think the woman might have had a glass of wine. But I can't tell you for *absolutely* certain. The police were here yesterday afternoon, you know, and asked me the same thing."

Oh, great. I should have known the cops would have wanted to talk to whoever had waited on Gino that night. And there's nothing like being interrogated by the authorities to make you start to waver in your story. "Well, could he have had something to drink before he came in? Did he seem drunk during dinner?"

The subject was clearly making her uncomfortable, and I could see why. For if the old man *had* been overly intoxicated when he left Solari's that night, she'd definitely be among those in the hot seat.

"No, I don't think so. Like I told the policeman, he was kind of loud, with all that bragging and stuff. And sort of rude, too, I thought. The way he kept talking about himself while she just sat there listening. But he didn't seem especially drunk to me." Cathy stopped and stared out the picture window, her forefinger tapping her cheek. "You know," she said, turning back toward me, "that just reminded me of something. The woman he was with had a pad of paper and was writing stuff down."

"Really?"

"Uh-huh. It was almost as if she was, like, interviewing him or something. I completely forgot about that till just now."

Which meant she hadn't given this piece of information to the cops. "Man, I'd sure love to talk to her, especially if she really was interviewing Gino. And think about it: she may very well be the last person to have seen him alive. Has she been back in the restaurant since then?"

Cathy shook her head. "Not that I know of. And that night was the first time I'd ever seen her in here. I don't think she's a regular or anything."

"Well, if she does come back in, be sure to tell me."

"Will do."

"And do see if you can dig up the guest check for their table. It would be great if we could prove we only served Gino one or two beers."

Elena had just seated several large tables for lunch and was shooting me a pleading look, so I released Cathy back out on the floor to help out. Watching her take the drink orders at table six, I considered what she'd just told me. The question of Gino's intoxication raised a much bigger one: How exactly had the old fisherman died? Had he in fact fallen over the side of the wharf, as Bobby and his friend apparently believed, because he was so drunk he couldn't walk straight? Or had something else happened?

But wait, I thought. *We don't even know* when *he died. How long would it take a drowned person's body to wash up on a beach?* For all I knew, he could have fallen off his fishing boat or something days after he ate at Solari's. Though the fact that he'd never shown up again at the restaurant after that night suggested otherwise.

Okay, so let's assume, then, that Gino did *die that night, sometime after leaving the restaurant.* If he wasn't drunk, as Cathy had said, how would he have ended up in the ocean? Even intoxicated, it would be hard to fall into the water, given the high railing that ran along most parts of the wharf to prevent such an occurrence.

And then I had an ugly thought: *Could he have been pushed?*

Maybe that's what the cops thought, and that was the reason they'd been interviewing people here yesterday. I was about to go in search of my dad to ask him about the police visit when the man at table eight caught my eye and waved me over.

It was Angelo, another one of Solari's regulars. He was hunched over a cup of coffee at the booth in the far corner of the restaurant, his usual spot. I slid into the red leather seat across from him and he reached out a hand, which I took. His grip was strong, notwithstanding the man's wiry build, and his skin leathery and smooth.

"You heard about Gino, I gather."

"Yes," he said, releasing my hand with a gentle squeeze.

"I'm so sorry. I know you were friends."

Angelo nodded and turned to look out at the empty bocce court and the steel blue water off Cowell's Beach beyond. "I haven't actually spent much time with him over the past couple months," the older man said. What was he—seventy, seventy-five years old? It was hard to tell; all that time out on the water setting lines and reeling in nets had no doubt taken its toll on the fisherman's appearance.

"Really? Why not?" I asked. "We certainly saw him here in the bar as much as ever."

"Yes, and that I think was the problem," Angelo said with a frown. "I don't know what was going on with him, but when I told him I thought maybe he should lighten up a little on the drinking, he got really angry and just cut me off. Like that." The fisherman snapped his fingers. "After all those years."

I reached out to touch his bronzed forearm. "I'm sure Gino didn't really mean it. He was just hurt." As was Angelo, obviously. And now the two friends would never be able to make it right.

"Sorry to interrupt, but here's your lunch." Neither of us had noticed Elena hovering with a sandwich piled high with meatballs and marinara sauce. Angelo smiled at the server and leaned back to allow her to set the plate before him.

"So, I was wondering if I could ask you something," I said as Angelo shook his red napkin out and spread it over his lap. "As I said, Gino was in here pretty much every afternoon, but he always just had his usual two Bud Lights. Do you think maybe he'd started drinking somewhere else as well? Or maybe at home?"

"Maybe. But it wasn't all that obvious. You wouldn't necessarily even have noticed it unless you knew him well. That's the way it often is with alcoholics. They're really good at hiding it. But he started getting angry a lot more. And he was getting into arguments with me—and other people—over stupid, little things. He'd be irrational. And mean. That's what did it for me, how nasty he could be." Angelo cut a meatball in two and stabbed half with his fork. "There's nothing worse than a mean drunk."

"So, do you believe it, what they said in the paper?"

The fisherman raised an eyebrow as he chewed his meatball.

"You know, that he was drunk when he left Solari's

that night. That he must have fallen and hit his head and then ended up in the water."

"It's possible," he said, after taking a sip of coffee to wash down his food. "But if so, it wouldn't be your fault. It's pretty near impossible to stop someone from drinking who wants to."

"I sure hope other people feel the same way as you." I recounted what Bobby and his friend had yelled at me yesterday, and Angelo just laughed.

"Stefano's boy has always been a hothead," he said. "I wouldn't worry too much what he says." He cut a slice of sauce-covered bread from his sandwich and chewed it while I contemplated what he'd said about Gino. If it was true that he'd had a drinking problem, was Solari's partly to blame?

FIVE

"So, what was Gino like?" I asked Angelo as he took another sip of coffee. "I only knew him as the old man who'd come in here every afternoon and stare out the window. He didn't talk a whole lot. Except when he was with a woman he was trying to impress, that is."

Angelo set his cup down with a *clunk*. "No, he wasn't generally one for many words when he was with the boys. He'd mostly just listen to others as they'd gab. But when he did open his mouth and speak, it was usually a gem."

"Like poetry, you mean?"

"Hardly. It was more likely to be profanity. But always spot on." Angelo shook his head and grinned. "He was a piece of work, was old Gino."

Elena started over with the brown-topped carafe to refill Angelo's coffee and I motioned for her to bring me one as well.

"Didn't you two used to fish together?" I asked once both our cups had been filled.

"Well, we never worked on the same boat, since we both had our own. But we'd go out together sometimes and fish the same spots."

"Really? You showed each other your spots?" Growing up in a fishing family, I knew how secretive folks could be about where to catch the best fish.

Angelo laughed again, and the sound of his deep, melodious voice made me smile. "Truth be told," he said, "I would never have voluntarily shown him my places, but back when I first knew him, about forty years ago, he'd wait for me to leave the harbor and then follow me to see where I'd go. I guess he'd heard I had pretty good luck finding the prime spots. I'd try to outrun him, but his boat was faster than mine, so it was useless."

"Whoa. That's not good form. I'm surprised that you became friends after that."

"Nah, it was okay. Back then there were a lot more fish to go around than now. And I kind of admired his *faccia tosta*—his, you know…"

"Chutzpah," I supplied.

"Right." Angelo chuckled and cut another bite of sandwich. "Anyway, it was actually nice having him out there. Even though he didn't talk much, we were good company for each other as we'd set our lines and wait for the fish to bite. That was how we ended up becoming friends. I guess we just kind of got used to each other."

I waited while he chewed his bread and meatball and then took another sip of coffee. "Were you two still going out fishing together, up until he cut you off?"

Angelo shook his head. "We hadn't gone out together in ages. Gino gave up his slip at the harbor about five years back, and after that he kept his boat on a trailer and would take it down to the launch ramp when he wanted to go out. I think that's when he started using Bobby, Stefano's kid, to help him crew. He couldn't handle the launching by himself anymore."

I could well imagine. The "Monterey" style boats the older fishermen around here tended to use—what they called *lamparas*, modeled after the Italian feluccas of the early nineteen hundreds—were fairly big and unwieldy and would be difficult for someone in his seventies or eighties to launch from a trailer all by himself.

"Wasn't Bobby also doing other stuff for him, too?"

"That's right," Angelo said. "Bobby's been quite the godsend to Gino over the past few years. Not just with his boat, which as you know requires a great deal of maintenance, but also around his house." The fisherman smiled as he took another sip of coffee. "You should see his place. It's a bit of a wreck."

"Where did Gino live?" I asked. "In the Barranca?" This is the old Little Italy neighborhood on the West Side of Santa Cruz, where the original Sixty Families had built their homes after arriving from Liguria.

"Uh-huh. On Gharkey, that yellow-and-white place near the corner of Lighthouse. His grandfather built it, I think."

Like my great-grandfather Ciro had done—probably around the same time.

"But his *nonno* would not be happy with it now," Angelo went on. "If it weren't for Bobby helping with repairs, it would probably be just about falling down."

"Were they close, Gino and Bobby?" I asked, thinking back to the accusation Bobby and his friend had shouted at me. "You know, after spending all that time together?"

"I'd say so. Gino had become pretty reliant on him over the years. Of course, I can't speak to the last couple months—you know, since Gino cut me off—but I do know he used to talk very highly of the boy. Almost like he was his son."

Angelo gazed out the picture window for a moment, watching a young man bait his hook and then cast the line out to the inlet that lies between the wharf and the cliffs beyond. After a moment he turned back to me. "Gino never had any of his own children, you know. In fact, he once told me he was going to give his boat to Bobby when he died, because, he said, no one else in his family would appreciate it as much as Bobby would."

DRIVING HOME AFTER my talk with Angelo, I pondered what he'd told me about Gino and Bobby. If they'd been as close as Angelo seemed to think, Bobby's venting of his anger about the old man's death would certainly make sense.

But, then again, if it was true that Bobby stood to inherit Gino's boat, the fisherman's passing also resulted in an enormous benefit for him. A boat like that would have to be worth a bundle. *Could Bobby have known of Gino's intended bequest?* I wondered as I waved my fob at the keypad at the end of the wharf and waited for the gate to rise.

Cruising through the roundabout, I headed up the hill onto West Cliff Drive and, after waiting for a pink spandex–clad woman with a jogging stroller to get through the crosswalk, turned right onto Bay Street.

I had to brake suddenly when a massive Winnebago lunged out of the Dream Inn parking lot right in front of me, and as I slowed, I noticed the sign for Lighthouse Street. I was only a couple blocks from where Angelo had told me Gino lived. Perhaps a quick detour was in order.

Several doors down on Gharkey Street sat a yellow-and-white bungalow with an old wooden boat on a trailer in the driveway—one of those "Monterey clipper" types so popular among the Italian fishermen of San Francisco and the Monterey Bay. "Bella Adella" was painted in dark green block letters on the boat's white bow.

This was clearly the place. I pulled over to the curb and surveyed the property: shades drawn shut, paint peeling and showing exposed wood in places, the lawn looking as if it hadn't been watered or mowed in ages. Angelo had been right about the house being in bad shape.

The boat, on the other hand, appeared perfectly maintained. It had fresh paint both top and bottom, with shiny hardware all over. Not a speck of rust, nor any barnacles or slime to be seen on its gleaming black hull. You could certainly tell what had been most important in the old fisherman's life, I thought with a smile.

I had just released the T-Bird's parking brake and was about to continue on home when someone called out my name. "Sally? What the hell are you doing here?" A man emerged from the boat's wheelhouse and peered down at me.

It was Bobby. But why would he be here now? It wasn't as if he was still working for his old boss. "I guess I could ask the same of you," I said.

"I'm just checking on Gino's stuff to make sure no one's messing with it. Now that he's *dead*." I couldn't tell for sure behind the mirrored sunglasses he wore, but I was pretty certain he shot me an accusatory look along with that last word.

"Look, Bobby," I said, opening the car door and climbing out. "I know what you think, but it isn't true. We're not responsible for Gino's death."

"That's not what I heard." He took another step forward and leaned on the wooden railing. "I heard he was so blotto when he left Solari's that he couldn't even walk straight."

"He only had two beers that night and ate a full dinner as well, so there's no way what we served him could have gotten him 'blotto.'" I crossed the sidewalk to stand below him. "But I have heard that Gino had been drinking a lot lately. At least that's what Angelo says."

Bobby didn't respond, and I thought maybe I'd set him off again. He stared at me for a moment but then let out a long breath. "Yeah, I think Angelo may be right," he said, pushing off from the railing and standing up straight. "I've been crewing for Gino for a few years now, but the past couple months I think he mighta been hitting the bottle more than before. I mean, he had always drank. We'd sometimes share a six-pack after coming back from a fishing trip an' all. But recently?" Bobby ran a paint-spattered hand through his short, curly hair. "I dunno. He seemed out of it a lot, I guess. Not all the time, but definitely sometimes."

"He still went out fishing, though, right?"

"I don't think anything would have stopped him from going fishing." Bobby walked to the stern of the boat, climbed carefully over the gunwale onto the trailer, and dropped to the ground. "And his drinking didn't seem to affect that at all. He always caught more than me. And then would brag about it the whole way home."

"But he needed your help on the boat…"

"For some things. Like, he had a hard time launching by himself. I'd usually back the boat down the ramp while he stood on the dock and tied up. But I know for a fact he'd sometimes go out without me." He laughed.

"I'm sure he drove the other people in line at the ramp nuts while they waited for him to launch by himself."

"So why'd he hire you to help, you think, if he could do it himself?"

"Well, even though he went fishing once in a while on his own, like I said, it was way easier if I was there to help. And I don't think he was hurting for money." Bobby gestured toward the house and then the boat. "So why not hire someone?"

I glanced down the driveway where he had pointed and saw that the side door into the building was standing wide open. "He gave you a key to the house?"

"Yeah. I've been helping him with boat maintenance and fixing things around the house for a while, too. You can see the place needs a ton of work." Bobby pushed up the sleeves of his sweatshirt, which I now noticed also bore splotches of dark paint. "The cops had that yellow tape up for a couple days after they found him, but it was gone yesterday, so I figured it was okay to come back over and check things out."

"Would you mind if I went inside? I heard the house was built around the same time as my dad's place, and I'd love to take a look around."

Bobby's manner had been laid-back up till this point, but now it changed. His fingers began to twitch and his eyes darted from me to the house and back again. "Sure," he said after a moment's hesitation. "I guess that'd be okay."

I followed him down the driveway and inside the building. The door led into a laundry room/pantry area, and from there we entered the kitchen. The first thing I noticed was the stove, which looked to be from the 1940s. It was one of those white enameled jobs with the griddle in the middle and a warming area. And it was in good shape—clean and obviously well loved. The tile counters were a sort of peachy-orange and brown, and the black-and-white checkerboard floor looked like the original linoleum, scuffed and faded as it was.

But my eyes were most drawn to the pegboard on the wall, upon which hung an array of cookware: cast iron skillets, heavy-bottomed aluminum pans, and a matched set of gorgeous copper pots. "Wow," I said. "Was Gino really into cooking? I had no idea."

"Yeah, he was always making something, it seemed like. Lots of pasta sauce and fish, mostly." Bobby had the freezer open and was pushing items around. After a bit he came up with a cellophane-wrapped burrito. "Lunch," he said, popping it into the microwave. He didn't offer me one, but then again, I would have declined if he had.

"I'm a little surprised Gino bought those," I said with a chuckle. "He doesn't seem the frozen burrito type, if you know what I mean." I gestured toward the cookware lining the walls.

"Gino didn't buy them, I did," Bobby said.

Oops.

But he appeared not to notice the implied criticism of his food choices. "I've been spending so much time over here working," he said, "and when I'd get hungry I didn't wanna always be eating his stuff, so I got these." He stared at the microwave and cracked each of his knuckles in turn as he waited for the ding, then pulled the burrito out. Gingerly opening the package so as to not burn himself on the released steam, he dumped the pasty white log onto a plate.

I watched him eat. He still seemed antsy, tapping

his foot rapidly and looking down as he chewed, not meeting my eye. But at the same time he seemed comfortable at the old man's house, slouching against the kitchen counter, then turning to rummage through the condiment cabinet for a bottle of hot sauce. He'd clearly spent a lot of time here.

"You and Gino must have become pretty good friends," I said, "hanging out as much as you did."

Bobby swallowed the enormous bite he'd just taken, walked to the sink, and stuck his head down to take a drink of water from the tap. "Yeah, I guess we did," he finally answered, wiping his face on a dish towel hanging from the door of the fridge. He had an outbreak of acne to the right of his mouth, I observed. Perhaps a change in diet would help his complexion.

"Gino didn't talk a whole lot," Bobby went on, "but I could tell he liked having me around. I think he kinda thought of me as family or something."

Just what Angelo had said. "Yeah, I could see that," I replied.

I was trying to get up the nerve to ask Bobby about inheriting Gino's boat when he wadded up the dish towel, gripped it tightly for a moment in his clenched hands, then threw it onto the counter. "Why'd he have to go and die?" he mumbled, striding from the kitchen back outside. I wasn't positive, but it looked as if he had tears in his eyes.

Maybe his grief over Gino truly was heartfelt.

SIX

I DIDN'T HAVE to be at Gauguin on Tuesday until four, so I called my new pal Marta to see if she wanted to go for a bike ride. She's Italian—from Naples—and super competitive, so I always get a good workout when we ride together. But she didn't answer either my call or my text, so I went without her. It was too nice a day to spend sitting around indoors.

Jumping onto West Cliff Drive, I cruised down to the Boardwalk and over the railroad trestle, then took East Cliff and Portola out to Capitola Village. After a quick stop at Gayle's Bakery for an apple–cream cheese Danish, I pedaled down to the water and perched on the cement seawall to enjoy my breakfast.

Today wasn't as warm as yesterday, but the little seaside town was abustle with activity—locals strolling with dogs along the restaurant-lined Esplanade, surfers rinsing off under the outdoor showers, and out-of-town visitors spreading hibiscus-print towels out on the warm sand. Across the way, Capitola's row of brightly painted bungalows gleamed in the morning sunlight, and in the shallow lagoon below, the stucco buildings took on the appearance of an impressionist painting as a pair of seagulls floated through their pink, yellow, and turquoise reflection.

I wonder if our plein air class will be coming down here, I mused as I savored my cheese and sugar-filled treat. If not, it would be fun to talk Eric into doing some painting here on our own, especially if the weather kept up like it had been.

After washing down the Danish with a drink of water from the fountain by the public showers, I clipped into the pedals of my Specialized Roubaix and turned my red-and-white steed back toward Santa Cruz. As I pumped up the hill out of Capitola, I thought about my agenda for the rest of the morning. I'd promised my dad I'd investigate the price of veal breast. *Oh, and I have to contact Javier about those bolete mushrooms, too.*

I was pondering how many pounds of porcini we would need to make enough of Dad's brown-butter-and-sage pasta dish for a hundred people when the light at 17th Avenue turned red and I had to roll to a halt. An SUV towing a small catamaran pulled up next to me, sending my thoughts back to poor old Gino.

Could he have gone fishing and fallen off his boat? That would explain how his body ended up on Its Beach, something that had been bothering me ever since I'd learned he was last seen on the wharf. Because, it had occurred to me, if he'd fallen into the water right after leaving Solari's that night, he would have washed up on Cowell's Beach.

Having spent many a summer as a kid swimming at Cowell's—which is where the wharf extends out from— I knew that the tide there washed *onto* the shore, not out and around Lighthouse Point to where Its Beach is. If, on the other hand, Gino had fallen from a boat on the other side of the point, it would make complete sense for Buster to have later sniffed out his kelp-entangled body where he did.

But in this scenario, I immediately realized, Gino's

boat would have been left unmanned out in the bay and would have either been discovered by another boater or run aground somewhere—which would surely have made the news. Someone else must have been with him on the boat, and either pushed him or chosen not to rescue the old man when he fell.

Someone like Bobby. He was the only one I knew of who'd gone out in a boat with Gino.

The light turned green and I fumbled with my right pedal trying to clip back in. Maybe Bobby had learned he was Gino's beneficiary and had taken the opportunity to hasten his inheritance. *If so, though, why did he seem so sad yesterday?* He obviously had real affection for the old man and wasn't acting like someone who was going to inherit any of his estate.

But what if it had been an accident? What if Gino and Bobby had been out fishing that morning and the old man had suddenly gone all crazy on Bobby? Given what Angelo and my dad had said about the fisherman's behavior of late, this was entirely possible. Bobby could have walloped Gino with an oar or something in self-defense and then, in a panic that he'd killed him, pushed him over the side of the boat.

If this were true, however, Bobby would have come back to the launch ramp alone. *Everyone knows Gino's Monterey clipper. Wouldn't they have noticed that he wasn't on the boat with Bobby?*

I thought back to the times I'd used the boat launch with my dad and his friends. There'd always been lots of people around, especially at midday and in the early afternoon, when fishermen tended to return from their outings. Plus, there were plenty of live-aboard vessels near the launch, whose residents tended toward the busybody variety, checking out all the comings and goings around the harbor. If Bobby had returned with Gino's boat and the old man hadn't been with him, it was a sure thing someone would have noticed and told the police by now.

And then I flashed on the security cameras they'd set up near the boat launch. One afternoon a few years earlier, my dad and I had been coming back after a morning out in the bay, me ready to jump onto the dock and tie off the boat. As we approached the ramp, Dad had held up a massive salmon he'd caught, mugging for the camera and telling me how impressed the guys in the harbor office would be by his big fish.

So if the authorities kept the footage from those cameras, it would be possible to see if Gino's boat had in fact gone out the morning after he went missing—and whether he was on board when it returned to the dock.

But I'd never get access to that footage; they'd only turn it over to someone like the police. And I was pretty darn certain they wouldn't be much interested in my theories regarding Gino's death.

And besides, I wondered as I flew down the East Cliff hill and cruised around Schwan Lake, *why—if Bobby were the one who killed Gino—would he have yelled at me about the old man's death the other day in front of Solari's?* None of it made any sense.

I really needed to take a chill pill and stop worrying about what had happened to the old fisherman. The cops would figure it all out in due course. If there was indeed incriminating footage from those security cameras, they would find it.

Forcing my brain to a cheerier subject, I contemplated the menu for dad's big dinner. Nothing like food to take your mind off the unpleasantries of life.

Once home, I let Buster outside and took a quick shower. Next, completely ignoring my own counsel to stop worrying about Gino, I left a message on Eric's phone asking if he'd heard anything around the DA's office about his having a will or trust. I knew the only sure way to stop fretting about this whole thing would be to take some sort of action.

Then, after shooting Javier a text about asking his Fungus Federation friend where we could get fresh boletes and how much they'd cost, I grabbed my laptop and sat down at the kitchen table. Pulling up the Quality Meats website, I scrolled down the price list and searched for breast of veal. There it was: $2.85 a pound. We'd need about a pound per person, since at least half the weight would be bone and fat. Not super expensive, but not cheap either, compared to ground beef or chicken.

Of course, it would cost quite a bit more if we were to buy pastured and grass-fed meats for the dinner, but so far I'd been unsuccessful in persuading my father that the ethical concerns outweighed the economics of the matter. But then again, it wasn't as if "pastured veal" even existed—not the kind with milky-colored flesh I knew my dad would want, anyway. You can get what's called grass-fed "calf" these days, but its meat is pink and the flavor closer to that of mild beef than to the delicate veal raised in tiny crates and fed only milk.

And then, the more I thought about it, the more agitated I became over the concept of serving veal at all at the sister-cities dinner. Why had I ever suggested it? Veal is pale in color only because the animals are not allowed to eat grass, which would provide iron to their diet and thereby turn their flesh red. To ensure white meat, the calves are kept anemic by feeding them only milk. Or, rather, "milk substitute," a mixture of formula and antibiotics made necessary by their anemia.

Plus, there was that whole crate thing, which was pretty horrible to even imagine.

Closing my computer with a snap, I stood up and crossed the living room to where Buster's leash hung from its hook. *How can people allow such treatment of animals?* The dog jumped up in response and followed me, tail wagging, to the front door. But I knew the answer: it's easy if you simply choose not to think about it.

Since I'd already raised my concerns over the mistreatment of farm animals with Dad on more than one occasion, I didn't think I'd get very far trying again. But he wouldn't question me if I simply told him I'd learned veal breast was hard to find or, better yet, too expensive.

WHEN I GOT to Gauguin, Javier put me straight to work parting out the case of ducks that had been delivered that afternoon. We'd be using the leg and thigh quarters for a confit and the breasts for a new dish we were calling Duck à la Lilikoi—seared rare, like steak, then thinly sliced and topped with a passion fruit glaze (*lilikoi* is Hawaiian for that tasty, tart fruit). We'd make a stock from the wings and bones, which would be reduced down to a *glace de viande* for the lilikoi glaze, and the fat from the backs and wings would be rendered to use for the confit. All very resourceful and economical.

As I was wrestling with one of the duck carcasses, pulling the thigh away from the back and poking my filleting knife inside in an effort to locate the ligament separating the bones, Brandon pushed through the swinging door into the kitchen.

"You seen Javier?" the waiter asked. "Gloria said he wanted to talk to me."

"Right. I think he wants to tell you about a change in tonight's seafood special. They didn't have any rock-fish, so we're doing the lingcod instead. But you can talk to him about it to see if it's a different preparation. He's in the *garde manger*."

"Great. Thanks." Brandon started across the kitchen but then stopped. "Oh, by the way," he said, turning back toward me. "There was a guy who called earlier to make a reservation and he asked about you."

"Oh, yeah?"

"Yeah. He wanted to know if it was true that you really found that fisherman's body on the beach. And I gotta admit, I'm kind of curious, too."

I set the knife down and wiped my hands on the side towel tucked into the ties of my white apron. "Yes, it's true. Actually, my dog found him first, but then I realized what it was he was sniffing at."

Brandon wrinkled his nose and swallowed.

"Sorry. It's not a very pretty image. So, was this customer…how did he sound when you talked to him?"

"Well, he kind of laughed when he asked the question, but I got the feeling it was mostly from embarrassment or something. I think he might have actually been a little freaked out by the idea of you finding the body. But I told him I didn't know anything about it except what was in the newspaper, and he did make the reservation—for Friday night at seven, in case you're curious. Party of two."

"Is he a customer you know?"

"I didn't recognize the name. I got the feeling he hasn't been in before." Brandon grinned. "Hey, who knows? Maybe we'll get a bunch of new customers hoping to meet the woman who found the body on the beach."

Or maybe they'll stay away instead, creeped out by the angel of death who owns the place.

ONE OF THE perks of being an ex-lawyer is that you no longer have to show up for work at eight am to commence the daily grind of cranking out those precious billable hours. Of course, the life of a restaurateur comes with the opposite problem: not finishing work until the grills are scrubbed, the range top is gleaming, and all the food is wrapped in plastic and stowed away in the walk-in fridge. Most nights it's well after midnight before I make it home.

But the new hours seemed to suit me—sleeping in till woken by the sunlight streaming through my green-and-white striped curtains, then getting to laze a while in bed, drifting in and out of consciousness, pondering the abstract mysteries of the universe.

Until a brown lump of a dog would jump onto my chest, that is, and stand staring at me, his hot breath smelling of kibble and dirt. Like this morning.

"Okay, okay," I said, grabbing Buster's neck in a wrestling hold and throwing him to the bed. The dog squirmed out of my half nelson lock and leaped up, assuming the downward dog, "oh, goodie—let's play!" position, tail wagging furiously. We tumbled about the bedclothes a few minutes, me trying to grab his paws as he artfully danced away and mock bit at my outreached hands, until I finally collapsed on my pillow, panting.

"All right, Buster. You win. Again." I rolled over to look at the clock on my nightstand and then fell back onto the pillow. Seven fifteen. *Way* too early to be woken when I hadn't gotten to sleep last night until almost one. Closing my eyes, I stroked the bristly fur behind the dog's shoulder, hoping to lull him back to sleep. It was starting to work—for me, at least—when a piercing bark made me flinch, banishing all hope of further shut-eye. He clearly needed his morning walk.

But not till I brewed some coffee. While the water heated and dripped through the grounds, sending a heavenly aroma through the house, Buster and I went out front to retrieve the morning newspaper from its usual place under the sprawling Mexican sage my Aunt Letta had planted years ago. Sliding the paper from its plastic bag, I smoothed it out on the breakfast table and did a quick scan of the headlines. Nothing more about Gino—or me—thank heavens.

My java wasn't yet done, so, ignoring Buster's pleading eyes and thumping tail, I sat down to flip through the front section. I was about to fold it back up when my eye was caught by the name "Solari's" in one of the letters to the editor on the opinion page:

A week ago, my wife and I had dinner at one of our favorite spots out on the Santa Cruz Municipal Wharf. After finishing our meal, as we were leaving the restaurant, we saw an older man who seemed rather intoxicated. I have now learned that this gentleman was Gino Barbieri, who had dined that evening at the same place as us, and whose body was found on the beach last weekend. No doubt he ended up drowning as a result of his drunkenness that same night.

So my question is, how could a restaurant justify serving liquor to an old man they knew to be in such a state of inebriation, and how could they allow him to leave in such a sorry condition? It seems like a clear case of negligence to me. I will now tell you that the establishment was Solari's, and I for one will from now on be taking my business elsewhere.

The letter was signed "Marvin Blanco." I knew the guy. He'd been one of our regulars for going on ten years. *Oh, lord...* This was precisely the sort of thing I'd feared.

My mood significantly altered from two minutes earlier, I poured coffee into my travel mug and headed for the front door, followed closely by the still near-manic Buster. Now I, as much as the dog, really needed some exercise to let off steam.

"Wanna go to Lighthouse Field?" I asked as I clipped on his leash. He knew the name well and responded with a series of sharp barks culminating in an excited whine.

Lighthouse Field is a thirty-seven-acre open space a few blocks from my house teeming with ground squirrels, gophers, lizards, and other scurrying critters. Doggy paradise, in other words.

The land is a potent environmental symbol in Santa Cruz, as the success in saving it from development in the mid-1970s emboldened the community and gave rise to the creation of numerous other green spaces around the county. But it isn't all that much to look at—just a swath of wild oats and other tall grasses, dotted here and there with unruly cypress trees. And for most of the year the parcel is far more brown than green, especially at the beginning of autumn, as it was right now.

Once at the field, I unhooked Buster and he set to work sniffing the scraggly vegetation lining the dirt path. Countless dogs frequent this park, all leaving their scent-laden calling cards along the way. After making his own mark on a series of shrubs, Buster trotted over to investigate an enticing collection of holes. Shoving his snout down each one in succession, he ensured that any animal lurking inside would immediately skedaddle down its tunnel to a location far away. Patience is not one of his strongest assets.

Bush by bush and hole by hole, Buster and I ambled across the park, me brooding about Marvin's letter to the editor and trying to decide what, if anything, could be done to put a cork in this whole fracas. Because that first letter was bound to result in a series of others. Nothing stirs folks up more than the chance to express their moral outrage about something.

And now that I knew from Angelo and my dad that Gino had in fact been drinking more heavily of late, it seemed more and more likely that the description in Marvin's letter was accurate. He had no reason to make it up, after all.

Yet Cathy had said that Gino wasn't drunk that night and that she'd served him only two beers at most. Could *she* be lying?

SEVEN

Bumping down the asphalt-coated planks of the hundred-year-old wharf, I imagined every eye to be staring at me, shooting silent accusations of negligence my way. Negligence is an ugly word—especially when you've worked on as many personal injury cases as I did during my stint as an attorney—and Marvin's use of the term in his very public letter to the editor made me nervous.

Those in the tight-knit circle of the Santa Cruz Genovese were no doubt already on edge about the suspicious death of the fisherman who'd essentially been their patriarch. For them, Gino had represented the last of the old generation—those who'd kept their *lampara* fishing boats out here on the wharf before construction of the yacht harbor in the early sixties, using mechanical davits to raise and lower the wooden-hulled craft to the water. And those who could still remember the days when sea bass, sardines, sand dabs, and sole filled the Monterey Bay.

No, I thought as I freewheeled my bike up to the back door of Solari's, many folks out here would not be pleased at all to hear that my family might have had something to do with Gino's death.

Dad wasn't in yet, so, after stowing my bike in the restaurant office, I went in search of Cathy. I no longer officially worked at Solari's—except in "emergencies," which my dad interpreted as meaning anytime someone called in sick. (We were still working that one out.) So I wasn't planning on staying at the restaurant; I just needed to discuss Marvin's letter with her and my dad and thought it best to do so in person. I also wanted to see if Cathy had found that receipt. It's no fun worrying that your new head waitress might be lying to you.

Heading down the narrow hallway outside the office, I ran into Sean, who was loaded down with a stack of dishwasher racks filled with clean water glasses. I followed him out to the wait station, where the busboy began arranging the glasses on a shelf.

"You know who old Gino is, right?"

He gave me a quick glance but didn't stop his unloading. "The guy who washed up on the beach? Sure, I know him."

"Well, do you remember him coming in for dinner the week before his body was found?"

"Yeah, I do." Sean set the empty rack on its side and turned to face me.

"And do you remember anything about him that night? Like, was he acting different in any way?" I didn't want to put words in Sean's mouth, but I could tell from his frown that he had noticed something about the fisherman that evening.

The teenager chewed his lip. "Uh…"

"Look, it's okay to tell me, whatever you saw. I just need to know the truth."

"Well, he did seem kinda…messed up."

"How so?"

"Just a little out of it. Like he mighta had a bit too much to drink."

"Was this when he first came in or later?" I asked.

"I didn't really even notice him till they were done

with dinner. But when I went out to bus the table he and that woman had been sitting at, he was talking real loud as they were leaving. She was trying to get him to quiet down, but he just laughed and said something that I could tell pissed her off. It was a little weird, actually, 'cause he usually barely even talked at all when he'd come into the bar in the afternoon." Sean shook his head, staring at the empty dish rack.

"Yeah, weird," I agreed. "So what happened next?"

"That's all I remember. They left at that point, and I just cleared their table and took the bus tray back to the dish room."

I frowned, staring out at the waitresses readying the dining room for the lunch service. *What Marvin said in that letter must be right, after all. Damn.* "Well, okay," I said, turning to go. "Thanks for being so honest with me."

He went back to unloading his glasses, but the teenager's eyes kept darting my way, as if he was nervous about something. Maybe there was something he'd avoided mentioning.

"By the way," I said, turning back as a thought occurred to me, "have you talked to anyone besides me about what Gino's condition was like that night?"

His body stiffened.

"You did, didn't you?"

Sean scrunched up his face, and I thought he might be about to cry. "I didn't know he had died," he said, his voice rising half an octave. "This was before anyone knew. I was just talking to this dude who came into the restaurant last weekend, and he told me he knew Gino but hadn't seen him in a while. So when the guy asked

if I'd seen him and how he'd been lately, I figured there
was no harm in telling him…"

Sean trailed off. And, given what I was thinking—
and that my expression likely mirrored the frustration I
was feeling about our blabbermouth busboy—I couldn't
blame him.

"I know," he said, bowing his head. "The guy was a
reporter. I figured that out the next day, after that article
was in the paper. Cathy showed it to me. I'm so sorry."

"It's okay. It would have come out eventually, anyway." Frustrating as Sean's blabbering was, it had
only hastened the inevitable. We were simply going to
have to deal with the facts as they were. I left the now-
contrite busboy to his water glasses and headed for the
dining room, where I'd caught a glimpse of Cathy walking by a minute earlier.

She was counting out today's cash for the till, and I
waited as she finished the twenties. "Did you see the
letter to the editor in this morning's paper?" I asked,
once she'd jotted the number down on the ledger.

"I did," she said, picking up the rubber-banded stack
of tens. "But I don't understand it. If Gino had been that
out of it, I surely would have noticed. Oh, and I found
the bill for their table. Here." She pulled up the register drawer and fished underneath, coming up with a
carbon copy of one of the old-school guest receipts Solari's uses. "See?" she said, handing me the bill. "Two
Bud Lights, along with a full dinner. How could he get
drunk on that?"

I studied the paper: two beers, one glass of Soave,
plus two fish specials. "Who knows," I said, pocketing
the receipt. I recounted to her what Sean had just told
me. "So I'm wondering, even though he didn't seem

drunk, if Gino maybe seemed upset or angry that night. Or maybe you saw him and the woman arguing?"

"No, nothing like that." The waitress sighed and picked up the stack of money once again. "I wish I could help you. I really do."

My DAD HAD now arrived at work; I could hear his raised voice as I walked back down the hall. I found him in the kitchen, where he'd cornered Emilio against the counter where the Robot Coupe sat.

"How could you not check the order before you signed off? We were supposed to get *two* cases of chickens and there's only one!" Dad shook the invoice in the line cook's face and then stalked off, muttering to himself about having to call the vendor himself.

He had clearly seen the morning paper. Now, don't get me wrong: my father has absolutely been known to lose his temper—on many occasions—but to physically accost a worker like that was not normal. His bad mood had to be the result of that damn letter to the editor.

I crossed the kitchen to Emilio and apologized on behalf of my dad, explaining why I thought he must have gone off on him like that. The cook waved it off with a laugh. "No worries. I'll just make him comp me an extra beer sometime."

I doubt he wants to hear about beers right about now, I thought as I followed my dad down to the restaurant office. He wasn't on the phone with the vendor. Instead, he was scowling at the Saeco cycling poster, fingers tapping out a rhythm atop the metal desk.

"Hey, Dad." Rolling my bike out of the way, I pulled out the folding chair and sat down. "I guess you must have seen the newspaper." And then I noticed that a copy was lying before him on the desk, open to the opinion page.

Dad stood up, turned around, and then sat back down again, like a dog who couldn't get comfortable in its bed. "How could Marvin do this to us? And right now, with that big dinner coming up? It's a disaster." He leaned forward with a moan and laid his forehead on the desk.

"We don't know that," I said. "Who reads the newspaper anymore, anyway? I bet most people won't even know."

"Not true," Dad said, head still on the desk. "I've already gotten a call about it."

"From who?"

"Wanda."

"Your neighbor?" I asked. "That busybody who calls about every strange car she sees parked on the street? Who cares what she thinks?" I reached over and shook him by the shoulder. "C'mon, it'll be okay. This will all blow over in a few days, just wait and see. And it's actually a good thing that dinner is coming up, because it's gonna be great publicity for Solari's. It'll make everyone forget about this thing with Gino." Hey, if I kept on like this, maybe I'd even make myself believe what I was saying. "So you wanna talk a little more about the menu?"

Dad lifted his head and sat up. "I've actually already decided on the menu."

"You have?" I gaped at him. So much for caring about my opinion. Apparently it was true that all he'd really wanted was another pair of hands to help out— someone he could guilt into working without pay. But I kept these thoughts to myself. Now was not the time for a big blowout with my dad. "I thought you were waiting for me to get back to you about those prices," was all I said.

"I've decided not to go with the stuffed veal breast, so I didn't need the price on that."

Well, that's one thing I don't need to worry about. "But what about the porcini? I haven't heard from Javier about them yet."

"I can use some other kind of mushroom if they're too expensive," Dad said. He folded up the newspaper and picked up a handwritten sheet underneath. "Here's what I came up with."

I took the paper from him and read the list he'd compiled:

antipasto (TBD), fugassa (cheese & onion, pesto)
tagliarini w/brown butter, sage & mushrooms
spaghetti w/mussels
braised meat in red sauce
chicken cacciatore
stuffed cabbage
Garibaldi cake/fried polenta
veg/salad
panettone w/gelato

I had to admit it looked like a great banquet menu. Lots of variety, but most of the items easy to prepare in advance. "Fugassa's a good idea," I said. That's what we call focaccia, a bread sort of like thick pizza dough, heavy on the olive oil and salt, often served with toppings similar to pizza. "And I like the mussels, too. Way better than *stoccafisso*." I handed the list back to Dad. "What kind of veg and salad are you thinking of?"

"Sautéed green beans or zucchini? And maybe a spinach salad with orange, fennel, and black olives."

"That sounds delicious."

"Oh, and I have this to show you, too." He flipped through a stack of papers on the desk, coming up with a glossy flyer that he held up proudly for my inspection:

**Celebrate Columbus Day at Solari's
With a Sumptuous Dinner
in Honor of the Mayor of Our Sister City,
Sestri Levante (Riva Trigoso)!**

"Oh, no," I said.

"What?" He turned the flyer over and studied its text. "Is there a typo?"

"Dad!" I wailed. "Columbus Day? *Really?*"

"What do you mean? Don't you see? It's perfect. When I realized that the dinner was going to be the weekend of October twelfth, it suddenly came to me: Columbus was from Genoa, which is the same province that Sestri Levante is a part of, so it's like it was meant to be." And then he lowered the paper and frowned. "Oh. I get it. It's those politically correct people that have taken over the town. You're worried about them."

"Not just me. Just about everyone in Santa Cruz— besides you, that is—would get that this is a bad idea. Nobody celebrates Columbus Day anymore."

"Italians do," Dad said, making an expression somewhere between a pout and a glower. "Especially the Genovese, like us. And you too should be proud of your heritage."

God, he could be so clueless sometimes.

"Look, Dad. You've got to trust me on this. We can't call it a Columbus Day celebration. That would cause *way* more flack than this whole thing with Gino. There are a ton of folks out there who find the holiday to be really offensive, and insensitive to the indigenous people who were already here when Columbus supposedly 'discovered' America."

"Well, it's too late to change it now," Dad said with a victorious smile. "I've already paid to have two hundred of these flyers made, and submitted it to all the local newspapers and a couple different magazines. So you and all your PC friends are just going to have to live with it being a Columbus Day dinner."

Live to regret it, more likely.

EIGHT

"You'll never believe what my dad's done now."

"Let me guess." Eric stretched out on the chaise longue in my backyard and kicked his flip-flops off onto the brick patio. "He's enrolled in a yoga class and has decided to switch Solari's to an all vegan menu."

"I wish that were it. No, instead he's decided that this big sister-cities deal is going to be a 'Celebration of Columbus Day,' and you can imagine how that will go over in this town."

Eric put his head in his hands. "Oh, no."

"Exactly my words. But Dad won't listen to reason. In fact, he's already sent the advertising copy out to all the local papers. So now we have two reasons for customers to boycott Solari's."

"Can't wait to see what kind of firestorm that stirs up," Eric said with a chuckle.

"Thanks for your support." Settling myself on the other lounge chair, I took a sip of my bourbon-rocks. "Sure you don't want a drink?" I asked, clinking the ice in an enticing manner.

"No can do. Marta might smell the liquor on my breath and then I'd never hear the end of it."

"I know. I'm just razzing you." Eric had stopped by my house after work to hang out for a bit, but he had to be at chorus practice at seven. I'd sung in his chorus over the summer and was well aware that Marta, the

choral director—as well as my new cycling buddy—
did not approve of any imbibing prior to rehearsals.
"Mmmmm. Delicious!" I said, taking another sip. I figured he deserved the teasing, given the lack of sympa-
thy he was displaying for my dad's colossal political
blunder.

"But I wouldn't mind a glass of ice water." Eric
leaned back luxuriously in his chair, extending a hand
to shade his eyes from the late-afternoon sun. "And
maybe a hat, too?"

"Fine." I got up again and went inside, Buster following after, and returned with the water and a straw
cowboy hat from my bedroom closet.

Eric accepted the hat with a grin. "Howdy, pard,"
he said, tugging at its wide brim. "Where'd this come
from?"

"It was Aunt Letta's. I think she got it in Mexico."

We sat without speaking for a few moments, enjoying the garden. My aunt, who'd lived here before me,
hadn't been an expert landscaper or anything like that,
but she did have a good eye for design. Along the edge
of the brick patio was a low box hedge (which I did my
best to maintain in its neatly clipped condition), interrupted at several points by brick planters overflow-
ing with red-and-yellow lantana, pink geraniums, and
purple salvia.

Beyond the hedge had once been a lawn, but with our
ongoing drought and resultant water restrictions, Letta
had let it die back. I was thinking of replacing the area
with some sort of xeriscape, perhaps a rock garden in-
terspersed with cactus and colorful succulents. But for
now, the dead grass wasn't all that bad. And the aging
fruit trees along its periphery, their oft-pruned limbs

reaching out like the gnarled fingers of some fairytale crone, were ablaze with autumn colors.

"Hey, you want to maybe paint for a while?" I asked. "Check out the orange fruit and leaves on that persimmon tree over there, and the cool shadow they're casting on the fence."

"Sure, why not? I still have over an hour before I have to leave."

I fetched paper, paints, brushes, and two tin plates and placed two jars of water between us—one for mixing paints and one for cleaning our brushes. Rather than messing with easels (I had only one, in any case), we simply set the paper down on our lounge chairs.

The sun was low, imparting a yellow patina to the world, and the sky was a rich, cobalt blue. But this magical lighting wouldn't last long; we'd have to work fast, painting sketches rather than full-blown landscapes.

Squeezing a ribbon of cadmium red gouache onto my plate, I glanced over to see what Eric had decided upon as a subject. He was roughing out what looked to be the ramshackle toolshed in the far corner of the yard, its weathered white boards glowing in the late-afternoon light. His lips were pursed in thought and he'd tipped Letta's cowboy hat back, allowing several strands of blond hair to spill out over his forehead.

"Did you know that Paul Gauguin used to wear a Stetson while painting?" I asked.

Eric looked up from his work. "Really?"

"Yeah. I read about it in that biography I told you about. He apparently bought it at the Wild West show they had at the world's fair in Paris—the same one they built the Eiffel Tower for."

"Well, I am in ze good company, zen," Eric said in a fake French accent.

I picked up my brush and dipped it in water. "I don't know how long he kept it, but I did read that he took it with him to Tahiti. The locals there apparently thought he was a pretty queer duck when he first came, what with his big ol' cowboy hat and long hair. In fact, the guy who wrote the book says they thought he might really be queer—*mahu*, they called it."

Eric laughed. "Well, they certainly got that wrong. Hey," he said, readjusting Letta's hat to a jaunty angle and striking a dramatic pose. "Maybe someday someone will unearth a previously undiscovered self-portrait of Gauguin in his Stetson hat."

"Oh, God, that would be awesome." I slapped my knee and had another drink of bourbon. "With palm trees and plumeria, and an idyllic, turquoise blue ocean in the background."

"Oh, and speaking of oceans," Eric said, "that reminds me. I heard from a woman at work this afternoon that, based on the autopsy, they think Gino's body was in the water for about four or five days."

I did the math. So that meant it probably *was* Monday night when he had died. The same night he'd eaten dinner at Solari's. Not good.

"And," Eric went on, "they did find salt water in his lungs, which means he was still alive when he ended up in the ocean. The coroner has ruled the cause of death to be asphyxia due to drowning, but they're thinking that as to the *manner* of his death, it was accidental. At least that's the buzz around the office right now."

"Really?" I lifted my brush midstroke from the outline of the tree trunk I was working on and set it on my palette.

"Yeah. They apparently found fragments of mussel shell embedded in that gash in his temple. The guys on the case won't make an official determination until they get the tox report back, but I gather that based on this new evidence, along with the eyewitness testimony that Gino appeared drunk when he left Solari's, they're thinking he must have fallen off the wharf. Then, once he was in the water, he got slammed by the surge up against the pilings—which, as you know, are covered in mussels and barnacles—and that's what gave him the abrasion and gave the skin there that purplish tinge. The report also said the blow was severe enough that it would likely have knocked him out. Hence his drowning."

"Well," I said, "that's good, I guess. You know, that there was no foul play."

But I didn't mean it. Because this finding would be sure to put the heat more on Solari's for letting a drunk old man leave the restaurant and then take a tumble into the ocean. If it were a homicide, on the other hand, *that* would be the story and folks would quickly forget that he'd been intoxicated when he left the restaurant.

Eric looked up from his paper. "Is that why you wanted to know about Gino's will? Because you think there was foul play?" He chuckled to himself and went back to filling in his shed with an undercoat of white.

"Well, you have to admit that a finding of murder would be better for Solari's. You know, that he didn't die just because we let him leave the restaurant drunk." I picked my brush back up and dabbed it in the smear of sepia paint on my pie pan. "'Cause right now's a really lousy time for any bad publicity, with the dinner coming up."

"Don't you mean the big *Columbus Day* dinner?"

"Ha, ha. Not."

"But seriously," Eric went on, "why would anyone want to whack Gino on the head? Wasn't he supposed to be this guy that everyone loved?"

"Well, I gather he'd become pretty crotchety of late. This other fisherman I was talking to the other day told me Gino had gotten really mean in the last few months, he thinks because Gino had been drinking a lot."

Eric frowned.

"Yeah, I know. Not so good for us. But that's why I asked about the will. Because I found out that Gino was supposedly going to give his boat to this guy, Bobby. And if he knew about it, that would provide a big-time motive to knock the old man off."

"Well, sorry to burst your murder bubble. I found out they did find a will, but it gives everything to a brother who's now dead. So this Bobby guy isn't going to inherit a thing. It'll all go to whoever's Gino's next of kin."

I sucked on the end of my paintbrush and contemplated a brown-and-orange skipper that had alighted upon the lantana bush nearest me. Angelo had obviously been wrong. And since Gino hadn't willed the boat to Bobby, he wouldn't have told him he was going to. Bobby's sadness at the fisherman's death must have been sincere, after all.

Dang. There went my prime suspect. So who else could have killed him?

SURE ENOUGH, THERE were two more letters to the editor in next morning's paper. One was in defense of Solari's from a woman who came in frequently for lunch. But since she hadn't been there the night of the incident, I doubted her plea would be all that helpful.

The other letter was from a guy who'd heard from a friend that Gino had been seen by someone else weaving down the wharf on the Monday night before his body was found, and who therefore blamed Solari's for his subsequent drowning. *Double hearsay*, I thought as I ate my banana and sipped my morning brew. Not that anyone would give a hoot just how unreliable that made the letter writer's accusation.

Tossing aside the newspaper, I set about making a list for my morning's shopping: tortillas, cheddar cheese, lettuce, onions, bread, milk, more bananas. *Oh, and stuff for Saturday night.* Nichole and Mei were going to be in town, so I'd invited Eric, as well as Allison and her husband Greg, to come to my place for dinner along with my pals from San Francisco. I was going to try out a recipe for black cod marinated in miso and sake that I'd recently read about in a magazine.

The grocery shopping didn't take long, but afterward I had to stop by the drugstore to pick up some vitamins and a packet of the special olive oil soap my grandmother liked and then swing by her place to drop them off. Then Nonna wanted to tell me in great detail about a parishioner who was having a spat with one of her fellow churchgoers and how the two women who'd once been close friends now no longer even sat in the same pew for mass. Although Nonna professed shock and sadness at this development, it was obvious she also took great pleasure in having such a juicy story to recount.

As a result, I didn't get home until after eleven. And

then, just as I'd picked up Buster's leash to take him for a walk, my cell buzzed. It was a text from the Solari's waitress, Cathy: "woman w/gino that night outside restaurant right now!"

"Sorry, Buster," I said, replacing the leash on its hook. "Change of plans."

After sending a quick text back, I grabbed my keys, gave the disappointed dog a biscuit (which did cheer him up), and ran back out to my car. If I could talk to that mystery woman, maybe—just maybe—I could get a definitive answer as to Gino's state the night the two of them had eaten together at Solari's.

Ten minutes later I pulled up in front of the restaurant and dashed into the dining room. "Where's Cathy?" I asked, interrupting Giulia as she took the lunch order at table two. The matronly waitress frowned her disapproval but nodded toward the wait station before turning back to her customers.

Cathy looked up from measuring coffee into a filter and frowned when she saw me. "Oh. I guess you didn't get my second text. She's gone already."

My face fell.

"Sorry. But you did tell me to—"

"I know, I did. And you were right to text me. So what was the woman doing? Just walking by, or talking to someone?"

"She was over there." Cathy pointed out the window at the line of benches facing the bocce court. "Sitting and talking with that man who's still there, the guy you were talking with in here the other day."

I squinted into the bright sunlight to make out who was on the bench she was indicating. It was Angelo.

"Really? How long were they talking, do you know?"

Cathy shrugged. "I have no idea."

Well, at least I could go find out from Angelo what he knew about the woman—and why they'd been talking together. What, did she have a thing for old Italian fishermen?

He smiled as I walked up and patted the place next to him on the bench.

"*Ciao,* Angelo," I said, taking the proffered seat. "Lovely morning. How come you're not fishing?"

"I went out yesterday and got skunked. Not one bite." Angelo touched his forefinger to his thumb, forming a zero. "*Niente.* Even down in Capitola, off the Slide, where I always find rockfish. So I decided to just take a few days off."

"We couldn't get any rockfish at Gauguin the other day either, so you're in good company." I shifted in my seat. "So I wanted to ask you about that woman you were just talking to. Do you know her very well?"

Angelo grinned. "Not as well as I'd like," he said, giving me a little nudge. "Though I have seen her out here before. She's a pretty hard gal not to notice."

Oh, boy. "Well, how did you meet her?"

"She just came up to me and asked if I'd be willing to talk to her. Said she wanted to find out about the old days out here on the wharf and that I looked like someone who might be good for that."

"Which means she thought you looked old," I said, nudging him back.

"True." The fisherman slapped his knees and laughed. "But I don't mind the age difference if she doesn't."

"Uh-huh. And is that what you talked about, the old days?"

He nodded. "She's writing a story for a newspaper about the history of the wharf and the fishing community out here. I guess people are interested in us now because of the hundred-year anniversary they celebrated a while back."

"Do you remember the name of the paper she's writing this story for? 'Cause I'd love to read it when it comes out."

"The *Santa Cruz Tribune*. She said it was one of the weekly papers."

I'd never heard of a publication by that name.

"But I could tell she was interested in more than just that," Angelo added with a wink. "I think we made a special kind of connection. She told me she wants to see me again—for dinner sometime."

And it would be Angelo's treat, no doubt. "What's her name? You know, so I can look for her byline?"

He smiled. "Anastasia. Isn't that beautiful?"

Boy, was he smitten. I made a mental note to ask Cathy who had paid for dinner when Gino came in with Anastasia, if that was indeed her name. Because I was starting to sense a pattern here.

"Well, when you do have dinner together, why don't you come to Solari's so I can meet this wonderful woman? I'll comp you the wine if you do."

"Why, that's awfully kind of you, Sally. Thanks. We'll do that."

It was my turn to smile. Even if Angelo and his femme fatale came in on a night I was working at Gauguin, as long as Cathy texted me right when they arrived, I'd have plenty of time to get down here before they finished their meal. So maybe I'd get to meet this mystery woman after all.

Angelo leaned his tall body back on the bench and stretched out his thin legs, which were almost lost in the baggy black canvas pants he wore. "Mario was telling me this morning about the big dinner he's hosting for that Italian mayor," he said.

"Did he tell you it's going to be a Columbus Day celebration?"

"He did. And that you weren't too happy about that. But I think your father is right. It's a good thing to honor our Genovese tradition. And the menu he's planning for it sounds *straordinario*. I think maybe I will have to buy a ticket myself." The old fisherman smacked his lips in anticipation. "You realize how important your heritage is to the Italian cuisine, don't you?"

"Sure. Pesto, focaccia, ravioli—they all come from Genoa."

"Yes. And don't forget *stoccafisso*," Angelo added, prompting a grimace from me.

"Oh, I think we can definitely forget the dried codfish stew our forebears used to eat. I am so glad Dad decided to opt out of it for the dinner."

"And remember that it was the Genovese Christopher Columbus who first brought the tomato to Italy from the New World," Angelo said.

I was fairly certain this wasn't true; I'd read that tomatoes hadn't arrived in Europe till later, after Cortez conquered the Aztecs. But I didn't bother arguing this finer point of history.

"And we all know how important the tomato is to Italian cooking," he went on. "My *mama*, she used to make her own *conserva*. Never bought it from the stores. I remember how she would grow the tomatoes in the Italian Gardens, up where the sewage treatment plant is now, by Neary Lagoon. Then, late every September, this same time of year, she'd get me and my brothers to pick and cart home the bushels of tomatoes from her plants, and she'd chop them all up and put them in a big wooden barrel with a spigot. She'd let the liquid drain out for a week or so and then strain out all the skins and seeds."

Angelo smiled at the memory and I pressed him to tell me more. I love hearing the old stories about food.

"Well," he said, pleased to have an audience, "then she'd pour the strained pulp into cloth flour sacks and hang them from the clothesline to drain even more. It would take days and days for the *conserva* to get thick enough and then, once it was done, she'd salt the purée, put it into jars, and pour olive oil on top. Preserved that way, it would last years without spoiling. And what a flavor. So intense."

"I remember my *nonna*'s sun-dried tomatoes," I said. "She didn't make her own *conserva*, but she'd slice and salt the fresh tomatoes and lay them outside on racks to dry. She stored them in crocks with salt and would soak them overnight in water when she wanted to use them. I think there are still a few jars down in her basement."

Angelo was nodding. "Yes, I remember those, too. In fact, Gino used to salt his tomatoes to preserve them and would sometimes give me some. He made the *conserva* too. You know he was a great cook, right?"

"No, I had no idea. But that explains his kitchen." I told Angelo about seeing the beautiful stove and copper pots the other day at Gino's house. "I wish I'd known he was so into food. I would have loved to talk to him about it."

"He never married," Angelo continued, "so he had

no wife to cook for him, and being Italian, of course, he loved his food very much and would not settle for store-bought pasta or *conserva*. He was very proud of his skills as a cook. But back when we were young, it was not so surprising to do one's own cooking like that, even for a man. All the Genovese here, they'd make their own fresh pasta and *conserva*, as well as bread, wine…"

"Yep, that certainly describes my family," I said with a laugh. "It's no wonder we all opened restaurants."

NINE

I ALMOST DIDN'T want to open the next day's paper, knowing what I'd find inside. Dad had told me Friday was when they'd be running his notice about the sister-cities dinner and, sure enough, there it was—a quarter-page full-color ad near the end of the front section. Not only did the words "COLUMBUS DAY" scream out in block letters, but Dad had included clip art line drawings of the *Niña*, *Pinta*, and *Santa María* floating through the ad copy as well as a pair of American and Italian flags top and bottom. Directly under the cartoon rendering of the sailing ships were the words "Hosted by Solari's Restaurant on the Wharf."

My landline rang before I'd finished my first cup of coffee, and I knew without even looking at the number that it would be Eric.

"Nice touch, those ships," he said. "I think Mario missed his calling as an ad man on Madison Avenue."

I sighed. "Do you have a reason for calling other than to taunt me in my misery?"

"Nope." Eric took a noisy sip from what I figured was the cup of Starbucks he bought every morning on the way to work. "But since I've got you, is there anything you'd like me to bring tomorrow night?"

"How about dessert? I hadn't planned on asking anyone else to bring anything, but since you're being such a brat, that can be your punishment."

"Fair enough."

"Nichole and Mei are coming down from the City, and Allison and Greg will be here, too, so we'll be six."

"Right; see you then. No, wait. I'll see you before, at class tomorrow afternoon. Where are we meeting, again?"

"On the wharf, at the old ship near Solari's."

"Oh, right. Okay, gotta dash; I have a witness interview in a half hour and I still have to read through the case file."

After hanging up, I returned to my newspaper. The autopsy results Eric had already told me about were finally in the news—that Gino had saltwater in his lungs and had died of drowning and that, pending the results of the toxicology report and "other evidence which may come in," the coroner's office was ruling his death an accident.

I closed the paper and pushed my chair back from the red Formica table. Yes, the ruling of accidental death was not good for Solari's, but it also made no sense from a practical standpoint. Even if Gino had been drunk when he left the restaurant that night, how could he have fallen over a railing that must have come up to almost chest height? And why would his body have washed onto Its Beach if he'd fallen off the wharf?

But if it was murder, who would have wanted to kill him? Bobby had seemed like the obvious suspect, but now that I knew he hadn't been a beneficiary in Gino's will, I could think of no reason for him wanting the fisherman dead. If anything, the opposite seemed true. Not only did Bobby seem to have genuinely cared for the old man, but he had been Bobby's employer. With Gino gone, Bobby no longer had a job.

There was also Angelo's new crush—Anastasia. She was the last person known to have seen Gino alive. And I couldn't help but think that her spending so much time with Gino and Angelo, men more than twice her age, was suspect. Could she have been trying to get money out of Gino? And now that he was dead, she'd switched her attention to Angelo?

I was going to have to find out more about the mysterious Anastasia.

GAUGUIN WAS COMPLETELY booked Friday night, with people on a waiting list hanging out in the bar hoping for no-shows. What a difference a rave review can make.

Javier had me on the hot line along with him, with Brian at the grill station and Kris on *garde manger*. "Two duck confit, two fish," I called out to the head chef, reading off the next ticket on the rail.

"I got the fish," Javier answered. He wiped down two sauté pans, set them over a high flame, and, once they were hot, poured a dipper of clarified butter into each.

I set about heating oil in two of my own pans and then grabbed a pair of duck leg quarters from the oven and laid them gently in the sizzling oil. While the duck was crisping up and browning, I took two plates from the warming oven and arranged the sides on them: potatoes *sarladaise* (fried in duck fat with garlic and parsley—yes, it's as good as it sounds) and roasted Brussels sprouts with an orange-balsamic glaze.

Brandon was waiting at the pick-up window as I set the golden-brown duck legs onto the plates, and he whisked them off to his customers. That's the thing about confit. The dish is almost a miracle with its fall-off-the-bone tender insides and crispy skin, but if you let it sit around for very long, it loses its magical crackle and crunch.

Two minutes later the server was back for the fish for the same table. While Javier arranged his orders of sole *meunière* on two plates and drizzled brown butter with lemon over the fillets, Brandon leaned through the pick-up window. "That guy who was asking about you finding the body?" he said. "Well, I thought you'd want to know he just came in. He's with a woman at table six."

After Brandon had taken the plates from Javier, I leaned through the window the other way to take a look at the man who'd asked about me. I'm almost six feet tall, so I was able to poke my head pretty far into the dining room. Which ended up being not such a great thing in this instance.

I spotted the guy, all right, but didn't recognize him. He was about my age—around forty, I'd guess—and had gray-flecked hair, cut short. Not bad-looking, actually. His eye must have been caught by the movement of a lanky woman in a white chef's jacket and black cap sticking half her torso out the pass window, because as I was giving him the once-over the man turned and met my gaze.

He looked away quickly, as one does in such situations, but I'm sure he could tell I was checking him out. I ducked back into the kitchen but continued to watch the man. He had turned back to his companion and was saying something to her as he nodded in my direction. *Great*. No doubt he was recounting how I'd discovered Gino's body on the beach and how corpses seemed to pop up wherever I went.

Seven tickets remained on the rail and I bent to examine them. No need to fire most until I heard from the servers, as those tables had ordered appetizers, which Kris and Tomás were working on in the *garde manger*. But two of the tickets had no apps, so I could start prepping their entrées.

"I got the veggie special and coq au vin for table two," Javier said.

"Great," I answered, wiping down a pair of sauté pans. "I'll do the scallops and duck for table five. Brian, you on those rib eyes?"

The grill cook raised his tongs above his head, revealing the orange-and-yellow flame he sported on the inside of his forearm. "Aye, aye, cap'n," he called back.

I had just set my seared scallops with potato-and-celery root purée onto the pass and was using the opportunity to take another look at the good-looking guy at table six when I heard a raised voice on the other side of the dining room.

"*Columbus* Day?" A woman with spiky black hair leaned back in her chair and let out an explosive laugh. "No way," she said, continuing to cackle. I didn't recognize her, but I did know two of the other people at the table: a professor at the university and her artist partner. They'd come into the restaurant before, with my pal Allison and her husband, Greg.

The professor—Louise, I think her name was—joined in the laughter, and I'm pretty sure I heard her say "Solari's" as she continued with the narrative that had triggered the other woman's outburst. After Louise finished speaking, the table turned as one toward the restaurant line where Javier and I stood with our pans at the Wolf range.

Looking down quickly to avoid their eyes, I returned

to my sauté cook duties. It was going to be a long eight days until that damn sister-cities dinner.

AN HOUR LATER, most of the second seating had been served their mains and the tickets were down to just four. Javier was stirring the beurre blanc reduction for the seared scallops, awaiting Brandon's call to fire the next course for one of the tables. As he tended his copper pot, the head chef whistled a tune that sounded a lot like Pharrell Williams's "Happy."

I wasn't surprised to see him in a good mood. His "friend" had been in again tonight, and Javier had just returned to the kitchen after visiting her for a few minutes out in the dining room.

"You certainly seem cheery," I said, leaning back on the stainless steel table that ran the length of the kitchen. "And I can't *imagine* why."

He glanced my way with a self-conscious smile.

I sidled up to the chef and poked him in the shoulder. "You're not still going to try to argue she's just some customer, are you?"

Javier knocked his stirring spoon against the lip of the pot and set it on the counter next to the stove. The self-conscious smile spread into an outright grin.

"I thought not," I said. "So who is she? Really."

"Her name is Natalie, and she's the pastry chef at the Full Moon Café." I knew this place well—a restaurant on the East Side of town, known for its desserts and baked goods.

"Oh, man, I *love* their baguettes! Good choice in a girlfriend, Javier."

"She's not my girlfriend," he replied. "Yet."

"Oh? Do tell."

"Well, I'm actually hoping to make some progress in that direction real soon. That is…" He turned to face me. "I was hoping you'd be willing to sub for me tomorrow night. She's asked me to go to a party with her. Even though we've known each other for a while now, this will be our first real date."

"Oh, man, I'm really sorry, Javier, but I can't. I'm hosting a dinner party of my own tomorrow. I've already got the fish marinating and everything."

His shoulders slumped. "Couldn't you maybe put it off till Sunday?"

"I have friends coming down from San Francisco and staying the night at my place, so that wouldn't work."

"Fine," Javier mumbled, and busied himself with adjusting the flame under the beurre blanc. His previous cheery countenance had now been replaced by a furrowed brow and pouty lower lip.

Damn. I hated disappointing him like this. His entire life was dedicated to Gauguin. There had to be a way we could work this out. Could Tomás maybe handle the *garde manger* on his own tomorrow so Kris could take Javier's place on the line?

I was startled out of my strategizing by Brandon's voice calling through the pick-up window: "Fire tables three and five!"

"Got it!" I answered back, and Javier and I set to work searing scallops, pan-frying pork chops, and deglazing our sauté pans with butter, chicken stock, and brandy. Neither of us spoke, and Javier kept his eyes focused on his cooking.

Once Brandon had taken all the plates out to the dining room, I cleaned my hands on my side towel and leaned once more against the stainless steel table behind me. Javier wiped down his pans and stacked them between sheets of paper towels, still refusing to meet my eye.

"Look, Javier," I said. "Maybe we could use—"

"It's okay," he interrupted. "I get it. You're the owner and I'm just an employee. Why should you have to change your schedule for me or, God forbid, work a little more?" Grabbing a damp cloth from the counter, he started cleaning the top of the Wolf range.

I stared at him, tears burning my eyes. Did he really think that?

"And besides," Javier went on, scraping at a patch of burnt matter with the metal spoon he kept in his chef's jacket pocket, "it's not as if *you'd* understand how important it is to go on a hot date."

TEN

"I BOUGHT A chocolate mousse cake for dinner tonight." Eric wrestled with the legs of his wooden easel, yanking them out, then lowering them back down again until they were the exact height he desired, and finally tightening down the wing nuts.

"Yum," I answered, and clamped a backing panel onto my already-set-up easel. Unlike Eric, who'd splurged on a fancy French job with its own built-in drawer for paints and brushes and other doodads, I'd gone for a bare-bones aluminum model. Mine might not have been as sturdy, but it took mere seconds to erect.

"I had to wait in line for about fifteen minutes this morning, there were so many people there, but it'll be worth it." Eric flipped his box-with-legs over, set it on the ground, and opened the lid. Raising the clamp, he attached his backing board to the easel, pulled open the drawer, and set about arranging his supplies.

"Where'd you get the cake?" I asked.

"The Full Moon Café."

"Oh."

I must have frowned, because Eric ceased his fiddling with brushes and paint tubes. "What? You don't like that place? Their German chocolate cake is amazing."

"No, it's not that. It just reminded me of something."

Javier's stinging words had kept me up half the night,

lying in bed trying to decide if he'd truly meant them or if he'd just been so upset that they'd flown out unintended. I wanted to believe that his reproof had no basis in reality, but my logical self reasoned that for those barbs to have come so quickly to the tongue, the issues must have been eating away at him for some time. Was I indeed a selfish boss?

Not until arriving at our plein air class out on the wharf had I been able to push the event from my mind. Listening to Omar expound on brushstrokes and complementary colors and negative space, I'd finally allowed myself to shake it off and focus on the moment: the sunlight sparkling on the water, the squawk of the gulls and gentle clack of bocce balls, the aroma of fried fish mingling with the harsh smoke of the old men's Toscano cigars.

But now Eric's comment had brought the bad thoughts flooding back.

He was clearly waiting for more of an answer, so I forced a light smile. "That's where Javier's new girlfriend works is all," I said. "And he and I had a little tiff last night about scheduling because of her." I wasn't sure if I even wanted to admit to Eric what the chef had said to me, and I certainly didn't want to discuss it here with all the other art students around.

This appeared to satisfy him, however, and he returned to his futzing. For today's painting, we'd been instructed to choose something on the wharf as our foreground, with the water and shoreline as the backdrop, and to concentrate in particular on the composition of our pieces. Most of the class, Eric and me included, had decided on the *Marcella* as our foreground subject, which was why Omar had chosen this spot for to-day's session.

The *Marcella* is an old Monterey-style "clipper"—just like Gino's—that's been refurbished and put on display out on the wharf. From the 1930s up until the Santa Cruz yacht harbor was constructed in the 1960s, these sturdy wooden boats constituted the Italian fishing fleet and would be hoisted up in inclement weather by the davits, or cranes, that used to line the wharf. Only a few of the old cranes remain—one used by the Coast Guard, the other two by private companies that rent wooden skiffs out by the hour to fishermen and tourists.

Doing my best to shake off the bad juju Eric's dessert choice had injected back into me, I concentrated on my composition. I selected a number four pencil from my paint box and sketched out the red, white, and green *Marcella*, choosing to omit the "Keep Off Boat Display" signs leaning against the wooden hull.

Next I roughed out my thumbnail of the water, sky, cliffs, and buildings beyond, once again taking artistic liberty and deleting the Dream Inn, which dominated the backdrop. I had decided to go for a vintage look, and the ten-story cinder block hotel hadn't been constructed till the early seventies. Digging through my lead tubes of gouache paint, I was searching for the ultramarine when I noticed that Eric had come to stand next to me.

"By the way," he said in a low voice, "I heard yesterday afternoon that the coroner's office is now thinking Gino's death might be a homicide after all."

"What? Why?"

"I don't know the details, but I guess the head wound was regular in shape—round, and not consistent with his being knocked against the piers. More like a baseball bat or something. So they're now thinking he was hit on purpose and then got the mussel fragments in the wound later, after whoever it was shoved him in the water."

"Huh." I chewed my lip, starting out across the inlet toward the surfers bobbing in the water at Steamer Lane.

"Yeah," Eric said. "So I just figured you'd want to know you may be right, after all, about there being foul play."

Was this a good or a bad thing? On the one hand, if true, it would take the pressure off Solari's for being what lawyers like to call a "proximate cause" of Gino's death. But on the other hand, the possibility that some-one had intentionally killed the old fisherman was a frightening thought.

I had finally located my tube of paint and was squeezing a line of the bright blue gouache onto my palette when I heard a shout from the direction of the bocce court, followed by a loud *thunk* and then a round of boisterous laughter.

I turned to see what had caused the commotion. An elderly man dressed in loose beige slacks and a white cotton shirt walked slowly from the bocce court toward the row of yellow rental skiffs leaning on their sides near the back of the Solari's building. He knelt down and then stood back up, a candy apple red ball in his bronzed hand, and the group back at the court cheered and applauded. But instead of joining in their laughter, the man glared at his fellow players and then, without warning, hurled the red ball their way, causing them to scatter like frightened pigeons.

Whoa, what a bad sport, I thought, and was about to return to my painting when I did one of those clas-sic double-takes. Because the natty gentleman with the silver hair and bad temper hadn't retrieved the ball from next to the row of rental boats, but rather from under the blue-and-white boat that sat next to them: my father's Boston Whaler 13-foot Classic. This was a limited-edition reissue of the 1960s version of the skiff, incorporating various modern amenities but retaining the cool, "retro" design and mahogany seats of the original. And my dad was gaga over the thing.

I waited until the men had returned to their game and then ambled across the courtyard to inspect the boat. Dad would not be pleased if there were now a ding in its immaculate paint job. Examining the hull and running my hand over its smooth surface, I determined that it was uninjured. *Good.*

As I stood back up, I glanced into the skiff and saw that one of its oars was out of place, leaning against the center bench. I shoved it where it belonged, next to the life jackets and rain tarp under the seat, and as I did so a piece of faded blue cloth poked out the other side of the bench. Was that a T-shirt of Dad's? Reaching down, I grabbed hold of the item, but immediately dropped it again as soon as I realized what I held in my hands. Definitely not a T-shirt.

It was Gino's fisherman's cap.

"WHAT WERE YOU doing over there?" Eric asked when I returned to my easel.

"Just checking on my dad's skiff. I wanted to make sure that guy's bocce ball hadn't put a hole in it. But it looks fine."

I didn't mention the cap. After checking to see that no one was watching, I'd tucked it under my shirt, where it still lay hidden. I waited for Eric to return to his painting, and once I was sure he'd lost interest in me, I pulled out one of the green plastic bags I always keep in my pocket (dog owners—at least responsible ones—will all relate). Facing away from Eric, I slipped the hat inside the bag and shoved it into my brown leather purse.

I know I should have told him about my discovery. But I was scared. Eric was a district attorney and would have been obliged, as an officer of the court, to turn over the evidence to the police. And since I'd found the cap in my father's boat—jammed under the seat as if it had been purposely hidden there—it looked bad. Real bad.

Up till now, the fact that Dad had scuffled with Gino and then ejected him from Solari's had worried me only because it showed knowledge of the old man's drinking problem. But with this new find, in conjunction with Eric's revelation that the cops were now treating Gino's death as a homicide, the altercation took on far graver proportions.

Had Dad even told the police about his fight with Gino? If he had, that, combined with the fisherman's cap being discovered hidden away in his boat, would certainly make them suspicious. And if he'd kept the information from the cops, once they found out it would look like he'd been trying to hide the event from them—even worse.

I had to talk to my dad before I did anything. No harm would come of my waiting a day or two to turn over the evidence. It was safely preserved in a plastic bag. Safer now, I reasoned, than it had been sitting unprotected in the boat.

Which just goes to show you can convince yourself of pretty much anything if you really put your mind to it.

THE ONE GOOD thing about discovering Gino's cap was that it served to supplant Javier's harsh words as my new current fixation. Nevertheless, I did my best to refocus on my painting and listened politely as Omar demonstrated how to wet our blank paper and then drop in a wash of white mixed with cobalt blue for what he called the "sky holes" between the puffy clouds rising up over the hills behind the city.

The dry, hot Diablo winds had finally dissipated and today was much cooler. I'd read in the paper that another storm would be moving in sometime the following week. We were now in that unsettled weather period between summer and fall when you never know if you should pack a tank top or a sweater and umbrella when you leave the house in the morning.

"As the paint diffuses and then dries," Omar said, "you can lay on some thicker white where you want the firmer edges of your cloud bodies to go." I did as directed, next dabbing in touches of gray and purple to add shadows to my clouds.

"Don't forget to keep stepping back from your work!" the instructor called out, and the class—as if the move had been choreographed in advance—simultaneously took several paces back from our easels.

Wow, that really worked. Up close it didn't seem particularly impressive, but from a little distance my white-and-blue splotches actually looked like a real sky.

As I moved on to my foreground subject, outlining the *Marcella*'s hull and then filling it in with a base layer of cadmium red, my eyes kept darting down to the leather bag sitting at the base of my easel. *Why would Gino's cap be in my father's fishing skiff?* The more I pondered this, the more I rushed through my painting.

It's hard to exercise patience when you know an article of clothing last seen on a dead man is hidden in the purse sitting at your feet.

By two thirty I'd completed my composition, a half hour before the end of class. We were supposed to have Omar assess our finished pieces before we took off, and I was worried I might get a lecture from the instructor about my slapdash work. But when I called him over to take a look, he nodded vigorously.

"Yes," he said, rewarding me with a broad smile. "It's nice to see you loosening up some, Sally. Your last two pieces have been rather tight, but this one is much more vibrant and alive. These brushstrokes here, for instance." Omar indicated the water, where I'd hurriedly slopped on a combination of blue, magenta, and gray, with some yellow and white for highlights, merely trying to get the painting finished as quickly as I could. "They show a real freedom of movement. Well done." He gave me a congratulatory pat on the shoulder and then moved on when another student called his name.

Huh. I stared at my work, trying to see it as he did.

"He's right, you know." Eric had come to stand next to me. "That's the problem with us lawyers. We're too controlling, which doesn't tend to translate well to making great art. But this really is good."

"Thanks," I said. "But I think it's only because I was trying to get it done quickly."

"Why? What's your hurry on such a beautiful afternoon as this?"

He was being so amiable that I was tempted to confide in him about finding Gino's cap. It always made me feel better to talk things through with Eric. Whereas my tendency was often toward excitability—especially these days with the hormonal changes I was going through—his default position was to consider the sensible and logical aspect of issues. So he was a good emotional backstop for me.

Should I tell him?

But then an image of my father and Gino grappling in the Solari's bar flashed through my mind, and I realized I couldn't tell Eric. Not yet. Not till I talked to Dad first.

"Oh, it's no big deal," I lied in answer to his question. "It's just that I need to talk to my dad about that stupid sister-cities dinner, and then I have to get home to make dinner for tonight, so I guess I'm just kind of feeling rushed for time."

He let it go at that, and I bent to organize my paints and brushes. Gouache dries quickly, so by the time I'd packed up my easel and supplies, my painting was ready to be slid into the portfolio I'd constructed for the class out of cardboard, duct tape, and string.

Waving good-bye to Omar, Eric, and the other students, I walked across the courtyard and pulled open the squeaky screen door into the Solari's dish room. Sean was at the sink, spraying down a stack of bus trays. "My dad still here?" I asked, and he jerked his head in the direction of the kitchen.

After dumping my gear in the office, I found Dad, not in the kitchen but in the dry storage room. He looked up from taking inventory of our red wines. "Hi, hon. How was class?"

"Well, no dead bodies today, so that's an improvement, I guess."

His mouth formed a smile not matched by his eyes.

"Sorry," I said, and took a seat atop a case of canned

San Marzano tomatoes. "But I actually did find something interesting today."

"Uh-huh?" He'd gone back to ticking off wines on his inventory list.

"Yeah. And I was wondering, when was the last time you took the skiff out on the water?"

He looked up from his clipboard. "Why do you ask?"

"I'll tell you after you answer." It broke my heart, having to interrogate my father like this, but I needed to hear what he had to say with no prompting from me.

Dad gave me a questioning look, but when I continued to hold my silence, he shook his head. "Okay, fine," he said, "be that way. It's been a while, a couple weeks maybe?"

"Do you know exactly when?"

He set the pen and clipboard on the shelf with the wine and then turned to face me, hands on his hips. "What is this, Sally?"

"Look, just bear with me. It could be important. Is there anything that might remind you of what day it was you went out?"

Sighing, he stared down at the floor as he considered. "Well, lemme see. It must have been a Tuesday morning, because I didn't have to get back for work. So, I guess the Tuesday before last. Satisfied now?"

The worst answer possible. At my slumped shoulders, his grin disappeared. "What?"

"That's the morning after Gino disappeared."

"So?"

"So I just found his blue fisherman's cap *in your skiff*. It had been shoved under the middle seat. I was out there for our painting class and noticed that one of the oars was out of place, and the cap slid out when I put the oar where it belongs."

"How do you know it's his?"

"C'mon, Dad. Everyone knows that cap. It's not like anyone else around here ever wore one like it." Gino's hat was what I believe is called a Genovese seaman's cap—kind of like a puffy beret with a wide brim at the front. And his was made all the more distinctive by the fact that its once-navy dye job had faded over the years to a sort of light denim color.

"But how could it have gotten in my boat?"

"That's what I'm wondering," I said. "And what the police will wonder, too, once they find out about it."

Dad's blue eyes grew wide as the implications of my discovery registered. "But you can't think I had anything to do with his death?"

"Of course not. But you've got to admit it looks bad. Especially since I just heard from Eric that they're now treating his death as a possible homicide."

"Oh, no," he said, his mouth going slack.

I considered Dad's Boston Whaler. There was definitely enough room to hide a body inside, and Dad kept a big tarp in the skiff to cover it during inclement weather. A tarp that could easily hide a dead body. "Look, even though I may not believe you had anything to do with his death," I said, the fear no doubt showing in my face as well, "others certainly could. Especially since you and Gino fought just the day before he went missing."

"Oh, God…" My dad sat—or more like collapsed—onto a stack of beer cases that had been delivered that morning. "What do you think's gonna happen?"

"So you never saw his cap in your boat?"

"No, I swear."

"Who knows you went fishing that morning?"

"Well, Johnny and Ralph, since they were operating the davit. But anyone who was out there when I left or came back would have seen me, too. So tons of people. It's not like I was trying to hide it from anyone."

"But I take it you didn't tell the cops about this fishing trip when they were at the restaurant?"

Dad shook his head, his blank eyes staring at the floor. "No, they only seemed interested in how Gino was acting that night at dinner and didn't ask about anything else. It seemed pretty clear they thought he must have just fallen in the water and drowned. So it never even occurred to me that my going fishing could be relevant."

"How about your fight with Gino? Did you tell the cops about that?" He didn't answer. "'Cause it's hard to say *that's* not pertinent."

"But it's *not*." Dad shot up off the beer cases, fists clenched. "That had nothing to do with his death."

"Well, that's probably more for the police to decide than you. If nothing else, it's evidence of him drinking too much on a previous occasion, and of his proclivity for fighting. And once they find out, they're going to also know that you withheld the information."

Perhaps I was being a little too hard on my father. He was, after all, no more guilty than I of withholding evidence. In fact, that was very likely the reason for my peevishness. We often react most strongly to the things in others that remind us of our own flaws.

But also, I had to admit, my irritation with him for dragging me once more back to Solari's wasn't helping. Yet every time I was tempted to finally have it out with him about this, something more pressing came up. How could I give him grief about some stupid dinner when I'd just discovered a murdered man's cap in his fishing skiff?

Dad slumped and his arms went limp. "You think I should go down to the police station and tell them?"

I considered a moment and then shook my head. "I don't think it would hurt if we held off for just a bit. I've been doing some poking around about Gino and who knows? Maybe I'll find out something that *will* make all of the stuff involving you irrelevant."

He smiled. "That's my girl."

ELEVEN

"YOU THINK IT'S warm enough to eat outside?" Ripping open a packet of shrimp crackers, I dumped its contents into the wooden bowl my guests had already cleaned out once. Buster sat at my feet, hoping for an errant treat to come tumbling his way.

Nichole and Mei, who'd driven all the way down from San Francisco, had arrived for dinner right on time at six o'clock, followed shortly by Allison and Greg, who'd come up from Aptos. Eric, however, whose condo is only about two miles from me, had finally waltzed in just ten minutes ago—almost a half hour late. Some things never change.

"Sure," Nichole called over the clatter of ice cubes striking glass. "We can always put on sweaters. And we might as well take advantage of the weather. There aren't going to be many more nights when al fresco dining is even a possibility." She snatched a cracker from the bowl and then went back to making our second round of drinks. We were a thirsty as well as hungry bunch.

Kneeling down to rummage in the cupboard under the silverware drawer, I came up with a large white tablecloth. "Okay, let's eat at the picnic table, then. And we can use this." I unfolded the cloth to display a 1950s-style map of the United States, complete with colorful line drawings of items associated with each region: a retro movie camera for California, several varieties of cactus for New Mexico, a red lobster for Maine, and two fishermen in a canoe for Minnesota.

As Nichole and I came back out to the patio, Buster following me and the bowl of rice crackers, Allison jumped up to help us set the table. "Typical guys," Nichole remarked with a snort as Eric and Greg remained seated.

"Hey, I always help with the dishes," Eric replied. "That's our job, right?"

"Right," said Greg, flexing his bicep. "It's what we manly men do."

Mei stretched out further on her lounge chair and sipped from her Martini. "And I researched and purchased the wine, and am therefore excused from all further labors tonight."

In Eric's defense, he's actually pretty good about stuff like this. So when I headed back inside twenty minutes later for the last-minute dinner prep, he followed me into the kitchen and asked what he could do to help. There wasn't much, as I'd planned a menu with little last-minute work, but I got him busy setting out plates and dishing into small bowls the pickled cucumbers I'd prepared that morning.

"Oh, man, I love *sunomono*," he said as he divided the thinly sliced cucumbers among the six bowls. "Is the whole meal Japanese?"

"Yep. Just to show how much I love you, even if you can be super annoying sometimes."

My black cod—which they call sablefish in the food biz—had now been marinating for two days in a mixture of sake, mirin, white miso, and sugar, so the sweet and savory flavors had fully penetrated the fish's delicate flesh. Scraping the excess marinade off the fillets, I pan-fried them in a blistering-hot cast iron skillet till their skin was a toasty brown, then flipped them over onto a roasting pan and set it in the oven. "These'll only take about five minutes," I said to Eric, "so you want to start corralling folks over to the table and open the wine?"

While waiting for the cod to finish cooking, I set about plating up the side dishes. I'd settled on steamed white rice with a little black rice added for texture and color, as well as roasted baby bok choy with a sesame-shoyu glaze.

Eric returned to the kitchen as I was arranging a small nest of pickled ginger next to each piece of black cod. "Perfect timing," I said, and we carried the plates out to the picnic table. I made Eric go back for the last one, since he does not possess my three-at-a-time skill gained from years as a waitress.

"To the cook!" Nichole said once we were all settled, and all five guests raised their glasses in a toast.

The table quieted down for an entire minute—long enough for everyone to taste their food and murmur "yum"—before conversation started up again.

Greg was the first to speak. "So tell us about discovering that the old guy washed up on the beach," he said. "I gather you have my lovely wife to blame for being there to find it?"

Allison swatted him on the arm. "She might not want to talk about it, you know?"

"It's okay," I said. "It's not as if it's not on my mind, anyway. And yes, I do place the blame a hundred percent on you, Allison, since you're the one who told me about Omar's class."

Nichole leaned forward, eagerness radiating from her round face and baby blue eyes. "Since you're willing to talk about it," she said, "he's someone you knew, right?"

"Uh-huh. A fisherman who used to come into the Solari's bar most afternoons. And as you probably know if you read the local paper, there's a bunch of folks who blame us for his death. They say he was drunk when he left the restaurant and that's why he fell in the water and drowned."

"But didn't he have a mark on his head?" Greg asked. "That's what I read, anyway."

"Yeah, he did," Eric answered. "So at this point—and this is in strict confidence, okay?" He waited for solemn nods from all of us before continuing. "Okay. So they're actually thinking it might be a homicide."

"*Dude*." Nichole said, and then turned and poked me in the ribs. "You gonna investigate, try to find his murderer?"

"All I said was that they think it *might* be a homicide," Eric repeated, "not that they're sure that's what it was."

But everyone at the table—except Eric, that is—continued to stare at me, waiting for an answer to Nichole's question. I took a sip of Gewürztraminer and savored its notes of lemon peel and ginger. Mei had chosen well for our meal. "Well," I finally said, setting down my glass, "I actually have been doing a little snooping around."

"I *knew* it." Nichole punctuated her exclamation with another jab to my midsection.

"*Ow*. Stop that, or I won't say any more." She bowed her head contritely and forked a piece of fish. "Anyway," I went on, "here's the thing. Gino, the old fisherman who died, had only two beers at Solari's that night, along with a full dinner. And the waitress who served him swears he wasn't drunk when he came in. But other people say he was acting weird after he left the restaurant. So it just seems like there's something fishy going on. No pun intended," I added when Nichole barked out a laugh.

"Maybe somebody slipped him a Mickey," Greg said, and then chuckled.

"That's actually not that far-fetched." I recounted what I knew about Anastasia, how she had dined with Gino the last night he was seen and how since then she'd been hanging out with Angelo.

"But why would she want to slip something in his drink?" Allison asked. "It's not like young women are known for drugging old men to take advantage of them."

Mei lifted her wine glass and studied its straw-colored liquid, now backlit by the setting sun. "There's a different kind of 'advantage' than what you're thinking," she said.

Several voices piped up in unison: "Money!"

"And I'm pretty sure Gino was relatively wealthy," I agreed. "He owned a boat, which has to be worth a bundle, and a house just a block from the water. If that was paid off…"

Everybody nodded at this. Anyone who lives in the Bay Area knows how pricey real estate is in Santa Cruz, especially houses near the coastline.

Allison set her fork down and reached for the wine bottle. "I still don't see how slipping the guy a Mickey could get her money, besides maybe what he had in his wallet that night."

"True." I ate another piece of fish (perfectly cooked, I was pleased to note—crispy skin, but tender and flaky inside) and considered the mysterious woman. "Angelo said she was writing a story for the *Santa Cruz Tribune*, but there's not a paper called that, is there?"

Eric pulled out his phone and did a search. "No," he said after a moment. "Nothing comes up with that name—no newspaper, magazine, journal, e-zine, anything." He slid the phone back in his pocket. "She's definitely up to something."

"Agreed," I said. "Pretending to be a journalist would be the perfect cover for asking lots of invasive questions. But what would she have to gain from that? Or from flirting like she did with Gino? A couple dinners out doesn't seem like enough reason. And now, just a week after throwing herself on Gino, she's doing the same thing with Angelo."

Of course, Gino was no longer in the picture, I mused as I cut a piece of bok choy. *Angelo must simply be her number two choice for whatever she's after.* And then I flashed on a film I'd seen years ago.

"Remember that movie *Black Widow*?" I asked. "You know, about the woman who marries rich, lonely men, gets them to name her in their will, and then kills them off? What if that was what Anastasia was up to? You know, she pretends to be a journalist as a way to meet the guys, then seduces them."

"Assuming that was her MO, I'd say she jumped the gun if she did kill Gino," Mei said.

"Not if he'd already put her in his will." Greg turned toward Eric. "Have they found one?"

Eric nodded as he finished chewing the enormous bite he'd just taken. "Yes, but he gave it all to a brother who's no longer alive. So it'll end up going to some distant relative."

"Unless…" Nichole had a gleam in her eye.

"Unless they'd already gotten married before he died," Mei finished.

"Ohmygod, maybe that's the reason Gino was so animated that night," Allison said. "Maybe it was a *wedding* dinner." She looked from Eric to Nichole to me—all the lawyers (or ex, in my case) at the table. "Those are public records, right, marriage certificates?"

"They are," I said. "And I know exactly where to find them. I think a visit to the county clerk's office might be in order for Monday morning."

TWELVE

"OF COURSE THEY had to use a permanent marker," Dad grumbled as he scrubbed unsuccessfully at the writing on Solari's front door. Someone had scrawled "COLUMBUS DIDN'T DISCOVER AMERICA, HE INVADED IT!" across the red paint, and it was not washing off.

"Here." He thrust the soapy brush toward Sean, who—along with the others who'd just arrived for work—had stopped to see what was going on. "You keep on trying to get it off while I go see if we have any of the right paint to cover this up." Striding past me and my bike, he refused to meet my eye. No one likes to be proved wrong, especially my father, Mario Solari.

I'd stopped by the restaurant to pick up a cannoli for a post-ride treat and had been planning on going directly home. But seeing Dad's frustration, I took pity on him and wheeled my bike around to the back of the restaurant and into the dish room. Maybe I could help him get rid of the graffiti before we opened.

He was in the storage room, poking around the shelf holding cans of paint and wood varnish, tubes of window putty, brushes, rollers, and rat traps.

"Don't you say it," he growled as I came into the room.

"I wasn't going to. I just wanted to see if you'd like me to paint that over so you can get the kitchen set up is all. And hey," I added, trying to diffuse the situation, "I've had a lot of practice painting of late. Maybe I can add some clouds to the door, or a boat or something."

Ignoring my attempt at levity, Dad reached for a small can near the back of the shelf and examined the paint splotches on the lid. "I think this is the right one," he said, handing it to me. "And thanks."

That was all I was going to get. But it was a lot, given the situation.

Taking a paintbrush, drop cloth, and a couple of rags from the shelf, I headed back out front. Sean hadn't had any more success cleaning off the felt marker than my father, so I thanked him for his efforts and told him he could go get to work inside. At least the door was now clean and ready for my paint. And as long as the marker didn't bleed through, it would be an easy job.

As I was putting on the last strokes, feathering them as best I could to match the texture underneath, a man walked up and stood behind me, watching. "Well, look at that," he said. "Who woulda guessed you're such a good little painter."

I wheeled around. It was Bobby, giving me what I took to be a superior, I'm-the-painter-you're-just-a-girl grin. I turned back to my work. "Haven't you got anything better to do than harass people?"

"What?" he said, actually sounding a little hurt. "It was a compliment."

"Uh-huh. I'm sure you would have said the exact same thing to Sean if it had been him painting the door." But then I remembered I wanted to ask Bobby if he'd known about Gino's will. *Better make nice with him.* "So, what brings you out to the wharf this fine morning, anyway?"

He kicked at the asphalt with his heel. "My dad asked me to come down and help out at the store. The guy that was supposed to be there with him this afternoon called in sick. And I could really use the money now, so I didn't really have the choice to say no."

"Bummer," I said. "I completely understand. Nothing like being part of a family business. You're never really off work, right?"

This time the smile seemed more genuine. "Yeah, totally. But it also sucks 'cause I couldn't get to sleep till really late last night and so I'm super tired." A large yawn confirmed this fact. "So how come you're painting the door? Some gangbanger tag ya?"

"Uh-huh," I answered, not wanting to further publicize the actual content of the graffiti. I wiped the edges of my paint can clean with a rag, buying time while I tried to come up with a story to go with what I wanted to ask Bobby.

Ah, got it.

"So, I actually had a question for you," I said, tapping the can closed with the end of my brush and then setting the brush on the lid. "I met this guy who's looking to buy one of those old-style fishing boats, and it occurred to me that he might be interested in Gino's. You by any chance know what'll happen to it?"

"I have no idea," he said. "I guess some relative will inherit it, right?"

"Right. If he has any, that is. I gather his will gave everything to a brother who's now dead, so his next of kin stands to get it all."

Bobby's expression displayed no surprise at this information. "Then I guess whoever that is might be interested in selling the boat to your friend. Unless they live around here, that is, and are into fishing. 'Cause it would be a pain to transport a boat like that anywhere far."

"I guess I'll just have to find out who does inherit it and then ask them," I said. "Does it surprise you to hear Gino gave it all to his brother?"

Bobby shrugged. "Not really. I never really thought about it."

"I only ask 'cause I thought that maybe since you'd been so helpful to him over the past few years with his boat and around the house, and since he didn't have any kids or anything, maybe he would have given you his boat."

"Why would he do that?" Bobby leaned forward and stared at me as if I were completely loony tunes. "It's gotta be worth a ton, and I'm not even related to him. No one would do something like that." He straightened up with a shake of the head.

"Well, you yourself said it seemed as if Gino thought of you almost like a son, so it wouldn't be all that weird, really. And it would also make sense if you were therefore maybe feeling a little, I dunno…bitter to find out that his entire estate is going to someone he barely even knew."

"You don't get it, do you?" Bobby shoved his balled fists into the front pockets of his jeans, arms stiff. But his right foot, I noticed, was tapping out a rapid beat. "The last thing I was ever thinking about was what would happen if Gino died. We were good buds—*and* he was paying me a good salary, too. The best work I ever had, actually. Now, not only have I lost a friend but I also lost my job, and so I gotta come in like some loser and work for my *dad*." He turned to glare in the direction of the gift shop three doors down from Solari's.

That was certainly one thing Bobby and I could agree on.

As I WAS heading for the Solari's office, a fat cannoli in my hand, Sean called out from the dish room. "You got a minute?" the busboy asked, and I motioned for him to follow me into the tiny room.

I took a seat at the desk and he found a spot between my bike and the metal storage shelf where he could lean against the wall. "What is it?" I asked, then took a large bite of the crunchy, cream-filled dessert.

"It's just that I remembered something else about that night when Gino had dinner here. I'd forgotten about it until this morning, when I saw these two bocce players arguing behind the restaurant." Sean took a step toward me and lowered his voice. "Seeing them reminded me that I saw Gino that night in that exact same place arguing with some guy."

"Really?" I set the cannoli down on the metal desk. "What guy? Tell me exactly what you saw."

"Okay." Sean took a deep breath. "So a while after Gino and that woman left the restaurant, I'm out back taking a break and I see Gino with this other guy, and they were really getting into it."

"What do you mean, 'getting into it'?"

"You know, like arguing an' all. I couldn't tell what they were saying, but Gino seemed kind of out of it. He was swaying, sort of, and his voice was a little slurred."

"Did you recognize the other man?"

Sean shook his head. "I knew it was Gino from his voice, and I could also tell 'cause he had on that hat he always wore. But it was too dark to see who the other guy was."

"Well, can you tell me *anything* about him?"

"Sorry," Sean said, shaking his head. "That's pretty much it. But since they were out by the bocce court, I'm thinking it coulda been one of those old Italian dudes who hang out there all the time. He was kinda hunched over, like an old guy."

I frowned, staring out at the servers readying the dining room for the lunch service. It sure sounded like whoever Sean had seen arguing with Gino that night could have been the last person to see him alive.

And therefore could also be his murderer.

I WAS AT the Solari's coffee station helping myself to a cup of regular to chase down that rich cannoli when I heard a familiar baritone laugh. Angelo was at his usual table, sipping from his own cup of coffee. As I watched, Giulia set a pair of to-go containers down on the table and poured him a refill. Once she'd left, I walked over to the red leather booth. "You're dressed awful spiffy today," I said, indicating his dark suit and red tie.

"I was at Gino's funeral this morning. Sit, please," he added, as I hovered over his table. "I'm meeting someone in a little bit, but I can stay and chat for a couple minutes."

Could that someone be Anastasia? I wondered as I complied, setting my coffee down before me. *A romantic picnic in some secluded spot, perhaps?* But I kept this thought to myself. "Oh," I said. "I didn't even know the funeral was happening or I would have attended. Was it a full mass?"

He shook his head. "Just a short service at the funeral home, but the parish priest was there. And the burial was private, so I didn't go. I think it's happening right now."

"Were many people at the service?"

"No, not many. A couple women from the church who go to all the parishioners' funerals, and a relative— a second cousin or something who came out from back East. Oh, and Bobby was there, too." Angelo drained his cup, then raised his arm to signal Giulia to bring his check.

"Huh." I sipped my coffee as I considered this. It made sense for Bobby to have been there, given how close he and Gino had been. "This cousin who was at the funeral, he was the only relative there?"

Angelo's eyes were following the rotund waitress as she crossed the dining room floor, but he turned back at my question. "As far as I know. He's the son of Gino's cousin, I heard someone say. And I think he may be the only living relation. He came out here to organize the funeral and deal with Gino's effects."

"I bet he's the one who's going to inherit his estate. Was anyone else there?"

"Just some of us old geezers who've known Gino forever—a few of his bocce buddies and several other fishermen."

"I didn't know he played bocce," I said.

"Well, he hadn't much lately. He made himself not all that welcome when he started cheating. Oh, thank you, *cara mia*." Angelo gave Giulia a wink as she set the bill down on the table, prompting a giggle from the waitress.

"Cheating? That seems kind of petty."

The fisherman smiled. "The way I heard it, Gino was nudging his balls closer to the *pallino*—you know, the little white ball you try to get your ball nearest to—when he thought the others weren't looking. Except they were, of course. And then he'd argue and deny it. After a while, no one wanted to play with him anymore."

"Well, you know what they say about Italians having a reputation for cheating and scamming, how they'll take advantage of you if you give them half the chance."

Angelo didn't join in my laughter. "Not so," he said, thrusting his chin forward. "At least not the ones here, who came from Liguria. We may be shrewd bargainers, but we've also always been respected for our integrity." He leaned forward, elbows on the table. "In fact, the Genovese down here in Santa Cruz were so well known for their honesty and paying their bills on time, my father could buy a whole year's supply of spaghetti, aged cheese, and olive oil on credit from the grocers up there in San Francisco."

"But what about all the rum runners I've heard about who were in Santa Cruz back in the twenties, you know, during Prohibition. They were Italian, right?"

"They were not from around here. And besides, their families were mostly from Naples and Sicily—not Genoa." Angelo chuckled. "Of course, I'm not saying all the Genovese were—or are—perfect. They could be very competitive, especially when it came to fishing."

"Oh, yeah?"

"Absolutely. And there's still lots of rivalry, mind you, over who catches the most fish, who makes the most money." Angelo picked up the check, examined it, then reached for his billfold. "I've even heard stories of lines and nets being cut by other fishermen."

"Whoa. That's not cool. Does it still go on, the line cutting and stuff?"

Angelo poked around inside, searching for the correct bills. In what seemed like slow motion, he finally extracted a twenty and a ten, smoothed them out on the table, and returned the wallet to his front pocket. "No," he finally said, his eyes on a new foursome that had arrived at the bocce court and were taking practice throws. "Those days are long gone."

THIRTEEN

NEITHER DAD NOR I mentioned the graffiti incident during Sunday dinner that afternoon. I didn't want to rub his nose in what pretty much confirmed the fears I'd expressed about the whole Columbus Day thing, but at the same time I took my father's silence as a sort of concession that I'd been right after all.

It was a hollow victory, though, as there was no going back at this point. "Let's just hope that defacing the restaurant door is the worst of it," I said to Buster as we pulled away from my grandmother's house.

Utterly stuffed from Nonna's Sunday gravy—and in Buster's case, all the tidbits she'd snuck him under the table—the two of us returned home after the meal for a nap. Like Bobby, I was also suffering from lack of sleep, since my dinner party the night before hadn't ended till almost one. Nichole and Mei had slept in and were only just getting ready to drive home to San Francisco when I'd gotten back from my bike ride and then the long detour at Solari's. After seeing them off, I'd had barely enough time for a quick shower and dog walk before heading off to Nonna's.

Buster and I dozed for about an hour, but at four o'clock I had to rouse myself to go to work at Gauguin. The dog, however, stayed put, shifting position just enough to roll over onto the warm spot I'd left by vacating the bed.

A half hour later, I pulled the T-Bird up to the side entrance of the restaurant, switched off the ignition, and stared through the *garde manger* window at Tomás, already at work on his dinner prep. I hadn't talked to Javier since our spat Friday night, and the prospect of seeing him again was making my palms sweat. Of course, it could also have been another hot flash. But the tightness in my shoulders and gut suggested otherwise.

The chef was up in the office, talking on his cell. I could tell from his giggles and animated voice that it was *her* on the other end—Natalie. Not wanting to eavesdrop (okay, so I did *want* to, but I restrained myself), I waited in the stairwell until all was quiet.

He was grinning at something on his laptop when I came into the room, but the smile disappeared when he saw me. "How was your dinner party?" he asked, closing the screen.

I didn't detect any sarcasm in his question, but then again, I was pretty sure he didn't want a detailed response either. "Fine," I said, and took a seat in the wing chair across from him. "Was it busy again last night?"

"Seventy-three covers," he said. "So, yeah, we were pretty slammed."

"Dang." Gauguin had only twelve tables for four, so that meant some had to have been double seatings. "How many reservations for tonight?"

"Eight tables so far."

I nodded. That wasn't a bad number for a Sunday. "So, look, Javier, I wanted to talk about what happened—"

"I know," he said, cutting me off. "Me, too. And I'm sorry I said what I did."

"Sorry you *said* it," I repeated. "Okay…does that

mean you really do feel that way, but you're just sorry you let it slip out?"

Javier didn't respond right away, instead picking up the small carved wooden tiki on the desk that he liked to rub with his thumb when anxious, much as a Greek might finger a set of worry beads. *Uh-oh, not good.*

He replaced the tiki and leaned back in his chair, lips pursed. "It's not that I don't think you're a good boss," he finally said, "because you are. You've been great, actually. It's just that, I dunno…" Running a hand through his fine, black hair, he exhaled slowly, like an athlete preparing for a feat of strength. "I guess maybe I've been thinking I don't want to have a boss anymore, even a great one. That maybe it's time to go off and, how do you say? Spread open my wings and start my own restaurant."

I gaped at Javier. *He can't have just said what I think he did.* But the combination of discomfort and elation he was displaying was answer enough. *Ohmygod. He did.*

You know how your face feels when you've experienced a shock—as if your muscles are frozen in place and all the blood has suddenly drained away? Well, that's exactly the sensation I had. And I must have looked as bad as I felt, because as soon as Javier finally glanced up to meet my eye, he started out of his chair.

"No, I'm okay," I said, waving him back. "Okay, maybe not *okay*…but I'm not going to faint or anything." I tried to smile but pretty much failed. A series of emotions were sweeping through me: disbelief, anxiety, anger. Ultimately, though, the one that overwhelmed all the others was fear.

No, more like abject panic.

What would I do if Javier left? The idea of running Gauguin without its head chef was unthinkable. Not only was he the heart and soul of the place, but I had no clue how I could possibly carry on without his experience and expertise. Plus, I knew I'd never find anyone I got along with or trusted as much as him. He was irreplaceable.

Neither of us spoke. And if my expression was reflecting even one quarter of the despondency I felt, I could see why Javier was hesitant to say any more. For my part, I was merely afraid that whatever I tried to articulate would come out as a wail.

After what seemed like an uncomfortably long pause in our conversation, I finally got it together enough to ask, "So, when…?"

"Not right away," he answered quickly. "It would obviously take a while. Me and Natalie have been talking, and she wants to get in a little more time at the Full Moon Café running the pâtisserie before she goes out on her own."

"Oh. So you're thinking of opening up a place with Natalie?" That explained things. But it also made them hurt all the more. How could he possibly choose someone he'd known only a few months over Gauguin? And over me…

Javier tried to hide it, but his eyes betrayed the excitement he felt at the prospect of starting a restaurant with his new flame.

"Uh-huh," he answered, bobbing his head vigorously. "I've been saving up for the down payment on a house, but if I move in with her I can use what I've saved for the restaurant instead. And she just inherited a little money, so we figure by combining our cash we should have enough—for a small place, anyway."

"Sounds like you're already decided, then. That it's not just a 'maybe.'"

I tried to hold his eyes but he turned away, just as Buster would have if he knew he'd done something wrong.

"So there's nothing I can do to get you to stay?" I was trying to control the trembling in my voice but was having a hard time of it. "'Cause I'll be better, Javier, I swear. You just need to tell me what to do to make it okay; I'll do whatever you say."

But he merely frowned and reached once more for the tiki.

THE SANTA CRUZ COUNTY offices are located in a concrete-and-glass edifice, designed in what's colorfully termed the "modern brutalist" school of architecture, a style favored by governments and other large institutions for projects during the late 1960s. Though flanked by soaring redwood trees that help soften its appearance, the blocky five-story structure isn't much to look at, in my opinion. But the view from *inside* the building, which overlooks the San Lorenzo River and adjoining park, is lovely.

I knew the place well from my days as a lowly associate attorney, for not only had I paid frequent visits to the county clerk's office to file and consult court documents, but I'd also passed many a long hour in the law library doing legal research for the memos, motions, and appeals I'd spent my days drafting.

Since the district attorney's office was on the second floor of the same building, Eric and I had sometimes met for coffee or lunch in the cafeteria, which was down in the basement along with the law library, when I had a research project at the law library. Their coffee wasn't all that great, but they always had a selection of doughnuts and other sweet treats, perfect for that much-needed three o'clock sugar rush to get me through the rest of the afternoon.

Today, as I found a spot in the two-hour section of the County Building parking lot, I thanked my lucky stars I didn't have to spend the morning in the fluorescent-lit library flipping through musty casebooks. Running a restaurant can be stressful and exhausting, but I wouldn't go back to pumping out those billable hours if you paid me the senior partner's salary.

Taking the stairs two at a time, I went up one floor and rounded the corner into the county recorder's office. The man at the receptionist counter was on the telephone, so I waited for him to finish his call.

"I'm sorry," he was saying, "but we can't take requests by phone. You need to either come down here in person or send in your request by mail if you want a certified copy of the deed." He listened a moment and then spoke again, the testiness in his voice now a notch higher. "No, it doesn't matter what company you represent; the same rule applies to everyone." A pause. "Yes. That's right. Good-bye."

He hung up the receiver and turned to me with a sigh.

"That must get old fast," I said.

"Yeah, and it's not even ten yet. So what can I do for you?"

"Well, my father is the head of the biggest construction company in the state, and I was wondering if you could print out for me free copies in triplicate of every lien against his corporation recorded in the county during the past six months."

His expression remained serious till about halfway through my sentence, at which point he laughed, slapping his palm on the black laminate countertop. "Good one."

"Nah, it was actually pretty lame," I said. "But I couldn't resist. So anyway, what I really want to know is how I can find out whether someone has recorded a marriage license in the county."

"Well, if it was after 1997, it's been digitized and scanned, and you can look it up on the index on one of those computers over there." He indicated a row of ancient computer terminals behind me.

"Oh, great. Thanks."

I took a seat at the nearest computer and, once I'd figured out how the index system worked, entered the name "Gino Barbieri." Nothing came up. The man had now left the front desk and was at a file cabinet flipping through manila folders. "Can I ask you something else?"

"Sure," he said, holding his place with his thumb.

"The name I'm looking for isn't there, but it occurs to me that it might be too soon to be in your system. How long does it take for a recorded marriage license to show up on the index?"

"It usually takes ten business days from the time the marriage officiant turns it in for it to show up in the system. You know when the officiant brought it down here?"

"I have no idea. In fact, I have no idea if the guy I'm looking for even got married or not. But thanks, that helps a lot."

I counted back ten business days from today: that would have been the Monday that Gino was last seen, the day he had dinner at Solari's. So if he and Anastasia had been celebrating their marriage by dining at Solari's that night, as Allison had suggested during the dinner party at my house, and the officiant had submitted the license the next day, today would be the earliest it could show up on the computer. Which meant I'd have to keep checking back if I wanted to know for sure.

But is it even worth it? I wondered as I logged off and gathered up my bag and sweater. Allison's idea had sounded terribly clever at the time, but now that all the bourbon and Gewürztraminer I'd consumed that night were no longer clouding my judgment, it seemed far more implausible than clever.

Once out into the corridor, I pulled out my phone and sent Eric a text: "Here in bldng. Meet for coffee downstairs?" The district attorney's reception desk was only about twenty feet down the hall from where I was standing, but if I went up and asked for him, all his co-workers would know he was playing hooky. This way, he could pretend it was business calling him away.

"Sure. Be there in ten," his answer came.

I was about to stow my cell back in my bag when a familiar figure emerged from the DA's office and headed for the elevator. The sight of the man's shaved head and burly frame triggered a wave of prickles across my shoulders and back. Spinning around to face the wall, I pretended to study the phone's screen, hoping he wouldn't notice me.

It was Detective Vargas of the SCPD, a man whose acquaintance I'd made under less than delightful circumstances the previous April, when (in his view, anyway) I'd poked my nose inappropriately into the investigation of my aunt's murder.

I never relished a conversation with him, but right

now I felt an extra need to avoid the detective. Ever since finding Gino's cap, I'd been feeling guilty about not turning it over to the police and instead stashing it in the bottom of my sock-and-underwear drawer.

I was planning to give the cap to the police. Just not yet. Not until I'd had a little more time to prove my father had no involvement in the old fisherman's death. Nevertheless, the idea of making small talk with Vargas, all the while keeping the evidence from him, gave me a severe case of the jitters.

The detective strode past without even glancing my way and punched the button for the elevator. I continued to hunch over my phone until the door had closed behind him and then hightailed it for the stairwell. *Bullet dodged. For now.*

Since I had at least fifteen minutes to kill (no way would Eric get down to the cafeteria as soon as he'd promised), I popped into the law library to say hi to the head librarian, whom I'd gotten to know well during my years as a frequent patron. She wasn't around, however, so instead I wandered the floor-to-ceiling stacks, enjoying the luxury of watching other research attorneys besides me pore through their pile of casebooks, searching for that elusive perfect legal opinion to prove their argument right.

As I strolled past a shelf lined with civil law treatises, one on wills and trusts caught my eye. Pulling down the heavy volume, I carried it to a nearby table and flipped to the section on omitted spouses. I knew there was a California statute protecting a husband or wife who had not been provided for in a testamentary document and was curious to see what the exact language was. Because, if the mysterious Anastasia *had* married Gino, he likely wouldn't have had time to draft a new will including her before he died.

The book summarized the law nicely: "In general, a surviving spouse who is omitted from a will or trust that was executed by the deceased spouse prior to the marriage is entitled to a statutory share of the deceased spouse's estate." There were exceptions listed (this is, after all, the law we're talking about), but none seemed likely to apply to Anastasia.

I returned the book to its shelf, walked back out to the cavernous basement hallway, and headed for the cafeteria. About a dozen people were in the place, but Eric was not one of them. They no longer sold doughnuts, so I bought a large coffee and a croissant and found a table in the corner where I could spot my tardy ex as he came in.

Watching a lawyer I recognized lean across the table to consult in a low voice with her clients, I considered the language I'd just read in the wills-and-trusts treatise. What it meant was that if Anastasia and Gino had in fact married, she would get all of his estate. Since the brother he'd willed everything to was no longer alive, Gino had, in effect, died without a will, and she'd therefore be the sole heir.

Could she have gotten the fisherman to marry her, and then knocked him out and shoved him off the edge of the wharf? It did seem more like a movie plot than real life, but I knew from my attorney days that fact could, indeed, sometimes be far stranger than fiction.

I'd finished all of my croissant and most of my coffee by the time Eric showed up. He flashed me a "just a sec" sign and got in line behind a group of women who'd come into the cafeteria just ahead of him. Five minutes later, he finally plopped down on the red chair across from me.

"Sorry," he said, setting his coffee and two blueberry muffins on the table. "Right as I was about to leave, I got waylaid by Nate, who wanted to talk about his new case—that guy who embezzled fifty grand from the Korean restaurant out in Capitola."

"Oh yeah, I read about it in the paper the other day. A bookkeeper with a gambling habit, right?"

"Yep. And he wasn't too good at it, either. The gambling, that is. Hence the need for cash. But, man." Eric shook his head. "I gather the guy had been with the restaurant for like twenty years. You'd think he'd have some sort of loyalty for the place after that amount of time."

"Uh-huh…" I said, then bit my lip and looked away.

"What?"

"Oh, it just reminded me of Javier, is all. The part about loyalty." I recounted what the chef had told me the night before, doing my best to keep my voice steady and my eyes from tearing up.

Eric frowned and took a large bite of his muffin. "That would be pretty cold," he finally said after washing it down with a slug of coffee. "After you saved his ass from jail last spring? And then promoted him to executive chef to boot?"

"Yeah, well, the restaurant biz can be awfully dog-eat-dog. And I guess I get it, his wanting to have his own place. It's pretty much every chef's dream." I stared past Eric, focusing instead on the table across the room where my attorney acquaintance was now flipping through a stack of papers, pointing out to her two clients where they needed to sign and initial each page.

Watching the lawyer and her clients reminded me of the probate law I'd just looked up in the law library. "So," I said, turning once more toward Eric, "I went to the recorder's office to see if a marriage license had been filed for Gino and that Anastasia woman, but no dice."

Eric shook his head and finished off the first of his muffins. "I gotta say I think that's a crazy idea," he said, mouth full.

"Yeah, me too, the more I think about it. But I did find out that if they *did* marry, she'd inherit his entire estate."

"And if I were to marry Jennifer Lawrence, I could quit my job and spend all my time surfing. Speaking of which, I was thinking of taking off a little early today. You up for some more painting this afternoon?"

"Sure. Gauguin's closed today, so I have the day off. How about going out to Wilder Ranch State Park? Those old farm buildings would make a great subject, especially in the late-afternoon—" But then I stopped. "Oh, wait. There's no dogs allowed. I don't want to leave Buster home alone. How about Capitola Village? I rode my bike out there last week and was thinking it would be a great spot to paint."

"No way. The traffic that direction in the afternoon always sucks. But we could go up to UCSC."

"No dogs there either," I pointed out.

"Well, shoot, let's just either do it at your house or at West Cliff, then. 'Cause my place allows dogs, but it wouldn't be that interesting to paint."

Eric was right about where he lives. It's a condo with no yard—only a balcony. And although the place is easy to maintain, it's not what you'd call an artist's dream subject.

"My house," I said. "If we're on West Cliff, Buster will have to be on a leash and just sit around while we paint. Plus, I can just see him tangling my easel and knocking the whole thing down. And that way we can have a drink while we paint."

"Not me," Eric said. "I have chorus at six."

"Oh, right. Well, I can at least offer you something to eat before you go to rehearsal. I brought some leftover coq au vin home from Gauguin last night."

At the mention of the restaurant, we both fell silent as our thoughts returned once more to its chef, Javier. Eric sipped from his coffee cup and I poked at the crumbs on my plate one by one and ate them off my finger.

"So what will you do if he does leave?" Eric finally asked in a quiet voice.

"I have no idea," I answered. Then, shoving the plate out of the way, I lay my head on the table and let out a soft groan.

FOURTEEN

AFTER TAKING BUSTER for a walk around the neighborhood so he could stretch his legs and, more important to him, search for morsels of food that had been
dropped on the sidewalk, the first thing I did after getting home from the County Building was pull the plastic
bag containing Gino's cap from the sock drawer where
I'd stashed it for safekeeping. Seeing Detective Vargas
had made me even more nervous about my "suppressing evidence," and I wanted to check whether the cap
did in fact contain any obvious clues.

Using a pair of clean tongs to extract the wool cap
from the bag, I set it on the newspaper I'd spread out
on the kitchen table. I examined the cloth inside and
out, and other than strands of the old fisherman's fine,
white hair—which were numerous—I saw nothing. No
blood, no bits of suspicious fabric, not even any dan-
druff as far as I could detect.

Of course, I thought as I poked the cap back into the
plastic bag with my tongs, that didn't mean it contained
no important information. I wouldn't be able to see
DNA evidence, or even such things as traces of blood
or individual strands of others' hair. But I wasn't going
to turn it over yet. *By the end of the week*, I promised
myself in an attempt to justify what was beyond doubt
unjustifiable behavior. *I'll turn it over to the police by*

*then if I still haven't found anything definitive to ex-
onerate Dad.*

After stowing the plastic bag back in its unoriginal
hiding place, I changed into my cycling clothes. A short
but vigorous workout seemed like just the ticket to rid
myself of the nervous energy now pulsating through
my body—a ride up Western Drive to High Street and
then back down the hill.

As soon as I started up the incline that is Western
Drive, however, I began to regret my decision. It's brutal, especially at the beginning. Santa Cruz is built on a
series of five sedimentary shelves, called "marine ter-
races," each higher than the next. And Western Drive
cuts straight up from the first terrace, where I live, to
the next with no respite.

I felt nearly spent within the first five minutes of the
climb, so, to take my mind off my pounding heart and
burning legs, I tried to concentrate instead on what I'd
learned so far regarding Gino's death and those who
might have had a reason to do him in.

First, I ticked off in my head, there was Bobby, who,
according to Angelo, was to have inherited Gino's fishing boat when the old man passed on. Even though I
now knew that Gino hadn't in fact given Bobby his boat,
it was still possible that Bobby had *thought* he was in the
fisherman's will. But given how genuinely sorry—and
sad—Bobby was that his good friend was now gone,
this scenario didn't really work for me. Plus, now that
Gino was dead, Bobby's gravy train had permanently
left the station without him.

Oof. If only I *had a train right now to drag me up
this damn hill.* I'd finally made it to the last grueling
stretch before summiting onto the upper marine terrace

and was feeling dizzy and lightheaded. I added to this wish a mental note to henceforth strike Western Drive from consideration for future rides, no matter how energized I might feel. *Okay, c'mon, Sal, you can do it. Just a few more pedal strokes. Concentrate on something other than that burning in the legs. Who else might have wanted to off poor old Gino?*

I wrested my attention from the fatigue in my calf muscles back to my list of suspects. Next up was Anastasia, who would absolutely have had a motive for killing the fisherman if they'd gotten married beforehand. But that was a massive "if." And the answer to that question was still unknown, so, other than checking back periodically at the records department, there was nothing more I could think of to do.

Okay, who else? There was also that old man Sean had seen arguing with Gino out by the bocce court the night he went missing. The more I thought about it, the more I liked him as a suspect. Maybe he was one of those old guys who played out there all the time and he'd been mad at Gino because of his cheating. *Wait. Maybe Gino was so out of it that night that he went one step too far and the guy just clocked him—with a bocce ball. That could certainly give you a big ol' welt on the head.*

I considered this scenario as I finally crested the hill and downshifted, exhaling a long stream of carbon dioxide from my overexerted lungs. The old bocce player wouldn't have necessarily intended to kill Gino. But once he'd struck out in anger, he might have gotten spooked and then shoved Gino over the side of the wharf in a moment of panic. Or maybe the guy had simply left him there and Gino—concussed and out of it to begin with—had wandered off and somehow fallen into the water all on his own.

But there was a major downside to this theory: I had no way of knowing who the old man might be. Sean's vague account could describe any number of old men who hung out at the bocce court.

Taking a long drink from my water bottle, I continued up the now gradual climb to the top of Western Drive until I reached the aptly named High Street at the base of the university, at which point I turned right, downhill. *Ah...*

As I cruised back home, enjoying the feel of the salt-laden ocean air on my sweaty face and damp cycling jersey, I could see tiny white triangles scattered across the Monterey Bay. The offshore Diablo winds had been replaced today by the more usual onshore variety, and numerous boaters were taking advantage of the breeze and the glorious weather.

Seeing the sailboats, however, sent my mood spiraling back down as I was reminded of Gino in his beautiful Monterey clipper. Why would someone have wanted to kill the old fisherman? And who could have had the audacity to actually carry out the deed?

THE FIRST THING I said to Eric when he showed up at my place three hours later was, "I have an idea about another possible suspect."

"Good afternoon to you as well," he responded, stepping into the living room. "And I'm doing just fine, thank you very much." Eric knelt down to give Buster a good long scratch at the base of his tail and behind the ears, then stood up and brushed the dog hair from his hands. "Okay, what is this new theory?"

I told him what I'd learned from Sean the day before—
how Gino had been arguing with some guy behind Solari's the night he disappeared. "And get this. I talked to
Angelo again yesterday, too, and he told me that Gino
had been cheating at bocce and getting into arguments
with the old men who play out there all the time. So, what
if one of those old guys finally had enough of him and
went ahead and whacked Gino with a bocce ball, then
shoved him into the water?"

"Huh." Eric scratched his chin as he considered
my theory. "Well, that would explain the shape of the
wound on his head."

"Of course, the huge problem with him as a suspect,"
I said, heading for the kitchen, "is that we have no idea
who it could be. There must be at least a dozen old guys
who play bocce out there all the time."

I led the way outside, where I'd already set up my
easel and laid out my paint supplies. While Eric wrestled with his fancy French easel, I went into the kitchen
and poured us each a glass of sun tea. Coming back outside into the bright sunshine, I crossed the patio and set
our glasses on the picnic table.

I had just opened my pad of watercolor paper when
I had a thought. "Wait," I said, turning to Eric. "Remember that man whose bocce ball hit my dad's skiff
during class on Saturday? And how pissed off he was
when the other guys laughed at him?"

Eric nodded. "Yeah. He hurled the ball back at them.
Not a nice fellow."

"So maybe it was him who was arguing with Gino
that night. I'll have to ask Angelo if he knows who he is."

"You do that, Miss Marple." Eric shook his head

and chuckled softly as he clipped a sheet of paper to his easel and selected a pencil from the drawer.

Neither of us spoke for a bit as we sketched in the blocks of light and shadows for the compositions we'd chosen. Omar called them the "big shapes." I was taking a second shot at the persimmon tree I'd painted the week before, and Eric had decided on the yellow rose climbing up the old wooden fence at the back of the property.

Buster had curled up on the far side of the patio, where a splash of sunlight was still warming the red bricks. "Leave it to a dog to find the last sunny spot," I said as I stepped back from my easel to examine my work.

Setting down his brush with a glance toward the sleeping dog, Eric removed his glasses and turned back to stare at his rose bush, eyes glazed.

"What are you doing?" I asked. "Something wrong with your prescription?"

"Remember when Omar told us to get in the habit of squinting, to make our eyes out of focus, so we can concentrate on the shapes and colors rather than the details of what we're painting? Well, it's easy for me. All I have to do is take off my glasses and everything's way out of focus."

Since I didn't need corrective lenses, I had to make do with narrowing my eyes and letting them go a little cross-eyed to achieve the same effect. "It's kind of like an Impressionist painting, huh? I wonder if Monet took off his spectacles to paint his water lilies."

"Maybe so," Eric replied, replacing his horn-rimmed glasses and once more taking up his brush. "After all, as Omar always says, 'We don't paint things'—"

"—'we paint shapes and colors,'" I finished for him.

This was a sort of mantra for our instructor. "Now, if only I could free myself up enough to paint like Monet. Or Paul Gauguin or Vincent van Gogh."

"I think you'd have to do some pretty heavy-duty drugs to get into the head space van Gogh was in," Eric said with a laugh.

"And Gauguin, too. That book I read says he went kind of crazy from syphilis toward the end of his life." I reached for my glass of sun tea and took a sip. "Oh," I said, setting it back down on the redwood table, "and did you know that Gauguin and van Gogh actually shared a house and painted together for a summer when van Gogh was living in Provence?"

"What a fun couple they must have been," Eric said. "Was this before or after Vincent cut off his ear?"

"Right before, I think. And pretty soon after that he moved up north and then killed himself."

"Well, that's what lead poisoning will do to you, I guess." Eric wiped the red paint off his brush with a paper towel and then dipped it in the jar of water. "Didn't he supposedly eat his paint or lick his brushes or something, and that's why he went insane?"

"I'm pretty sure the current thinking is that he had some sort of mental illness like schizophrenia. Man, talk about painting 'what you see, not what you think.'" This was another of Omar's favorite sayings. "He probably *did* see all those swirls in the sky and the fields, and all those super-saturated colors, too."

"Well, I'll take my mental health any day," Eric said, dabbing blobs of yellow gouache onto his paper. "Even if it does mean I'm destined to be a mediocre artist."

We painted together for another half hour or so, and while we worked, I mused about what Eric had said regarding van Gogh and his lead paints. For although I knew this had been pretty much debunked as the cause of the painter's insanity, the mention of lead paints had gotten the wheels turning in my head about someone other than Vincent van Gogh.

"What if Gino had lead poisoning?" I asked, breaking the silence.

"What?" Eric looked up from his palette, where he'd been mixing a muddy gray for his fence posts.

"Well, think about it. He'd been a fisherman all his life, and if he was like all the other fishermen I've known, he must have painted and repainted his boat over and over again over the years, well before they outlawed using lead in paint. So maybe the reason he was acting so weird the past few months was because of lead poisoning."

Eric frowned. "It's an interesting idea, actually. Here, let's see what the symptoms are." Pulling his phone from the front pocket of his chino shorts, he entered a query and then scrolled through the results that appeared on-screen. "Okay, found it," he said after a moment. "Conditions associated with lead toxicity include anxiety, arthritis, blindness, hair loss, convulsions, fatigue, irritability, vertigo and dizziness, disorientation, poor concentration, mood swings, hallucinations, memory and speech impairment, impaired muscle coordination…" Eric looked up at me. "It goes on, but…"

"Yeah. A lot of that behavior could easily be seen as drunkenness by someone who didn't know better. Plus, plenty of those symptoms would explain his irrational behavior, his getting into fights with people. You gotta wonder if that was the reason he was killed. He got so weird he just pushed someone too far."

Eric slid the phone back into his pocket. "Well, a test for heavy metals will certainly be part of the tox report, so we'll find out soon enough if it was lead poisoning that made him so wonky."

"Soon isn't exactly how I'd put it," I said. "Doesn't it take at least a month to get the report?"

Eric just shrugged and went back to his painting. But I was thinking, *It sure would be nice for Solari's if there were a way to find out earlier.*

FIFTEEN

As soon as Eric left for his chorus rehearsal, I sat down at the kitchen table with my laptop and typed "lead poisoning test" into the search box. Scanning the first page of results, it immediately became clear that a booming online business existed based on hair analysis for lead toxicity as well as for other heavy metals. *Gino's cap had a lot of his hair on it*, I recalled. *How much do they need for a test?*

I clicked on the link to a site called "Speedy Hair Analysis" and scrolled down till I came to the requirements for the sample. A hundred and twenty-five milligrams was best, it said, but the test could be done with as little as fifty mg of hair—about a teaspoonful.

Jumping up, I strode to my bedroom, where I pulled the green plastic bag from its hiding place under my socks. I brought the bag out to the kitchen, once again extracted the fisherman's cap with tongs, and examined its cloth, inside and out. There was indeed a *lot* of hair. Far more than I'd originally realized. Several clumps were hidden deep inside the wool cap in addition to the strands I'd noticed before. And then I remembered the list Eric had read earlier: hair loss had been one of the symptoms of lead poisoning.

I sat back down at my computer and searched the Speedy Hair Analysis website until I found instructions on how to submit a sample for analysis. The hair needed to be placed in a trace metal-free plastic bag or container, and they wanted it cut from near the scalp. Well, I certainly couldn't do that, since this hair had fallen out of Gino's head. But I'd just send along what I had and see what happened. No need to tell them it had come from a man who was now dead.

Under the heading "Expedited Service," I read that by paying an additional fee I could get one-day service for the analysis. That meant that if I used overnight delivery both ways, I could get the results of the test as soon as Thursday. What time was it now? Five thirty, my computer said. And the UPS store was open only till six.

After printing out a copy of the submission form, I filled in the required information along with my credit card number, carefully inserted one of Gino's locks of hair into an unused zip-top plastic bag, searched Letta's old desk until I found a manila mailing envelope to put it all in, and then ran out to my car, Buster at my heels. I made it to the store with a full three minutes to spare and startled the young sales clerk—who had her back turned and was sorting through a stack of cardboard boxes—by dashing up to the counter and slapping my package down.

With the hair sample successfully on its way to the lab, I breathed a sigh of relief. Maybe this would solve the mystery of why Gino had seemed so sloshed when he'd had hardly anything to drink.

Of course, lead poisoning couldn't have been what *killed* him, I mused, returning home at about half my outward-bound speed. The coroner had ruled the cause of death to be drowning, plus there was that blow to his head, which the cops now thought was probably caused by something like a baseball bat.

But from what it said online about its symptoms, lead

toxicity could certainly have caused him to behave ir-rationally and act like a complete jerk. And the more I thought about it, the more it made sense that Gino had simply provoked someone—by arguing, or cheating, or picking a fight—to the point where he or she had sim-ply lost it and decked him with a nearby object. Some-thing like a bocce ball.

Or the oar from Dad's skiff, I thought glumly as I pulled into my driveway and let Buster jump out of the car. *The skiff he took out fishing the day after the old man disappeared.*

THE NEXT MORNING, as soon as I'd brewed a pot of coffee, I sat down to make a list of the tasks that still needed doing for the sister-cities dinner. Top on the list was to confirm all the rentals and their delivery time: plates, serving dishes, flatware, wine and water glasses, table-cloths, napkins, tent, tables, chairs. Since the guest list now stood at one hundred thirty-two, no way did So-lari's have enough table settings for everyone, so Dad and I had decided to go ahead and rent everything. That way they'd all match.

Next I wrote down "confirm w/wharf admin. set-up time." We'd arranged to have the dinner portion of the event outside in the area behind the restaurant under the big tent, since Solari's could only legally seat eighty at a time, and I needed to make sure we had use of the public space for the entire day, starting the morning of the big dinner. I was pretty sure that setting up one of those enormous tents wouldn't be nearly as easy as they made it look in their ads. Plus, we'd have to put out all the tables and chairs and get the tables completely set well before the start time of five o'clock.

Tapping my pen on the kitchen table, I considered a moment and then jotted down "wine." My dad was ordering all the food for the dinner, but I'd asked to be in charge of the wine, since I cared way more about it than he did. Left to him, we'd likely end up with boxed "hearty red" and "classic white." I'd just made a note to check the wine prices at Costco when the *Hawaii Five-O* ringtone rang out from my cell. Eric.

"Hey," he said, mouth full when I answered the call.

"More muffins?" I asked.

"Sorry." Eric swallowed before going on. "I didn't think you'd pick up so quickly."

"You caught me making a list of things to do for Dad's damn dinner," I said.

"Has a nice ring to it, that: DDD."

"Certainly better than Columbus Day dinner, that's for sure."

Eric laughed and I could hear him take a drink of what was no doubt his morning Starbucks. "You know," he said after bit, "if there's anything I can do..."

"Yeah, well, I'm not sure what help you could be. It's not like you've got a whole lot of banquet experience."

But it was sweet of him to offer. I couldn't put my finger on it exactly, but it had seemed that Eric had been going out of his way to be nicer to me of late. Doing stuff like agreeing to take that painting class, and listening to my wild theories about Gino and lead poisoning without making fun. And he'd been surprisingly amenable to tracking down information about the will and the coroner's findings and then passing it along to me—even though such activity could probably lose him his job if his boss found out.

But there were little things, too: the way I'd started

catching Eric looking at me when he thought I wasn't watching, and his calling when he had no real reason to do so. Like now.

Was there more to this recent behavior than mere friendship? Not that I'd call what we had a simple "friendship." Our relationship had always been far more than that, even after we called it quits as a couple. But did he now want more? Was he starting to regret the decision to break up?

If so, I wasn't at all sure how I felt about it.

"So, was there any more graffiti at Solari's today?" Eric asked, rousing me from my thoughts.

Great. Way to remind me of something else besides the possibility of my dad being arrested for Gino's murder and, now, potentially complicated relationship issues. "Not that I've heard," I said, "but it's closed on Tuesdays, so I doubt anyone's been down there since last night."

"That's good." Eric cleared his throat. Maybe our conversation had seemed a little awkward to him as well. "Anyway, I guess I should get back to work. I don't have to keep track of billable hours, thank God, but we government lackeys do need to take the occasional glance at our case files."

"Uh-huh." I knew Eric to be a highly conscientious worker, but he preferred to present the carefree surfer dude image over that of serious district attorney.

After we'd hung up, I filled my thermos cup with coffee and called out to Buster. "Wanna go for a ride in the car?"

The dog came careening and skidding across the hardwood floor from the dining room into the living room, then sat eagerly at my feet while I searched for my car keys at the bottom of my bag.

I'd had an idea while talking to Eric. Thinking about the information he'd gotten me from the DA's office had set me wondering who exactly the police might have interviewed now that they considered the case a possible homicide. Had they tracked down Marvin Blanco, the man who'd written that first letter to the editor? Because, I realized, he had to have been one of the last people to see Gino alive, besides Anastasia and the old man Sean had watched arguing with him behind Solari's.

In any case, there was no reason I couldn't have a chat with Marvin, too, right? Since he was a Solari's regular—or had been, at least, before writing that letter—his phone number was probably in the Solari's reservation book. Maybe if I talked to him, he'd remember something that could help us.

The T-Bird's ragtop was down, but even though today was much cooler than yesterday, I left it as it was. The morning paper had said another storm was coming in toward the end of the week, and this could be one of the last days of the season that cruising around topless was a possibility.

And then it hit me: the end of the week was when the sister-cities dinner was happening. *Oh, boy...* Although we'd ordered a big tent, it would still be a royal pain if we had to be carting food from the restaurant out to the diners during a rainstorm.

Oh, well, I thought as I pulled out of the garage. At least that was one thing I couldn't fret about too much, because I certainly wasn't going to be able to change the weather. We'd deal, whatever the situation.

I pulled up in front of Solari's ten minutes later and, telling Buster to stay in the car (dogs aren't allowed on the wharf, either), headed for the front door. No signs of graffiti, thank goodness. And no bleed-through from my paint job of two days earlier. I went around to the back of the restaurant and let myself in the door to the dish room.

It was strange, being in the place all alone. No clatter of plates being stacked in the dishwasher, no raised voices coming from the kitchen. The unusual silence was disquieting. Kind of eerie, in fact.

As I passed by the office, I heard a *clunk* and started at the noise, nearly falling over a case of beer somebody had left in the hall. *What the hell could that be?* No one should be here on a Tuesday morning. Had I imagined it? Heart thumping, I crept toward the office. And why was the door closed? My dad and I always kept it open. If you didn't, the tiny room quickly became stifling for lack of ventilation.

There it was again. Could there be a burglar in the office? We had an old computer in there, as well all our checkbooks and financial records, but nothing a high-class burglar would want. I hesitated outside the door a moment, trying to decide whether or not to call 911.

But then something smacked against the inside of the door, shaking its wood frame. *What the...?* Without stopping to think, I threw the door open, hoping to knock whoever was inside to the floor.

No one. The office was empty.

But at a muffled, fluttering sound, I turned. There on the floor lay a bird. A blackbird of some sort, or a starling. As I watched, it righted itself, fluffed its feathers, then flew up to perch at the top of the metal storage shelf. Above the shelf was a small window—wide open.

It took another fifteen minutes to corner the bird and convince it to fly back out the window, during which time I tried to calm the nerves that had overtaken me out there in the hallway. Had I overreacted? Although it turned out to be nothing but a stunned bird, I'd had no way of knowing that. There could have been an ax-wielding madman in the office for all I knew, right?

But deep down, I had to admit that this whole Gino thing was starting to get to me.

Walking back down the hall and through the wait station, I crossed the dining room and opened the reservation book sitting on the hostess stand. Now to find Marvin's contact information. I'd tried to talk my dad into switching to one of those online reservation systems, but his response had been, "I hate those things, and if I hate them, then it's a sure bet a ton of our customers do too." So we'd stuck with the old-school leather-bound book.

Which was good, in this case. All I had to do was turn to the Monday night Gino and Anastasia had eaten here, and there was Marvin's reservation for two, along with his phone number.

I pulled out my cell and punched in the number. "Hello?" a man's voice said.

"Is this Marvin Blanco?"

"Yes…" I could tell he thought I was a telemarketer. But when he found out who it really was, he'd be even more annoyed.

"Oh, hi. This is Sally Solari, from—"

"I know who you are."

Yep. Definitely not happy to hear from me. "Okay,

look, Mr. Blanco, I know you're pretty upset with Solari's right now, but I was wondering if you'd be willing
to talk to me about it. Just for a minute or two."

"I can't say I have much to add to what I wrote in that
letter. It's obvious that the man I saw that night—the
one who ended up drowned—had had way too much to
drink, and that you people not only sold him the alcohol but then let him walk home. What you should have
done was call him a taxi."

"I hear what you're saying, Mr. Blanco. And it's true
that we did serve Gino two beers. But that's all he drank
here, and he had a full dinner as well. Plus, the waitress who served him swears he wasn't acting drunk
during dinner."

"Well, that's not what I saw," Marvin said, his voice
gruff. "Look, I appreciate that you're worried about
a lawsuit or something, but I really don't want to talk
about this any further."

"Wait. Please don't hang up. There's something I
need to tell you."

This got his interest. "And what might that be?"

"As I said, we've had contradictory stories about
Gino's behavior that night. The waitress says he wasn't
intoxicated, and you—and our busboy as well—say that
he did seem drunk, or at least really out of it."

"Okay…"

"So I've been trying to figure out how these various people could have seen such radically different behavior. And the only thing that makes any sense is if
Gino in fact *had* been acting in different ways over the
night—first sober, and then all of a sudden intoxicated."

"And your point is?"

"I think Gino might actually have been suffering

from lead poisoning." Marvin didn't respond, so I went on. "He was a fisherman all his life, and would have painted his boat pretty much every season. And the lead that used to be in that boat paint back in the old days, if you didn't take the proper precautions like wearing a mask and stuff, it could be super toxic—especially if you were exposed to it year after year."

"Huh." I could tell he was considering the possibility.

"And it turns out the symptoms of lead poisoning can be similar to being drunk—dizziness, disorientation, speech and muscle impairment. Which would explain why he could seem fine one minute and completely out of it the next, because I read online that the symptoms can come and go."

"Well, wouldn't the police know if that were the case?" Marvin asked.

"They will know eventually how much liquor he had in his system, but it takes at least a month to get the toxicology report back from the lab. I'm not sure if they do a test specifically for lead, though." I wanted to tell him about sending in Gino's hair for my own private analysis but couldn't risk his wondering where I got the hair. "So, anyway…"

"Okay, look." Marvin paused and drew a long breath. "There's something I guess I should tell you."

Yes. He seemed to be softening his stance.

"As my wife and I were driving down the wharf that night after dinner, we saw the man, Gino, again. This was just a few minutes after we'd seen him at the front of the restaurant. He was down near that boat that's on display, along the side of Solari's, and he wasn't alone."

"He was with the woman he'd had dinner with, right? The one you mentioned in your letter?"

"I assume it was her, but I couldn't guarantee it. And, well, they were…uh…"

Now he had my full attention. "They were what?"

"Kissing. My wife was the one who spotted them, and she said it looked like he was really coming on to her. I considered stopping to make sure she was okay, but then it became obvious that the woman wasn't objecting. So we went on our way. My thought was, well, at least he's got someone to help get him home."

"Did he still seem drunk then?" I asked.

"I don't see how he could have sobered up in that short a time. But it was dark, and they were leaning against the wall of the restaurant, so I couldn't tell you for certain."

"Right." I stared out the Solari's window at a souped-up '57 Chevy cruising down the wharf. It had been painted a metallic blue and was jacked up on its axles, but even with these nonstandard features, the car was cherry. "So, I was wondering, Mr. Blanco, if you wouldn't mind telling me, did the police talk to you?"

"Yes," he said, "they contacted me after I wrote that letter to the paper. And I of course told them about this incident. But I hadn't felt it necessary to put it in my letter, out of respect for the old man. Especially since he isn't around anymore to defend himself."

But what if Marvin's first impressions were correct? I wondered as I ended the call and slid the phone back into my bag. *What if Gino had been assaulting the woman, the mysterious Anastasia, and she'd been the one who needed defending—from a man deranged by lead poisoning? Defending to the point, perhaps, of knocking him out and pushing him over the side of the wharf…*

SIXTEEN

ONCE BACK HOME, I sat down again at the kitchen table and studied my list. *Better check on all the equipment we're renting first.* I dialed the number for June's Party Rentals and a young woman picked up after two rings.

"Hi, I'm calling about a bunch of stuff I have ordered for this Saturday, and just want to confirm that you have it all down and that we'll get delivery first thing Saturday morning."

"Sure," she said in a breathy, perky voice. "Who's it for?"

I gave her my name and, after she'd pulled the order up on her computer, read the items from my list: plates, serving dishes, flatware, wine and water glasses, tablecloths, napkins, tent—

But when I got to that last item, she cut me off. "Tent? I don't see any tent here on the order."

"No tent? What do you mean? It's the most important thing. I'm sure I ordered it."

"I'm really sorry," she said, "but there's no tent listed here."

"Okay, well, let's just add that to the order then. I need one of those big ones, with sides. Thirty by fifty I think is what I ordered."

"Let me see…" I heard clacking in the background as the woman typed something into her computer. "Oh, dear," she said after a bit. "It looks like the only thing we have available for this coming Saturday is one of those small pop-up tents, ten by ten. Everything else is already rented."

"You're kidding."

"No, I'm afraid not. I'm so sorry."

"Okay, look," I said, "I'll call you back later about the other stuff. I gotta deal with this ASAP."

No way could we do without a tent for the dinner—not with the rainstorm that was predicted to hit the Monterey Bay area at the end of the week. Opening my laptop, I Googled tent rentals for the Santa Cruz area. Six different vendors came up and I called each one of them in turn. No dice. Either they had only small tents or their big ones were already rented. Next I tried places in Monterey and Salinas, and even a few in San Jose, but still no luck.

Oh, nooo... I let out a long moan, prompting Buster to jump up from his doggy bed in the corner and come sit at my feet. Stroking his silky ears, I fought the panic that was starting to overtake me. Was it really possible that I'd forgotten to order the tent? This could be a disaster of monumental proportions. And how would I tell my dad?

I couldn't, was the answer. I simply *had* to find one.

Maybe someone I knew had a tent, or knew someone who did. Turning back to my computer, I logged on to Facebook and composed a plea to all my friends (since Dad had no interest in social media, he'd never be the wiser): "Help! I'm in desperate need of a 30 × 50 foot party tent with sides for this coming Sat. Let me know if you have such a thing or know someone who does, and please DO repost. I'll be boiled alive with my dad's spaghetti if I don't find one!"

That done, I took Buster for a walk and tried to calm myself down. But it wasn't easy. Not with so many different things to worry about. The tent had now jumped to obsession number one, but there were plenty of others: the possibility of my dad becoming a suspect in Gino's murder, Javier leaving Gauguin, the threat of a boycott against Solari's because of Gino *and* for celebrating Columbus Day...

Not even the sight of three humpback whales spouting and cavorting less than fifty yards offshore in Mitchell's Cove was sufficient to vanquish the dark mood that had settled in my bones.

THAT NIGHT AT GAUGUIN, Javier was in high spirits, which only served to further dampen mine. Although he was not happy about my being absent this Thursday, Friday, and Saturday so I could help my dad prep for and then host the sister-cities dinner, his displeasure was tempered by the prospect of opening his new restaurant with his new love, Natalie.

"We're thinking of calling the place 'le Bar Zinc,'" Javier said to Brian and me as we tended our sauté pans at the hot line. "After those shiny metal bar tops that used to be so popular back in the 1930s in France. What do you think?"

"Great idea," Brian answered. "Santa Cruz could so use a traditional French bistro. They do great up in San Francisco."

"It was Natalie's idea," Javier continued. "She lived in Paris for a year when she was a student. The plan is she'll make traditional French pastries and I can be in charge of the classic French dishes like steak au poivre and pot-au-feu and coq au vin."

"Just don't go stealing the Gauguin recipe for the chicken," I said. It was meant as a joke but came out harsher than I'd intended, and Javier looked up from his two orders of duck breast to give me a questioning look.

"You found a place yet?" Brian asked, oblivious to the friction between Javier and me.

"No. We're just at the early planning stages at this point," Javier said, turning back to flip his duck breasts and then stir the pan of lilikoi glaze that would be drizzled over their thinly sliced, medium-rare meat. "And besides, I need to give Sally time to find my replacement."

Ouch. Now *that* was harsh.

"Hey," he went on, with a grin directed at Brian, "maybe you could be the next head chef at Gauguin. What d'ya think, Sally? I bet, with a little work, he could do the job."

Brian laughed and swatted at Javier with his side towel, but I could tell from the flicker of hope that crossed his face that he liked the idea.

Javier changed the subject at this point, perhaps sensing that he might have gone a little too far with his teasing. "So how are the preparations going for the big dinner at Solari's this weekend?"

"Oh, God," I said, shaking my head. "It looks like we might not have a tent for the event. Either because I forgot to order it, which I strongly doubt, or because the rental company blew it and didn't get my order entered in their system. Either way, we're screwed."

"Dude," Brian said. "Isn't there supposed to be a storm coming in this weekend?"

"Yes, there is," I answered, wiping clean the pan I'd just used and slamming it down onto the Wolf range.

"And I called every single company within a fifty-mile radius, and all their tents are already rented for this Saturday. I don't suppose any of you happens to own an enormous party tent?" I asked the kitchen at large.

No one replied, but then again, who besides a rental company—or a circus—would possess a thirty-by-fifty-foot tent?

The kitchen was unusually quiet after my outburst, but it took only a couple of minutes for conversation to start up again. Kris had come in from the *garde manger* to fetch more green onions from the walk-in, then stopped to talk with Brian about a party they were going to after work.

Javier plated up his duck breasts and set them on the pick-up window. "Order up!" he called out, and Brandon scurried over to retrieve the entrées. "By the way," the chef asked, reaching for the next ticket on the rail, "did you ever get those porcini mushrooms from that Fungus Federation guy I connected you with?"

"Yeah," I said, "he dropped several enormous bags off at Solari's yesterday. And there's even enough that we can use them for the chicken cacciatore as well as the tagliarini with brown butter and sage. So thanks for that."

"What else are you having?" Javier asked, and I described the menu in detail. We might be having our differences right now, but the subject of food never failed to get the two of us going.

"Tomorrow," I said, once I'd told Javier and Brian about the dishes we were serving, "Dad's going to bake all the panettones and the fugassa and freeze them till the morning of the dinner. Then Thursday we'll cook the Sunday gravy, and Friday we'll prep the chicken cacciatore, the stuffed cabbage, the zucchini, and the salad."

"You hiring extra staff for the event?" Kris asked. "'Cause I have a friend who's looking for some part-time work until she finds a permanent gig."

"Not for any of the prep, but the day of the dinner we're using some servers Dad knows who have banquet experience. He didn't want to hire any extra cooks, but I think that's a mistake. Who's this person you know?"

Kris described her friend—a woman who'd just moved to Santa Cruz from New York City. "I went to cooking school with her back East," she said, "and she's the real deal."

"I doubt she'd be thrilled with working at Solari's, then. But hey, if she's looking for a one-day gig, I'll talk to my dad about using her."

"Cool." Kris found the woman's contact info on her phone and sent me a text.

"Speaking of needing temp work," I said, swiveling around to face Javier, "we have to figure out how we're going to deal with my being gone from Gauguin at the end of the week. Especially since we still seem to be getting bigger-than-normal crowds from that review."

I knew this was a sore subject with him, but I couldn't simply ignore the fact that the hot line was going to be one cook short for three of our biggest days of the week.

Javier, however, just waved me off with a grin. "Don't worry, I've got it covered. Natalie's going to come in and work those nights."

"Natalie? But isn't she a pastry chef?"

"She is," he answered, reaching for the bottle of sherry to deglaze his pan of chicken with artichokes and pancetta. "But she worked the hot line for a while before switching to desserts. And since she does pastries for the Full Moon Café, she doesn't work nights. So she's free to come in here and help out."

"Oh. Well that's good, then."

"And this way," Javier continued, "me and her can get a feel for how we work together. You know, so we can figure out how it's going to work at our new restaurant."

"Right." I focused on my two orders of sole *meunière*. No way did I want Javier and Brian to see the moisture collecting in my eyes.

SEVENTEEN

I'D JUST LOGGED off Facebook on Wednesday morning to see if anyone had responded to my plea for a tent (no one had, though I'd gotten a slew of sympathetic comments) when my cell rang. It was the Solari's business number.

"You gotta get down here," Elena shouted as soon as I answered. "There's a bunch of protesters out front and Mario's gone ballistic. He's threatening to go out there and throw them all off the side of the wharf if they don't leave by the time we open."

Which was fifteen minutes from now, my phone screen informed me. *Damn.*

"Okay," I said, "I'm on my way. And go tell my dad I said to cool it about throwing people off the wharf. Talk like that, even in jest, is not a good idea right now. Not with what happened to Gino."

"Agreed. But I'm not sure he's in the mood to listen to what anybody has to say."

"Well, do your best. I'll be there in ten."

I grabbed my bag and ran out the front door, not even taking the time to give Buster his usual "see you later, be a good dog" treat. I'd just have to make it up to him when I got back.

I spotted the protesters as soon as I got to the point in the wharf where it bends to the right. There were about a dozen of them, most with handwritten placards. As I pulled into a parking spot across the street

from the group, I saw that all the signs were of the anti–
Columbus Day variety. At least that was one thing to
be thankful for—none of them seemed to be claiming
Solari's was to blame for Gino's death.

The front door to the restaurant was still closed and
the protesters were doing a good job of blocking access thereto. As I walked behind them to go around the
corner of the building to the back entrance, I could see
Cathy peeking out from behind the neon Amstel Light
sign in the front window. Seeing me, she bared her teeth
and then grimaced.

I found my dad in the kitchen, where I was immediately hit by the heavenly aroma of something baking. *Right, he's making all the panettone and fugassa
this morning.* Dad was standing by the oven, hands on
hips, as Elena spoke. "They have a right to picket," the
waitress was saying. "It's in the Constitution. Right,
Sally?" she added, seeing me come in.

"Yep. The First Amendment allows them to exercise
their rights of free speech as long as they're on public
property and as long as it's a peaceful protest."

"But they're completely blocking the entrance!" Dad
bellowed. "They're going to scare off our customers!"

"Which they are *not* allowed to do," I responded in as
calm a voice as I could muster. "Look, I'll go out there
and talk to them. Try to get them to move aside and not
harass anyone who wants to come into the restaurant.
And if that doesn't work, we can call the authorities.
But only as a last resort."

Mollified for now, Dad waved us both out of the
kitchen and hollered at Emilio—who had stopped chopping a pile of yellow onions to listen to our exchange—
to get back to work.

It was now eleven o'clock, so I unlocked the front door and walked outside toward the group of protesters. I didn't recognize any of them, which was good. It was embarrassing enough having to deal with Dad's Columbus Day blunder without having any of my friends participating in the protest of our family restaurant.

I approached the guy with the biggest sign, which read, "Columbus Was an Imperialist Invader!"

"Hi," I said, "I'm Sally Solari. My dad owns this restaurant."

"Maybe you should give your father a history lesson about genocide and mass murder," he responded.

"Look," I said calmly, "I absolutely agree that the arrival of Columbus opened up the continent to the subsequent slaughter and subjugation of the Native Americans. And I also agree that Columbus Day probably shouldn't be something that we, as Americans, celebrate. Because what it symbolizes isn't something we should be proud of.

"Here's the thing, though." I lowered my voice to convey that what I was about to tell him was important—and perhaps even confidential—and the man leaned in to hear what I had to say. The others in the group were now also listening intently to our conversation. "My dad is kind of naïf. I *tried* to talk him out of the whole Columbus Day thing. For exactly these same reasons," I said, gesturing toward the placards the group held. "Because you're right. But even though my dad grew up in the sixties, he was pretty much sheltered from all the political awareness that was going on then because of being from such a conservative, traditional family. So, on some basic level, he just doesn't get why an Italian-

American shouldn't be proud of the Italian who supposedly discovered this country."

"Well, he should learn then," a young woman with a mane of burgundy-colored hair piped up.

"I agree," I said. "And I'm actually thankful that you all are here, because I think he *has* learned something. I think his eyes are finally being opened to the fact that it's not really 'discovering' a country if it's already occupied by another culture."

Most of the sign-holders were now nodding in agreement. *Good.* I'd succeeded in creating some sort of rapport. Now for the tricky part.

"And I think it would be a good thing for you to stay, as well," I said. "To show just how much you care about this issue. But…" I turned back to the man with the big sign. "It's not going to work if you block the entrance and make it hard for customers to go in and out of the restaurant. You're just going to piss people off if you do that, including my dad, who I know you'd love to sway to your way of thinking. And you'll annoy all the old-timers who want to come in for lunch, too."

I indicated two elderly Italian women who had been standing behind the group, trying to figure out what to do, and the crowd backed off a few paces, allowing them to come forward. "But if you're friendly and polite to folks," I said, after the ladies had entered the dining room, "you might just convince them. You know, catch more flies with honey than vinegar and all that?"

The woman with the red hair whispered something to the gal next to her, then turned to me. "Okay," she said. "As long as you're not trying to make us leave or anything."

"No way," I said, raising my hands, palms out. "You absolutely have the right to be here. And I encourage it."

"All right, then." The two women stepped back and the others followed suit, creating a wide space between them for people to enter and exit the restaurant.

"Great." I beamed a friendly smile and started back inside. "Oh," I said, stopping and turning back to the group. "And if any of you need to use the restroom or want a glass of water or something, feel free to come on inside."

"Uh, thanks," several murmured in response. They were holding their signs, I noticed, just a little bit lower than before. *Catching flies with honey, indeed.*

BACK INSIDE THE dining room, I winked at Cathy, who had been monitoring my discussion with the protesters from her spot behind the neon beer sign, then headed for the kitchen in search of my dad.

I found him in the dish room, examining the spray valve for pre-rinsing stuff before it goes into the dishwasher. He peered into the nozzle and then pressed the trigger lock a few times, directing a powerful stream of water into the large stainless steel sink.

"I think it's okay now," he said, handing the hose back to Miguel, the Solari's dishwasher. "Probably just had some gunk in it that was making it stick."

I filled my father in about my talk with the protesters out front. "So I don't think they'll be too much of a problem. I bet they get bored and go home before lunch is even over. And I'd be surprised if they came back again tonight."

"Well, let's hope so." Dad stared out the screen door, and I followed his gaze. Four men had started up a

game of bocce, and I could hear them arguing amiably
about whose ball was closest to the little white *pallino*.
I looked for the guy who'd thrown the ball against my
dad's skiff but didn't see him among the group of players. Angelo, however, was sitting on the bench by the
bocce court, watching the game. "Did you and Angelo
ever fish together?" I asked my father.

"No, but Nonno Salvatore did. I remember him talking about Angelo working on his *lampara* a long time
ago, before Angelo got his own boat." And then Dad
laughed.

"What?"

"Oh," he said, "I was just remembering a story my
papà used to tell. Back in the day—this was before I
was even born—the guys would head out to the fishing grounds in the afternoon, because of the northwest
trade winds that come up then. They'd stay the night out
there and then return in the morning with their catch.
And to keep themselves amused during the evenings,
they used to sing out on the boats."

It was a lovely image, my grandfather's boat floating out there in the silence of the night, the moonlight
reflecting off the still, black water. And I could well
imagine him regaling the other fishermen in his rich
tenor voice with the old songs like "La Carolina" or
"The Boatman's Farewell."

"Sure," I said, "I remember Nonno talking about
that. How you *had* to sing, and if you didn't know any
songs you had to make one up."

"Right. Well, you asking about Angelo just now reminded me of one story in particular that my father told.
They were out there one night with a young fisherman
who I'm pretty sure was Angelo, and the kid refused to

sing. He said he didn't know any songs, or that his voice was bad, or something like that. I suspect what was really going on was that his voice was changing right around then, and he was embarrassed about the cracking. Well, anyway..." A wicked smile formed on Dad's lips. "You can imagine how the other guys responded to *that*. They told him if he didn't sing, he wouldn't get anything to eat that night, and then they all laughed."

"And what did Angelo do?" I asked. "Did he sing?"

My father shook his head. "He still refused. And when they continued to pressure him, the boy jumped up, grabbed hold of one of the men—not your *nonno*, I'm sure, or he would have never repeated the story—and threw him over the side of the boat into the water."

"Whoa."

Dad chuckled as he gazed out the window at the old fisherman lounging in the sun on the wooden bench. "And I don't think he's changed all that much, really," he said. "Angelo is a warm and generous man, but he can still have quite the temper."

"How so? Have you ever seen him get really angry?"

"Just once. But it was a doozy. This was years ago, when he was still selling a lot of his catch to the old West Side Grocery before it closed. The buyer had brought his refrigerated truck out onto the wharf and was checking out Angelo's fish, and I happened to be walking by when I heard them start to get into it. The grocery guy was accusing Angelo of trying to pass off old fish as today's catch, and Angelo did not take kindly to the accusation. But when the other guy refused to buy anything, Angelo just lost it. He took one of those big ol' cannonball sinkers they use for deep sea fishing and just went for the guy's head."

"No way."

Dad nodded. "It was pretty scary, actually, 'cause the grocery buyer went straight down. I thought he might even be dead. But I guess the blow hadn't really connected. It only just barely glanced off him, so it turned out he was okay. I don't think he even pressed charges. But I bet there was some sort of under-the-table payoff."

"Man." I studied Angelo, now clapping and cheering a well-executed bocce throw. He hardly seemed the type to belt someone with a two-pound lead weight. But then again, most anyone can snap if pushed far enough.

Was it possible he could have been pushed that far by something Gino had done? Angelo had said that the two of them had fallen out. But was it a bigger deal than he'd admitted?

Thinking back to my last conversation with Angelo, I remembered what he had told me about guys cutting each other's nets and lines. Although he'd said it no longer happened, it struck me that there was no particular reason such aggressive competitiveness would suddenly disappear. And I couldn't help but notice at the time how the fisherman had avoided my eye when telling me those days were long gone.

Could that be the real reason Angelo and Gino fought? Had one of them been cutting the other's lines? If it had been Angelo doing the cutting, it made sense that he would concoct a different story for their falling out.

But what if Gino had been cutting Angelo's lines? Such belligerent behavior, I now realized—along with all his recent fighting and cheating—could easily be explained by lead poisoning. And if he had cut Angelo's lines and the other fisherman had been pushed to the brink and done something truly horrible, it would make sense for him to want to keep what Gino had done to provoke him a secret.

It would also explain why Angelo was telling folks Gino had been drinking heavily of late, to supply a reason he might have simply fallen off the wharf and drowned. And it would explain, as well, Angelo's desire to redirect suspicion to Bobby, by saying that he was going to inherit Gino's boat.

As I watched the fisherman through the window laughing and calling out gibes to the bocce foursome, it suddenly came to me: *Ohmygod. Maybe* Angelo *is the old man Sean saw arguing with Gino that night behind Solari's.*

EIGHTEEN

AN IMMENSE BLACK cloud loomed in the distance, filling me with dismay and dread. No, I'm not referring to a figurative, metaphorical cloud—though such imagery would indeed have been descriptive of my current mood—but an actual thunderhead, its edges so dark and laden with moisture that I was amazed it hadn't yet started to pour.

"C'mon, Buster," I said, pulling the reluctant dog away from a scent-saturated tree stump. "Let's hustle our bustle and get on home."

We'd taken a morning stroll out to Lighthouse Point, and above us the sky was the color of cerulean blue gouache paint, interrupted here and there with mere wisps of cottony clouds. It was only when we got out to where you can watch the surfers up close as they catch rides at Steamer Lane that I noticed the ominous thunderhead. The black cloud was creeping up from behind the low mountains that separate Santa Cruz from Silicon Valley to the north and, to the east, from the Salinas Valley.

So much for a leisurely walk home. I was already in a foul mood, and the last thing I needed right now was a thorough drenching.

Although my logical self knew it was completely unrealistic, my Pollyanna alter ego had been certain someone would write me by this morning—two days before the big sister-cities dinner on Saturday—to inform me that they miraculously had a massive party tent tucked away in the corner of their garage. Guess which self proved right.

So now I was trying to decide which was worse: the prospect of serving a four-course menu to a hundred and thirty unlucky people sitting outdoors in a blustery downpour, or the prospect of telling my dad we'd have to do so.

The rain started to pelt Buster and me when we were still a block from the house, and we made a mad dash to cover that last short distance. I shook out the old towel that I kept by the front door and rubbed down the soggy dog before letting him indoors. He immediately jumped onto the living room couch, circled three times, then curled up and closed his eyes. I could hear his soft snoring before I even made it to the kitchen.

Taking my half-drunk coffee to the microwave, I reheated it for thirty seconds, removed the mug, and took a sip as I pondered my day. First, I wanted to go back down to the county recorder's office to see if a marriage certificate for Gino had yet been filed. Before talking to Marvin, I'd pretty much convinced myself that this theory was far too preposterous to be taken seriously, but his revelation that he'd seen Anastasia and Gino kissing after their dinner at Solari's had served to resurrect it as a possibility. I'd been planning to bicycle down to the County Building, but that was now out of the question. I detest riding in the rain. The roads are slick and dangerous, visibility sucks, and your brake pads get worn down super-fast when they're wet. I'd just have to drive instead.

After that, I needed to spend a few hours going over

Letta's old Gauguin manual. When she'd hired Javier over ten years before, she'd compiled a sort of instruction book regarding the restaurant for him to use as a guide, which included all sorts of details about the day-to-day running of the restaurant, like information on ordering, food-costing, recipes, kitchen setup and *mise en place*, and staffing.

I'd of course read through the manual when I inherited Gauguin, and had also occasionally consulted it when I'd had a specific question about something. But now that it looked as if Javier was going to be leaving, it seemed like a good idea to really study the book. It would not only help give me an idea of what to look for in his replacement, but it would also make me truly face the fact that I was soon going to have to run Gauguin without its longtime head chef.

Which was the main reason I'd been putting off the task.

Then, at around three, I had to head down to Solari's. I'd promised my dad I would spend the evening helping him with the braised meat course and anything else that needed doing for the Saturday dinner. Since the restaurant would be open tonight and tomorrow for its regular dinners, having an extra pair of hands there to work on the sister-cities meal was pretty much a necessity.

The recorder's office was unfortunately once more a bust. Nothing had been filed in the past three days in Gino's name. I considered texting Eric to see if he wanted to meet me again for coffee but decided against it. Better to go home and get to work reading that Gauguin manual.

Buster jumped up and smothered me with kisses as soon as I came through the front door, even though I'd only been gone about a half hour. Dogs are wonderful for the self-esteem of their caretakers.

I'd just sat down and opened Letta's manual when the doorbell rang, setting Buster off once more—this time barking as if every criminal from *America's Most Wanted* were trying to break down my door all at once.

I peeked out the window to see who it was. *Ah, the UPS guy.* No wonder he was excited. Dogs *love* to bark at delivery people. It's something about the uniform and the big, loud truck. Plus, you have to admit, the tactic works: every time they bark at those uniformed people who come to your door, the folks immediately leave. So why not continue with such successful behavior?

I opened the door just wide enough to accept the package, keeping the frantic dog inside with my legs held stiff, then examined what he'd given me. It was from Speedy Hair Analysis.

Hot diggity dog! I'd forgotten that the report on Gino's hair was supposed to arrive today. Sitting down on the couch, I ripped open the envelope and pulled out the papers it contained.

There was a long paragraph of introductory text: "…not for clinical diagnostic purposes…we cannot be held liable for mistakes contained in this analysis, or any damages arising therefrom," blah, blah, blah. Skipping over this, I turned to the next page, which contained a chart with the results. A list of toxins, heavy metals, and essential elements ran all down the page, but I zoomed in on the one I was interested in.

There it was: "**LEAD** (Pb)—Result: 8.7 $\mu g/g$; Reference Range: < 5.0 (children), < 10.0 (adults)." I wasn't positive what "$\mu g/g$" meant (something per gram?), but I could see that Gino's levels were within what was considered normal limits for adults, even if they were a bit on the high range of the norm.

Damn. So much for my theory.

I dropped the report on the coffee table and got up to make myself some lunch. Locating a can of tuna in the pantry, I mixed the chunks of albacore with chopped celery, cumin, garlic powder, mayo, and salt and pepper, then made myself a sandwich with soft, white bread and lots of crispy lettuce.

I set the plate down on the kitchen table, took a seat, and opened my laptop. How hard was it to get lead poisoning, anyway? A website about the toxicity of heavy metals told me that small children were particularly at risk for lead poisoning because of eating paint off old toys or eating chips of old paint around the house. But, the article noted, since lead had been outlawed for most paints since 1978, the frequency of this sort of toxicity was far less than it used to be.

The page went on to discuss other heavy metals that can be toxic at high levels, including arsenic, mercury, copper, and cadmium. Laying my half-eaten sandwich back on the plate, I went to the living room to fetch Gino's hair analysis report. There'd been a list of other elements tested for besides lead. Could any of those levels have been elevated?

I sat back down and read through the list of elements and Gino's results as I finished my sandwich: aluminum, antimony, arsenic, beryllium, cadmium, calcium, copper—

Wait, that one was slightly high: "**COPPER** (Cu)— Result: 137 µg/g; Reference Range: 10–100." I dropped the paper and turned once more to my computer.

The same website I'd consulted for lead poisoning

had a section about copperiedus (i.e., copper toxicity). Tainted drinking water was one of the primary causes of high copper levels in the body, and birth control pills (estrogen) as well as IUDs were considered culprits by some in the online community.

I hadn't heard that Santa Cruz had a particularly high level of copper in its water, and besides, if that were true, we'd *all* have had copper toxicity, not just Gino. And he clearly hadn't gotten it from birth control. But then I read the next paragraph of the article: "Copper cookware, when not lined with a non-reactive metal, is a common cause of copper toxicity, particularly if used to cook or store highly acidic foods, as the acid can cause copper to leach into the food."

I stopped reading and thought back to the rack of gorgeous copper cookware I'd seen hanging from the pegboard in Gino's kitchen. They hadn't been simply copper-bottomed, like Revere Ware pots, but were copper all over. More like the kind Julia Child famously had hanging in her kitchen.

I knew that most all-copper pots generally had a thin lining of tin inside to protect the copper from leaching into food. But what if the pots were old—as Gino's no doubt were—and the lining had worn off, exposing the copper underneath? Angelo had told me that Gino used to make salted tomatoes as well as *conserva*, both highly acidic. If he'd prepared pasta sauces with these tomato preserves in his copper pots and the tin in the pots *had* worn off, that could easily explain the high levels of copper in the hair sample the lab had tested.

I went back to the copper toxicity article and scrolled down to the part about symptoms. There was a long list, similar to the lead poisoning symptoms Eric had read that day in my backyard. Many of them could be mistaken for intoxication and could also have caused Gino to become ornery and combative: confusion, fogginess, insomnia, irritability, lack of concentration, memory loss, mood swings, nausea, paranoia and hallucinations, spaciness.

So maybe I wasn't that far off after all. Maybe Gino *had* suffered from long-term poisoning—just from copper rather than lead.

I had to tell Eric.

I pulled out my cell and was about to press "Call" for his contact number when I had a thought and set the phone back down. If I told Eric about the results of the hair test, I'd have to tell him about the hair. Which meant I'd have to tell him about finding the cap and not turning it over to the police. Not only would he be furious with me for suppressing evidence, but he'd force me to take it down to the police station immediately.

And if I did turn over the cap, I'd be obligated to tell them not only where I found it, but also about Dad taking his boat out fishing the morning after Gino disappeared. Not to mention his altercation with the old fisherman just two days earlier.

Even though I knew my father couldn't possibly have had anything to do with Gino's death, the police would never take such a generous view. There was no getting around the fact that this evidence made Dad an obvious suspect.

No, I couldn't tell the police—or Eric—about the cap yet. I needed just a little more time to figure out what had really happened to Gino.

SEVERAL HOURS LATER I locked up the T-Bird out at the end of the wharf and dashed across the street. Taking cover under the Solari's awning, I shook the rain off the hood of my yellow rain slicker.

No sign of the protesters, thank God. I'd have to ask if they'd been here during today's lunch. Dad had emailed me in the morning to say that they had shown up last night, but that they'd been well behaved and had kept out of the way of the customers. As I watched other people darting through the rain to and from their cars, it occurred to me that maybe they'd been scared off by the storm.

But this thought, instead of cheering me up, only served to remind me of that damn tent, which in turn sent my mood spinning downward once more. Because without a tent, we—far more than the demonstrators—were going to be in a world of hurt if the rain continued through the weekend. What I really needed to do was march right inside and tell my dad that there was a good chance we'd be serving dinner to a host of waterlogged customers come Saturday night.

That's what I should have done, but I couldn't. Instead, I was just going to have to find a tent, even if it killed me. Because if I told Dad, that's pretty much what would happen, anyway.

I was mulling my dilemma and psyching myself up to greet my father when I saw Bobby jump out of his enormous truck. He locked the door and made a run for the shelter of the Solari's awning, coming to stand beside me.

"Damn," he said, brushing the water off his hair. "Was this storm even predicted? I'd been planning on going fishing this morning, but that sure didn't happen."

"Yeah, it was in the newspaper. They think it's supposed to last a few days, but hopefully not into the weekend."

"Oh," he said. "Is that dinner thing this weekend? My parents are going to it."

"That's nice." *And you might want to warn them to bring slickers and umbrellas.* "So, you been working at the store again today?"

"Uh-huh," Bobby said, aiming a kick at a paper plate someone had dropped on the ground. "Just got off my lunch break." He stared out at the rain for a moment, then let out a slow breath. "I guess I should be heading back there."

"Before you go, there was something I wanted to ask you."

"What?" He continued to stand under the awning, but the rapid tapping of his foot signaled that he was anxious to get going.

"I'll be quick," I said. "It's about Gino. You know all those copper pots that are in his kitchen?"

"Yeah."

"Well, I was wondering if he used them much. Did you ever see him cook anything in those pots?"

"Why the hell do you care about that?" Bobby asked. The tempo of the tapping had increased.

I told him my theory that the old fisherman had gotten copper poisoning from using his cookware, and how that would explain his behavior over the past several months—being more out of it and seeming intoxicated even when he hadn't had much to drink.

"And get this," I added. "One of the other symptoms of copper poisoning is erratic and irrational behavior. It can even make you have hallucinations. So my thinking is, maybe Gino was acting totally deranged that night he disappeared. And maybe because of that, he ended up getting into a fight with someone. The busboy at

Solari's saw Gino arguing with an old man that night behind the restaurant. Maybe, if Gino did have copper poisoning, he got so crazy that he attacked that old guy."

Bobby stared at me for a moment and then burst out laughing. "Really? You think he might have been poisoned by his *pots*?"

"Okay, I know it sounds weird, but if a pot is old and worn away so the copper comes through on the bottom, and if you cook a lot of acidic food in it—something like tomato sauce—you really can get copper poisoning, I swear."

The tapping stopped and Bobby's eyes got wide. "Gino did use those copper pots a lot," he said, "especially for red sauce. Like almost every day."

NINETEEN

Now I *HAD* to call Eric.

As soon as Bobby went on his way to his dad's gift shop, I dashed out to my car where I could talk in privacy. But once the phone started to ring, I realized my choice of location for the call had been a mistake. The rain pelting the T-Bird's canvas ragtop sounded like my high school marching band's percussion section pounding out a drum cadence six inches from the top of my head.

"Hi, Sal," Eric said.

"Hey, you. So, I have an update about Gino."

"What's that noise?" he asked. "It sounds like you're inside a machine shop."

"I'm in my car and it's kind of raining out there, in case you hadn't noticed."

"You're not driving, are you?"

"No, Mr. DA, I'm parked outside Solari's. I just didn't want a bunch of people hearing what I have to say."

"That good, is it?"

"You tell me. It looks like Gino was suffering from copper poisoning when he died."

I wasn't positive, because it could have been the wind howling outside my car windows, but I was pretty sure Eric's response was a long, exasperated sigh. "Okay, I'll bite," he finally said. "And why, exactly, do you think this?"

Now for the tricky part. Was there any possible way I could tell him about the hair analysis test without mentioning how I'd found Gino's wool fisherman's cap?

No, there wasn't. Nothing for it but to jump right in and hope Eric didn't immediately home in on that portion of my story.

"Okay, remember how we talked about the possibility of Gino getting lead poisoning from painting his boat? Well, I sent some of his hair to—"

"His hair? Where the hell did you get any of Gino's hair?"

So much for his not homing in on that fact. "Hold your horses; I'll get to that in a sec. Anyway, so I sent it to one of those online labs to test it for lead, and the results came back today."

"But wait, you said copper poisoning, not lead."

"I did. Because the analysis showed his levels of lead as being within the normal range. But his levels for *copper* were kind of high. And when I looked up copper poisoning online, I found out that a bunch of the symptoms are similar to lead poisoning and would explain a lot of Gino's behavior of late—his acting drunk, getting angry, just generally being really out of it. And here's the kicker: one of the most common causes of copper poisoning is using copper pots to cook highly acidic food, and I have it on good authority that Gino used to cook tomato sauce all the time in his copper pots."

"You know those online hair analysis tests are considered to be exceedingly unreliable," Eric said in his lecturing voice, "if not out-and-out scams. They just take your money and—" He stopped. "Hold on. Don't think you can sidetrack me from the important question here. Where *did* you get this hair sample, anyway?"

"Uh, yeah… I'd been hoping you wouldn't ask that."

"Okay, Sal, fess up."

"It was in Gino's cap. Which I, uh…found…"

"Oh, Jesus." There was a pause, and I had an image of Eric laying his head on his office desk as he silently cursed my name. "You mean to tell me you found Gino's cap—a piece of highly relevant, possibly *vital* evidence—and did not turn it over to the police? What were you thinking?"

"I know, I know. But it's only because of where I found it."

"And where, pray tell, did you find it?" Eric asked in that way people do when they're pretending to be patient and reasonable but the opposite is actually true.

"In my dad's fishing skiff, shoved under the middle bench. I found it that day we were out there painting with Omar's class and I went over to see if that guy's bocce ball had dented the boat. I was so freaked out about finding Gino's cap there that I didn't tell anyone."

"But I don't get it. Why would you be freaked out by that?"

"Because it turns out Dad went fishing in that boat the morning after Gino disappeared. So, with finding the cap lodged under the seat like that, it looks like Gino must have been in the boat. And I'm afraid the police will take it one step farther and accuse Dad of killing Gino and then using his skiff to take the body out to sea and dump it."

"Whoa, girl. That's making an awful big jump. Why on earth would the cops suspect your father of killing Gino?"

I told Eric about my dad forcibly ejecting Gino from the Solari's bar the day before he disappeared, and how Gino had thrown a punch at him in front of several witnesses. "And then the morning after Gino disappears, my dad goes fishing early in the morning, after which Gino's cap is discovered hidden away in the boat? Not good."

"Oh, boy." Eric was quiet a moment. "Look," he said, "the cops aren't going to suspect Mario just because he threw Gino out of the bar. It's a pretty weak motive for a murder, after all. And besides, you know they have to have other far better suspects by now."

"You think so? Have you heard anything around the office?"

"No, not really."

"Oh." So he was just trying to be sweet. Which was nice, actually, because right about now I could truly use some support. But what I needed far more than emotional support was a real live suspect—other than my father.

"That doesn't mean they haven't got other suspects, though," Eric added. "It's not my case, so I wouldn't necessarily hear."

"Yeah, I know. But here's another thing that makes it look even worse for Dad. I know you said the cops think that Gino was knocked on the head by someone and then thrown off the wharf, because of the mussel shell they found in his wound. But that doesn't make any sense to me. If that's what happened, how could his body have ended up on Its Beach? The wharf tides wash into shore, to Cowell's, not around the point."

"Hmmm…" Eric considered this a moment, and I listened to the sound of the rain on the ragtop, which had thankfully now decreased from its previous pounding to a mere patter.

"Wait," he said, jarring me from the meditative state

the rhythmic percussion had lulled me into. "This was the Monday night he disappeared, right? And just a few days later we got those Diablo winds."

"So?"

"So, they're *offshore* winds. If Gino ended up drowning in the water off the wharf, he would have pretty much immediately sunk after he died. The body would then have stayed where it was for at least several days until the gases that form inside after death made it float back up to the surface."

"Yuck," I said.

"Yeah, sorry. Anyway, let's assume it took four days for that to happen, which I think is realistic, given the temperature of the ocean this time of year. By then, the offshore Diablo winds had come up, which would have caused the current to reverse, taking Gino's body out to sea. After that, it could easily have washed up on Its Beach."

"Really? Are you sure? How come you know so much about ocean currents?"

"I'm a surfer, remember? A huge part of surfing is understanding currents and tides. So, yeah, I'm sure."

"Wow, that's great! At least for my dad, anyway. Maybe he won't now immediately be bumped up to suspect number one. Since it *does* make more sense for Gino to have knocked his head against the piers, which means he wasn't in a boat at all."

"Maybe," Eric said. "But don't you think for one second that this digression about where Gino's body washed up is going to let you off the hook for suppressing that evidence, young lady. Where is the cap right now?"

"At home in my sock drawer."

"What an original hiding place. Good thing no one's broken into your house since you found it, or it would have been for sale on Craigslist by now." Eric chuckled to himself before going on. "Now I know I don't really have to tell you that as soon as we hang up, the next thing you're going to do is take that cap down to the police station, correct?"

"I guess…"

"And that if you don't tell them, I will?"

"Okay, fine. But if they haul my dad off to jail in handcuffs because of this, I'll never ever forgive you."

"Hey, once you tell the cops your theory about the copper poisoning and all about the super-professional online lab that procured the results, they're going to get down on their knees to thank you for discovering such a crucial piece of evidence in the case. They're gonna be so thrilled, in fact, that they'll completely forget all about your dad."

So much for the sweet, supportive Eric. "Ha, ha. Very funny."

"That's why I'm laughing." And he was. A lot.

TWENTY MINUTES LATER, after swinging by my house to retrieve Gino's cap, I was standing in line at the Santa Cruz Police Department's reception desk. As I waited for the woman ahead of me to finish her discussion about obtaining a permit for a protest march downtown, I sent my dad a text telling him I wouldn't be at the restaurant for another half hour. Hopefully he wouldn't ask me the reason for my delay.

"Hi," I said when I stepped up to the counter. "I'm here because I have some evidence that may relate to the Gino Barbieri case."

"What sort of evidence?" the woman asked.

I held the plastic bag up for her inspection. "This." But then, realizing she'd have no idea what was inside, I added, "It's Gino's cap, which I found out on the wharf. I put it in this so it wouldn't get contaminated." The manner in which she was eyeing the dark green bag suggested she had a dog and knew what its normal purpose was.

"Okay," she said, and picked up the phone. "Let me get a detective to come down and talk to you. What's your name?"

I told her, and the woman spoke for a moment to someone and then replaced the receiver. "Detective Vargas will be down shortly."

Great. I took a seat on the wooden bench in the lobby and waited, trying to keep my jimmy legs to a minimum. *Why couldn't it have been someone else? Anyone but him.*

Sooner than I expected, Vargas's burly frame emerged from the door that led into the police department offices. He stood there a moment without speaking and then motioned for me to come inside.

"When Erica said it was you, I thought it best that I come down," the detective said as we mounted the steps to the investigation department. "Since I'm accustomed to your, shall we say, proclivity for trying to help us do our job?"

I didn't respond to this, instead following him silently into the small interview room that I'd gotten to know quite well over the past six months.

"So what is this evidence you have?" the detective asked after we'd both gotten settled, me on the small couch, him on the armchair across from me.

I lay the plastic bag on the coffee table between us. "I found this on the wharf. It's Gino Barbieri's wool cap."

Vargas took the pen from his shirt pocket and used it to open the bag. "How do you know it's his?" he asked.

"Everyone knows that cap," I said. "It's a Genovese-style fisherman's cap, and no one else wore one like it. Plus, you can tell from the faded color that it's Gino's."

"Uh-huh." The detective took the bag by its bottom and dumped the cap out onto the table. "Where exactly did you find it?"

"Uh…it was in my father's skiff, the little boat he keeps behind our restaurant for fishing. I found it jammed under the seat."

He poked at the cap for a moment with his pen and then sat back in his chair. "And when did you find the cap?"

"Well, it was a few days ago, actually. I've been meaning to bring it down to you, but…"

"When, *exactly*?" He'd now leaned forward again and was giving me a "cut the crap, lady" look.

"Last Saturday," I said, almost in a whisper. The small room was becoming claustrophobic as I felt the heat build up under my long-sleeved T-shirt. Not a good time for a hot flash.

"Last *Saturday*?" he bellowed back, jumping from his chair. "It took you five days to turn over evidence relevant to a possible homicide investigation?" The detective glared down at me, and I did my best to shrink into the recesses of the couch. "Why the hell would you wait so long? Oh, wait, I get it." He smiled, but the smile wasn't of the jolly, friendly variety. "It's because of where you found the cap—in your father's boat. So, tell me: What do you know about your father that would cause that discovery to make you so nervous?"

I didn't answer right away. It was one thing to merely fail to volunteer information, but to tell an actual, bald-faced lie to a police detective would be a giant step toward the criminal—as in, "making false statements to an officer of the law" kind of crime.

"I...well..."

"Yes?" The smile grew even broader. The detective was enjoying this.

"Okay. I found out my dad took his skiff out fishing the morning after Gino disappeared, and I was afraid you'd think he had something to do with Gino's death since the cap was found in his boat."

Vargas shook his head. "No matter how tiresome I might find your insistence on getting involved in police matters, I would never allow that to cloud my judgment in a case. And I hardly see how the mere fact that the hat was found in your father's boat would lead us to suspect him of killing Mr. Barbieri. It could have just fallen off and ended up there."

And then got itself miraculously hidden away, jammed under the seat? But since I'd already mentioned where in the boat I'd found the cap, I saw no need to repeat this tidbit of information.

The detective had finally sat back down, but he was still eyeballing me. "I'm thinking there's something else, too. Am I right?"

I had to hand it to the guy. He did seem to have a knack for reading people's thoughts and body language.

"Uh-huh," I said. "There is one more thing. My father eighty-sixed Gino—you know, kicked him out of the Solari's bar—the day before he went missing. And they kind of got into a scuffle over it. Gino was pretty mad and apparently threw a punch at my dad."

Vargas frowned, then picked up a pad of paper that was sitting on the small table next to him. Clicking open his ballpoint pen, he jotted something down and set the pad back on the table.

Definitely not good that this merited a note. Time to divert his attention to something other than my father.

"So there's another piece of evidence I need to tell you about, too, and this one I only just found out today."

The detective leaned back in the chair, hands clasped behind his head. "Uh-huh?"

"Well, you need to know first that a bunch of people have been talking about how Gino had seemed to be drinking a lot over the past few months and that he was acting different in other ways, too. Picking fights with people—"

"Like your father," Vargas said.

"Yeah, like my dad, and other people, too. Anyway, as you know, there are witnesses who say he was acting drunk that night he came into Solari's before he disappeared, but his tab from the meal shows he only ordered two beers with dinner."

The detective glanced at his watch, and I decided I'd best get to the point quickly. "So I got this idea that maybe something else was going on with Gino, and then got to thinking about how he was always painting his boat, and it occurred to me that maybe he was suffering from lead poisoning."

"Oh, boy." Vargas sat forward impatiently.

"So I took some of his hair and sent it to this place to get analyzed."

"You what?"

Now I had his interest back. I explained how the test had come back negative for lead (at which point the detective smiled) but how his copper levels were higher than normal. Pulling the report from my purse, I handed it to Vargas, who studied the paper while I went on.

"I heard from Bobby, the guy who's been working for him, that Gino used to cook tomato sauce in his copper pots all the time, which could totally give him copper poisoning, and which would explain his weird behavior over the past few months."

Vargas lowered the report. "I fail to see how his having copper poisoning, even if true, would help us determine *how* he was killed, which is all I'm really concerned about at this point."

"But don't you see? If Gino was all of a sudden acting totally irrational because of copper poisoning, that could have been the *reason* someone did it. So at least it gives you a motive for his killing."

"Right." But Vargas did not appear convinced. "Where did you get this hair sample, anyway?"

"I…from the cap. There was a ton of hair in it, so I figured it couldn't hurt if I took a little bit…"

The detective stood up again and pointed to the door. "Out," he commanded. "Get out right now, before I change my mind and have you taken downstairs and booked not only for suppression of evidence, but for tampering with it as well."

TWENTY

WELL, THAT DIDN'T go well. But then again, I hadn't really expected it to. At least Vargas hadn't hauled me or my father off to jail. And he had kept that hair analysis report. Maybe he'd mention the copper poisoning angle to the coroner, who could then make sure they included that along with the other things they tested for in the tox report.

The rain was steady as I darted out to my car in the police station parking lot, but nothing like the previous deluge. Once inside, I checked my messages and, seeing one from my dad, tapped the screen to open it: "Can u stop by Ggn and pick up large heavy pot for gravy? We only have 3 here."

"Will do," I texted back and fired up the T-Bird.

It was a little after four by the time I got to Gauguin, and Javier and Brian were already in the kitchen prepping for dinner, along with a woman I recognized as Javier's new flame. Brian was tending to the grill station, turning chicken quarters in a pan of marinade, and Natalie and Javier were at the line, whisking sauces and arranging the row of stainless steel inserts with ingredients for tonight's *mise en place*.

"What are you doing here?" Javier asked, looking up from his sauce—our Thai curry, I guessed from its turmeric-yellow hue. "Aren't you supposed to be helping your father tonight?"

"Yeah, but he asked me to swing by and pick up an extra pot on my way over there." I turned to Natalie. "Hi, I'm Sally. Great to finally meet you. And thank you so much for coming in tonight and saving my butt."

She let out a deep laugh and, after wiping her hand on her side towel, took mine in a firm clasp. "You're very welcome. I think it's going to be fun, getting to work in this gorgeous kitchen. And I have to say I kind of miss the frenzy of working the hot line, so I'm actually looking forward to the next three nights."

"Even though you have to get up at like, what, four am tomorrow morning?"

"More like six, but yeah, that is one drawback of working back-to-back shifts. Luckily I can get by on not much sleep." Natalie chuckled again, and I found myself understanding Javier's attraction. From the streaks of gray in her dark, shoulder-length hair and the laugh lines around her eyes, I guessed her to be older than Javier, but there was an exuberance about the pastry chef that was almost irresistible.

I knew I should have been happy for my head chef to have found this woman who held your gaze in a manner that suggested she truly cared about your thoughts, your feelings. But it just made it all that much harder. If she'd been a grouch or a shrew, at least I could have consoled myself with the prediction that he'd regret his decision soon.

"So tell me," Natalie said, returning to her organization of the hotel pan inserts, "how many people are you expecting for this big dinner on Saturday night?"

"Over a hundred and thirty," I said.

"Wow." She dropped a pan of diced red onions into one of the slots and turned to face me. "I didn't realize

Solari's could hold that many. Is there a banquet room I don't know about?"

"No, we're going to hold the pre-dinner reception inside, but the sit-down portion of the meal is going to be outside, behind the restaurant." I slumped back against the stainless steel table that ran down the middle of the kitchen and stared at my feet, tasting the acid that had risen to the back of my throat.

"You still haven't found a tent yet, have you?" Javier said.

I shook my head. "And now I've got to go over there and tell my dad the horrible news."

"What tent?" Natalie asked, and Javier explained how Solari's needed a huge party tent for the sister-cities dinner but that all of them were already rented.

"And so we're going to be royally screwed," I added in a moan, "especially if this storm keeps up for another two days."

A slow smile was forming on Natalie's face. Maybe there was a shrew aspect to her personality, after all, if she found my abject misery to be amusing. But, no.

"We have a tent," she said. "The Full Moon Café, that is. We use it for special events, like big wine tastings and when we cater weddings." She pulled a phone from the pocket of her black chef's pants. "Here, lemme call the owner and see if she'd be willing to let you use it."

Natalie stepped into the dry storage room to confer with her boss in private.

"Ohmygod," I said to Javier. "That would be awesome!"

He grinned as he squeezed lime juice into his curry sauce and tasted it. "Yep, she's a keeper," he said, and added another squeeze to the pot.

Natalie emerged from the storage room nodding vigorously. "She said yes."

I pumped my fist, then danced across the kitchen to envelope her in a hug. "Thank you. You have no idea the hell you have just rescued me from."

"I actually think I might," she said with a laugh. "I've worked in the restaurant business for many years." She shoved the phone back in her pocket. "So here's the deal. You can come get it tomorrow, and you'll need your own truck to move it. We always rent a truck, because the thing really is huge, but if you know someone with one of those enormous pickups, I bet that would work. And you'll also need at least three other people to help you set it up and take it down. Have you ever used one of these tents before?"

"No," I said. "But I'll figure it out."

Because, as everybody knows, necessity is the mother of saving yourself from having to serve tagliarini and chicken cacciatore to scores of customers in the pouring rain.

"No, no, wait. You have the wrong part facing down." I dropped my corner piece and trotted over to the opposite corner of the unconstructed tent. Sean, the Solari's busboy, stepped back, and I showed him how the piece was supposed to sit as Bobby and Emilio, the line cook, looked on. "This part, with the B—for bottom—goes down," I said, flipping the piece over and inserting the long aluminum pole into the short inward-facing pipe.

It was ten o'clock on Friday morning and we had just picked up the Full Moon Café's thirty-by-forty-foot party tent. It was a little smaller than I'd wanted, but at this point I was thrilled to have anything at all. We'd make it work.

Remembering Bobby's mammoth-sized pickup, I'd stopped by his family's gift shop before heading to Solari's the previous afternoon to see about using it to transport the tent. He'd been reluctant at first, but had enthusiastically agreed once he knew I was offering two hundred bucks for the use of both the truck and his brawn to load the thing and help set it up and then break it down again on Sunday.

The rainstorm had finally blown through, and today was blustery but mostly clear. The forecast, however, was for another front to move in sometime tonight or tomorrow. *Thank you, Natalie,* I said to myself for the hundredth time since her offer of the tent.

The metal poles, corner pieces, and vinyl top and sides were laid out on the ground behind Solari's in a rough approximation of where the enormous tent would eventually stand, and we were in the process of assembling the roof. Angelo and several bocce players were on the benches scattered around the area, following our progress with amused interest.

"So how come you know so much about putting together tents?" Sean asked as I returned to the corner piece I'd been working on before I noticed the busboy's error. "Have you done it before?"

"Nah," I said. "I just watched a YouTube video this morning is all."

"You can learn a lot from those videos," Angelo piped up from his spot on the wooden bench that sat against the Solari's back wall. "I learned how to change the ink in my computer printer last week by watching one of them."

The white-haired man seated next to him asked what YouTube was, and I bent down with a chuckle to attach my pipes as the fisherman showed off his knowledge of the Internet to his fellow seniors.

We'd just finished raising the roof, which now had its vinyl cover attached, and were about to start attaching the sides when the strains of a surf guitar sounded from my jeans pocket.

"Let's take a quick break," I said to my helpers. "I'd like to answer this." The three guys had no complaints and wandered off while I took the call. "Hey, Eric. What's up?"

"Just wanted to find out how it went yesterday down at the police station. You *did* go, didn't you?"

"Yes, I went." Glancing around to see if anyone was within earshot, I walked around the corner of the Solari's building and stood facing the wall. "And as you can imagine, Detective Vargas was not pleased that I'd waited so long to turn the cap in to him."

"You admitted when you found it?"

"C'mon, Eric. I may have taken longer than I should have to do it, but I'm not going to lie to the cops about something like that."

He was chuckling. "Well, that's good. I was starting to have my doubts."

"It's not funny," I hissed. "I also had to tell him about my dad's interaction with Gino, as well as where I found that damn cap." Detecting movement behind me, I glanced back. But it was just Sean walking from the Solari's back door to the area where we were setting up the tent.

"Interaction?" Eric asked.

"Don't you remember? I know I told you. About how the two of them got into that fight."

"Oh, right."

"And I gotta say, the detective seemed particularly interested in that information. Anyway, I better go. We have to get this tent up and—"

"You found a tent? Great!"

"Yeah. At least one thing seems to be working out. Anyway, I'll talk to you later, okay?"

I ended the call and headed back to the tent construction site. Bobby was standing a ways off, checking his phone, and Sean and Emilio were leaning on the wharf railing, checking out the storm surge sloshing noisily against the piers. As I rounded the corner of the building and passed Angelo and his friend on their bench, I realized that they had stopped chattering and were eyeing me as I walked by.

Had the two men heard any of my conversation with Eric? And then I realized with a jolt that the man with Angelo was the guy who'd hit my dad's skiff with his errant bocce ball throw. Same natty pressed slacks and cotton shirt, same head of silver hair. And he was slender and slightly hunched over. *Yes, he could definitely be the man Sean described arguing with Gino the night he disappeared.*

I stopped to talk to them, eager to learn something about the old bocce player. "I don't think we've ever officially met," I said, extending my arm. "I'm Sally, Mario's daughter."

"Frank." The man took my hand in a strong grip. "Very pleased to make your acquaintance."

"Frank only moved here last year," Angelo said,

"down from San Francisco, to be closer to his daughter who lives here."

"Ah." I nodded. "I pretty much grew up on the wharf and know most of the folks who hang out here—that explains why we haven't met. But I've seen you playing bocce a lot lately."

Frank smiled, producing rows of creases on his tanned face. "That's one thing I miss from the old neighborhood," he said. "My bocce club was one of the best in the Bay Area. Down here, well, let's just say they don't take the competition quite as seriously."

And I can imagine you don't take kindly to cheaters, either, I thought, remembering what Angelo had said about Gino, and also how this man had reacted to the ribbing of his fellow bocce players. But I kept this observation to myself. No reason I couldn't ask him in general terms about Gino, though.

"So, did you know the man who died a couple weeks back, Gino Barbieri? He used to play bocce here."

The smile vanished from Frank's face. "Uh-huh, I knew him," he said, but didn't elaborate. I was about to probe him further but, seeing a look of surprise from Angelo, who was staring at something behind me, I turned to see what had caused such a reaction from the old fisherman.

"Ms. Solari, just who I was looking for. May I have a word?"

It was Detective Vargas. And two uniformed officers were with him. *Damn.*

The detective held out a piece of paper for me. "I have a warrant to seize your father's boat," he said. "Could you show me where it is?"

I took the warrant and scanned it to make sure the

document was properly dated and signed by a judge and that it was indeed for my dad's skiff. No procedural errors I could see, alas.

I handed the warrant back to Vargas, trying to ignore Angelo's and Frank's gape-mouths and wide eyes. "It's over here," I said. The detective followed me to the other end of the Solari's building and we stopped at the Boston Whaler. "This is it."

"Thanks." He studied the boat for a moment and then asked, "How does your father transport it? Does he have a trailer?"

"No. When he wants to take it out, he borrows a dolly from the boat rental folks to move it over to their davit, and they lower it into the water for him."

Vargas frowned and then turned to his two cohorts. "Okay, Mark, you stay here and secure the scene, and Lisa, you go back to the station and find a trailer so we can transport this thing."

"You got it," the gal said, then trotted back out to the front of the building.

I watched her go and then turned to the detective. "You need anything else? 'Cause I really should get back to work helping put up that tent." I nodded toward the metal frame and pieces of vinyl scattered across the asphalt, and to Emilio, Sean, and Bobby, who were staring our way with the same bewildered expression that Angelo and Frank wore.

"Yeah, there is one more thing," Vargas said. "Is your father here? Because I'd like him to come down to the station with me to answer some questions."

TWENTY-ONE

THE DETECTIVE STARTED for the back door of the restaurant, and, after giving a "just a sec, be right there" sign to the guys by the tent, I followed him inside. We found Dad talking to Joe, the new prep cook, five cases of whole chickens stacked next to them.

"Part 'em all out, cut the breasts in two, and throw the backs, skinned, into this pot for—" Dad stopped when we came through the door. "What's this?"

"I'm Detective Vargas of the Santa Cruz Police Department, and I have some questions I'd like to ask you pertaining to Gino Barbieri."

Dad looked from the detective to me, his eyes initially registering confusion but then changing to understanding as they came to rest on mine. "Oh," he said, and his shoulders wilted. "Okay, I guess I can give you a few minutes. Let's go into the office."

Vargas bit his lip. "I'd actually prefer it if you came down to the station with me."

"Is he being charged with anything?" I asked, cutting in. "Because if he is, then he's not going to say anything without an attorney present. A criminal defense attorney, who hasn't gone inactive with the bar," I added, when Dad raised his eyebrows as if to suggest I might be that attorney.

"No, you're not being charged," the detective said to my dad. "We're just trying to figure out what happened and feel that you might have information relevant to the case because of where that cap was found."

"So that means you don't have to talk to him if you don't want to. And I recommend that you don't."

Vargas glared at me but, since he knew I was right, remained silent.

Twisting the side towel hanging from his apron into a giant knot, Dad swallowed and blinked a few times. "Well," he finally said, "I guess I'm willing to talk to you, if it could really help with your investigation."

The detective smiled, but I groaned. "Oh, Dad…"

"No, it's okay, hon," he said. "I didn't do anything wrong, so what's to worry about?"

Lots, I thought, but kept this to myself. I didn't want to further antagonize the man who would shortly be grilling my father like a flank steak on the Gauguin charbroiler. Besides, I knew full well that once my dad had decided on a course of action, it was nearly impossible to get him to change his mind.

He untied his apron and tossed it on the counter. "I'll go down to the police station with you, but can I drive myself?"

Vargas nodded. "Yeah, I guess that will be okay. I'll follow you."

"I'll be back soon," Dad said to me. "If I'm not back by the time you get that tent up, why don't you and Emilio get started on the chicken cacciatore. And once that's cooking, you can get going on the cabbage rolls. Emilio knows the recipes for both of them."

I watched my dad go out the front door with a tightening of the gut. Why did he always have to be so stubborn? Why couldn't he listen to me just this one time?

Because although the police weren't charging him with any crime right now, that didn't mean they wouldn't later.

SEAN, EMILIO, AND BOBBY were standing back from the crime tape that had now been strung around Dad's skiff, watching the cop, who'd put on latex gloves, cover the boat's top with plastic sheeting.

"C'mon, guys," I said, clapping my hands, "back to work," and the trio reluctantly turned away from the engrossing scene and followed me over to the half-constructed tent.

"How come the cops are interested in your dad's boat?" Emilio asked.

"It's 'cause I found Gino's cap in it," I said. No point keeping it a secret any longer, now that Vargas knew. "You know, that faded blue fisherman's cap he always wore? So they think there might be more evidence in the boat, too. And my dad's gone down to the police station to see if he can provide any information that might help them out with the case," I added, pleased at this spin I'd come up with to make my father the good guy rather than the suspect.

At eleven, I sent Emilio inside to cook the lunch orders, with the prep cook, Joe, as his second. Hopefully Dad would return before the usual rush began at noon.

A little while later, three police officers came around the side of the building, one of them dragging a large dolly. The cop who'd been guarding Dad's boat helped them lift the skiff onto the dolly and then push it around to the front of the restaurant where they no doubt had a trailer waiting.

After a couple more minutes, the first cop came back

and handed me a sheet of paper. "It's a receipt for taking the boat," he said.

"Do you know how long you'll keep it for?"

The man shrugged. "Who knows? It depends on what happens with the case. Oh, and you might want to know there's a group of people out in front of the restaurant with signs protesting something."

"Great. Like I haven't got enough to worry about right now. But thanks for telling me." I pocketed the paper and turned back to my tent construction.

It took Bobby and Sean and me about an hour to finish setting up the tent, but once we were done, I was pleased. The sides looked stable enough to withstand even strong gusts of wind and would surely keep out any rain that fell during the dinner.

"It looks like the circus has come to town," Sean observed.

Circus, indeed. Between the protesters, the rain, and the possibility of my father being arrested for Gino's murder, the analogy was not that far off. "Let's just hope no one falls off the tightrope between now and tomorrow night," I answered, eliciting blank stares from my two helpers.

Dad and I had devised a plan for lighting the inside of the tent, which involved running heavy-duty orange extension cords and clamping aluminum reflector lights all over the place inside. Probably not up to code, but I was hoping the fire department wouldn't come round to do an inspection between now and tomorrow night.

After getting Sean and Bobby started on the lighting, I headed out front to take a look at the protesters. There were only five, and they were standing well back from the restaurant door. Nodding thanks to the man

I'd spoken to before, I went inside. The dining room was about half full, which normally would be a piece of cake. But without my dad here, it meant Emilio was probably going nuts.

I was right. "I'm totally in the weeds," the cook shouted when I came into the kitchen. He had six sauté pans going as well as several steaming pots of pasta and sauces bubbling on the range top.

"Where's Joe?" I asked.

"In the prep room chopping more zucchini. We ran out and I've got eight tickets on the rail right now."

"Okay, I'm on it," I said, donning a chef's jacket and washing my hands at the stainless steel sink. *What could be taking Dad so long?* This was not good.

At one thirty the lunch rush finally tapered off and I was able to turn my attention to the chicken cacciatore for tomorrow's big dinner. I'd just gotten the flour-dusted chicken pieces browning in olive oil and was chopping up a case of bell peppers when my father shuffled into the kitchen and sat heavily on the stool in the corner by the Robot Coupe.

"Thank God," I said, setting down my knife and rushing over to give him a hug. "It was taking so long I was worried they'd—"

"Arrested me?" Dad let out a short laugh, but the accompanying frown belied any actual humor. "No, they didn't arrest me. But the way they kept at me, asking the same questions over and over again in different ways, I was sure at some point they were going to snap the cuffs on and cart me off to jail."

"But they didn't," I said.

"No. They did tell me not to leave the area, though."

It was my turn to let out a sarcastic laugh. "That's just posturing, Dad. You're either under arrest or you're not. The police have no right to keep you from leaving town. So what did they ask you about?"

"Mostly about my eighty-sixing Gino. What exactly happened, who hit who, was I angry at Gino, why did I let him in the next night if I'd kicked him out the day before?" Dad shook his head impatiently. "I swear I told them the same story about a hundred times."

"That's what they do. They figure if you have to re-peat it and it's a made-up story, you'll slip up at some point and say something that proves you're lying. Did they ask about your taking the skiff out the morning after he came in for dinner?"

He nodded, staring blankly at the mound of green bell peppers on the counter. "They wanted to know what time I left and came back, where I went fishing and what I caught, who saw me go out." Dad sat up straight, hands on his knees. I could see beads of sweat forming on his temple and upper lip. "They can't really think I did it, right?" he asked, twisting on the stool to face me. "That I took him out in my boat and…"

I knelt at his side and took his rough hand in mine. "They're just doing their job. They have to cover all the bases. And since Gino's cap somehow ended up in your skiff, it makes sense that they'd ask you about the last time you used it. But I bet they also asked whether you noticed anything odd about the boat or around the area where you keep it, right?"

"Uh-huh. They did."

"See? So they're not focusing only on you." I stood back up, giving his hand a squeeze before I let it go. "And the most important thing is, they let you go after questioning you. If they really thought you could have done it, they'd have kept you there."

"I know." Dad ran a hand through his short, salt-and-pepper hair and forced a smile. "So, how did lunch go? I saw that those people are still out front."

"Yeah, but they seem to be behaving themselves, at least." I caught him up on all that had transpired in the three hours he'd been gone, including the fact that his beloved Boston Whaler had been taken into custody.

I detected a tightening of the jaw, but he didn't say anything. Even Dad had to recognize that in the grand scheme, this was a minor issue.

"But at least the tent looks like it's going to work out well," I said, "so there is some good news."

After going out back to inspect the tent and the lighting that Sean and Bobby had run, Dad and I returned to the kitchen to work on the dishes for tomorrow's dinner. By six o'clock we'd finished the chicken cacciatore and all the cutting and chopping for the sautéed zucchini and the salad, and I was ready for a break.

As I poured myself a glass of iced tea from the pitcher in the wait station, I checked out the early dinner crowd. A husband and wife in their sixties who were regulars sat at table three, and four much younger people—tourists, by the look of the men's form-fitting T-shirts and pressed blue jeans—were at table five. Most of the booths along the picture window were filled, which was not surprising, since they have the best view in the house.

But who was the tall woman in the far corner with the perfectly coiffed raven hair? As I peered out at the dining room to get a better look, she bent over to reach for something in her purse and I saw that her companion was Angelo, in his usual spot. It had to be the mysterious Anastasia!

Setting down my iced tea, I strode across the dining room. "Good evening, Angelo. How nice to see you here." I turned to the woman, who I now saw had on lipstick in a shade Sophia Loren might have worn in one of her early films. A perfect match for the crimson bolero jacket she wore. "Hi, I'm Sally Solari."

"Oh, pleased to meet you," she answered with an enthusiastic smile to match the flaming red lipstick. "I'm Anastasia."

Bingo.

TWENTY-TWO

I CHECKED OUT her left hand: no wedding ring. But that didn't necessarily mean anything. Was there any way I could casually bring up the subject? *So, I was just wondering, did you by any chance happen to marry Gino right before he ended up drowned?* Probably not the best way to start a conversation.

Small talk was a better idea. "I see you still have your menus," I said, "so you haven't ordered yet. May I recommend the Albacore Steak Florentine, which is tonight's special? The tuna was caught just this morning, and we're doing them like a traditional *bistecca Fiorentina*, grilled with olive oil, garlic, and a hint of rosemary. We're serving it with cannellini—those small white beans—and sautéed chard."

"Oooh, that sounds delish!" Anastasia crowed. "I'll have that."

"Make that two," said Angelo, directing a loopy smile at his dinner partner.

"Great. I'll go tell your server. And would you like any wine to go with it?" Anastasia responded with a vigorous nod. "Red or white?"

She looked at Angelo, who shrugged. "Whichever you want, my dear."

"White, then, I guess. Since it's fish, right?"

"Good choice," I responded, though I actually thought a light red would pair better with the bold flavors of the garlic, rosemary, and tuna. "I'll bring it right out." Gathering up their menus, I headed for the wait station, filled a glass carafe with the house white, and returned to their table. "The wine's on us by the way," I said with a wink at Angelo, who flashed me a subtle thumbs-up.

"Wow, thanks!" Anastasia raised the glass I'd poured for her in salute, then took a sip. "Very good. Nice and smooth," she said, setting the wine daintily on the red tablecloth.

"Yes, I like this Pinot Grigio more than the Soave, which I think you had last time you were in."

Anastasia pursed her lips and looked down at her glass, and Angelo frowned. I knew neither probably wanted to be reminded right now of her previous dalliance with Gino, but I needed to get some information out of her if I could. Maybe a change of tactics was in order, though. "So, Angelo told me you're writing a story for some newspaper about the history of the Italian fishermen out here on the wharf."

That did the trick. Her head popped back up and the sparkle returned to her eyes. "I am, for the *Santa Cruz Herald.* You know, that new weekly paper?"

Aha. Angelo had said the *Tribune*, not the *Herald.* Maybe she was legit after all. "Well, it sounds like an interesting subject, if I do say so myself—being the daughter of one of those Italian fishermen."

Anastasia laughed and took another sip of wine. "It really is, though. I've lived in Santa Cruz almost five years, and I had no idea about the whole Italian culture that still exists on the West Side—and how *friendly* they are." She touched Angelo's forearm flirtatiously, and the old fisherman ducked his head in response. Had it not been for his tanned, olive complexion, I'm sure we would have seen a flush of red jump to his cheeks.

"I guess that must be why you had dinner here with Gino, then. Because of your article."

"Right. And he was very helpful. He had so many fascinating stories about the old days." She looked down once again. "It's so sad about his death."

I studied her face for signs of guile or deceit, but all I could detect was genuine sorrow. "I don't know if you know this," I said, "but you were probably one of the last people to see Gino."

Her head jerked up, accompanied by a quick intake of breath. "Really? I had no idea. It was days after our dinner that he was found, wasn't it?" And then her hand went to her mouth. "Ohmygod. Does that mean I'm a suspect? I mean, no one's tried to contact me or anything."

If she was faking this reaction, it was an Oscar-worthy performance.

"That's probably because they didn't know how to find you," I said. "But I bet the police would very much like to talk to you."

From the blanching of her face, it appeared that this possibility disturbed her even more than the prospect that she might be a suspect in Gino's death. *Could she in fact have something to hide from the police?*

And then I had an idea how I could get information from her without sounding like some interfering busy-body. "You know," I said, leaning in toward the table, "if you wanted to tell me about what happened that night, I have connections with the police and could talk to them for you. And then they'd only have to contact you if they needed anything more."

This was most certainly false. The cops would obviously want to talk to her themselves, not to mention that Detective Vargas would be apoplectic once he found out I'd been interrogating an important witness before he had the chance to do so. Oh, well.

"Yeah, maybe..." Anastasia said, taking a breadstick from the basket and breaking it in two.

"Do you mind?" I asked, and nodded at a chair sitting at an unoccupied table.

"Please." Angelo jumped up to help me get seated at the end of the booth.

"So..." I cleared my throat as I tried to figure out where to start. "There are some people who thought Gino appeared rather...intoxicated when he left after dinner that night."

Anastasia nodded. "Yeah. He seemed fine at the beginning of dinner, but by the end he was pretty out of it. I figured he must have been drinking before we met up."

"Did it come on all of a sudden, or was it gradual?"

She thought a moment. "I think it was kind of sudden, actually. Because one minute he's telling me about his parents, and then he stands up to use the restroom and I notice he's kind of unsteady on his feet. He'd already paid the bill, so I waited for him out in front of the restaurant. I thought maybe the fresh air would sober him up and it did seem to help, 'cause once he'd been outside for a bit he said he wanted to show me this old boat they have on display."

"The *Marcella*," I said, "behind Solari's."

"Right. And Gino was acting more normal now, so I said okay and we walked around the building and stood and looked at the boat for a few minutes, him going on about the huge fishing fleets they used to have here in the bay."

She stopped to take a sip of wine, then glanced at Angelo with a quick frown.

"And…" I prompted her, pretty sure I knew where this was going.

"It's okay, honey," the old fisherman said. "Whatever it is, you can tell us."

"Okay." Anastasia smiled uncomfortably. "It's just kind of embarrassing. We were standing there looking at the boat, and then all of a sudden Gino turned and grabbed me and started kissing me. It caught me totally off guard, and it took a minute for me to react and push him off."

"Once you made it clear you weren't interested, did he stop?" I asked.

Angelo was staring intently at her, waiting for the answer to my question.

"Oh, yeah, he did. And he even apologized, too. But by this point he'd gotten kind of out of it again. His balance was off and he was sort of slurring his words. So I hung out with him for a bit longer to make sure he was okay. But after a little while he told me to go, that he wanted to sit and look at the moon and think. I asked him if he'd driven to the restaurant—I certainly didn't want him driving home—but he swore he lived nearby and that he'd walked. So I left him there."

Anastasia took another drink of wine and turned to look out the picture window. I followed her gaze. The forecasted rain hadn't yet arrived, but gusts of wind were now buffeting our big party tent. I was glad I'd taken Bobby's advice to anchor heavy weights all along its sides, because the structure seemed to be holding fast.

At the sight of Giulia approaching with plates of grilled albacore, I stood up. "Well, I should let you eat in peace. I do appreciate you telling me all this, and I'll make sure the information gets to the police."

Anastasia nodded absently, brows furrowed. She bit her lip, opened her mouth as if she were about to speak, then closed it again.

I waited till Giulia had set down their dinners and then left again to fetch a pitcher to top off their water glasses. "Was there something else?" I asked. "Did you see Gino again after you left?"

She shook her head. "No, but I did see someone else."

"What do you mean?"

"It was as I was heading back out to the street. I realized there'd been someone watching us, standing behind that kiosk—you know, the thing with those photos and stuff about the Italian fishing fleet that's right near the boat?"

"Sure, I know it," I said. "Could you see who was watching you, or what they looked like?"

"No. It was too dark, and he was hunched over behind the kiosk. The whole thing seemed kind of creepy, and I just wanted to get away."

"So it was a man you saw."

"Yeah, I'm pretty sure. I mean, who else but a man would do something like that?" Anastasia glanced up at Angelo with a quick smile, as if to say, "Not that all men would act like that, of course."

But it took a second for the fisherman to return the smile. And in that short moment, I glimpsed a hardness in his eyes I'd not seen before.

BACK IN THE KITCHEN, Dad was working with Emilio on the dinner tickets, but when he saw me come in he hollered over the din of the exhaust fan and banging

pots and sauté pans that I should get started on the cabbage rolls. He'd left instructions in the prep room, so I
headed in there with my iced tea and read through the
handwritten sheet of paper.

First off, I needed to get the ten heads of cabbage
simmering for the wrappers, but since four of the six
burners on the stove were already in use, I'd have to do
them in separate batches. I got two stock pots of water
heating up on the back burners, then started prepping
the ingredients for the filling: more cabbage, onions,
garlic, and potatoes. These would be sautéed—also in
several batches, after the cabbage heads were done—
then mixed with ricotta cheese and chopped basil and
parsley and wrapped in the cooked cabbage leaves.

As I chopped my way through a pile of yellow onions, I thought about what Anastasia had just told me,
wondering who could have been watching her and Gino
that night. *Was it the same guy that Sean saw arguing
with Gino just a little while later?* It seemed likely, especially given how both Sean and Anastasia had described
the man as being hunched over. Maybe whoever had
watched Gino and Anastasia had not been happy about
what he'd seen and had confronted Gino afterward.

Then Angelo's expression as Anastasia had been telling her story—those cold, steely eyes—came back to
me. I would never have described the old fisherman as
being hunched. He tended to carry his slim form ram-
rod straight, shoulders back. But it was obvious that
he'd fallen hard for Anastasia.

What if he'd already become smitten with her before
she started hanging out with Gino? Angelo had made it
clear he'd been checking her out for a while before they
actually met. How would he have reacted if he'd seen

his old friend, with whom he'd recently had a bitter falling out, coming on hard to the woman of his dreams?

Setting down my chef's knife, I walked from the prep room to the wait station and poked my head around the corner. Angelo and Anastasia were still at their table, and Angelo was nodding and smiling at something his companion was saying. He didn't appear to be upset or unhappy, and as I watched, he poured both of them another glass of wine.

My view was temporarily blocked as Giulia arrived to take their dessert order, but when she'd retreated I saw that Angelo was now leaning forward and had taken Anastasia by the hand. Since she was facing away from me, I couldn't see her expression, but she didn't pull her hand away.

Interesting, I thought as I made my way back to the prep room. Was she leading him on or merely being polite? Or was it possible that the affection went both ways?

The last step for the cabbage rolls was to make a red sauce. Once stuffed, the rolls would be arranged in roasting pans on a bed of the sauce to be chilled overnight. We'd bake them tomorrow afternoon, then finish off the dish by topping the cabbage rolls with grated Pecorino cheese and bread crumbs, broiled to a crispy, golden brown.

It was a slow process because of having to share the range top with my father and Emilio, but by a little after seven the dinner orders had slackened and Dad was able to come back to the prep room and help me out. In a sort of mini assembly line, I spooned filling onto the leaves and then he'd fold each one into a burrito-shaped packet and place it on the tomato sauce–lined baking

pan. With two of us now working, we made quick progress and had a hundred and forty rolls ready for baking
in under a half hour.

After wrapping the filled pans with plastic and stowing them in the walk-in fridge, I poked my head around
the corner to check out the dining room once more. Angelo and Anastasia had finished their dessert and the
fisherman was examining the check. He pulled several
bills from his wallet and laid them on the tip tray, and
the two of them stood to go.

As I watched the couple leave the restaurant, laughing and chattering, I made a snap decision. Crossing the
dining room, I opened the front door and followed them.

TWENTY-THREE

ONCE OUTSIDE, I peered up and down the sidewalk that runs along the shops and restaurants on the wharf, trying to spot which way Angelo and Anastasia had headed. No sign of the pair.

Shoot. How could they have disappeared so quickly?

But then my eye was caught by a flash of red on the other side of the street—Anastasia's crimson jacket. It looked as if they were headed for Bobby's giant pickup, which sat across from his dad's gift shop. But no, they'd stopped at the blue sedan next to it.

Realizing how conspicuous I must be, standing there gawking at them (the food-spattered apron I'd forgotten to remove didn't help), I ducked behind an SUV parked in front of the restaurant and continued to monitor the couple through its windshield.

Anastasia dug around in her bag and extracted a set of keys, then leaned back against the driver's side door of the car. They continued to chat, Anastasia nodding and smiling at whatever he was saying, but after a few minutes she pushed off from the car—clear "okay, I've gotta go now" body language. Angelo took a step closer, then leaned in to give her a kiss. It looked as if he was aiming for her mouth, but at the last second Anastasia turned her head so that his lips landed on her cheek instead.

Opening the car door and sliding into the seat, she

started the engine and pulled out of the parking space
with a quick smile and wave good-bye. Angelo watched
as the blue car sped down the wharf, then turned and
directed a kick at a seagull pecking at a pile of French
fries at his feet. The gull hopped out of the way, then
immediately returned to its dinner.

The fisherman glanced my way but didn't appear to
notice me crouching behind the black SUV. With one
last look in the direction of Anastasia's car, he crossed
the street back toward Solari's, then turned the corner
of the restaurant toward the rear of the building.

Keeping a safe distance, I followed Angelo. He made
his way across to the bocce court, where a group of
players were gathering up all the balls scattered about
the crushed granite surface and packing them into their
canvas cases. I hid myself behind the *Marcella* and
watched as he approached a tall, lanky guy with his
back to me. *Frank, the bocce player with the temper,* I
realized when I caught sight of his profile.

The two spoke for a few minutes, then Frank leaned
toward Angelo, said something into his ear, and let out a
bark of a laugh. Angelo stared briefly at the other man,
then gave him the Italian version of the finger (raised
clenched fist, hand on bicep) and strode off.

I was torn. Should I continue to follow Angelo or
stay and see what Frank was up to? But then I noticed
that from my vantage point, I could keep an eye on both
men, at least till Angelo rounded the corner. So I stayed
put, hidden behind the red-and-green Monterey clipper.

Frank was now laughing in earnest. Pulling on a
dark brown jacket to match his slacks, he gestured toward the retreating Angelo as he held court with three
other guys who'd come over to see what all the fun

was about. I could well imagine what was being said about poor old Angelo, who must have made the mistake of confiding in the other about being rebuffed by his young lady friend.

I left them to their gossip and hightailed it after the fisherman, who'd turned the corner out of my line of sight. As I emerged onto the sidewalk in front of Solari's, I spied him crossing the street once more. Angelo threaded through the cars to the far side of the parking area, then took a seat at one of the wood benches sprinkled along the edge of the wharf. Stretching his long legs out before him, he leaned back, arms crossed, and gazed out across the water.

He didn't look as if he was leaving anytime soon. The bay between the Boardwalk and Cocoanut Grove was now awash in orange and pink from the setting sun, a vista that even the dejected fisherman had to appreciate.

Better go back inside to see if Dad has anything else for me to do.

I felt a little sorry for Angelo. At the same time, however, he'd started to give me the heebie-jeebies. Not just that hard look in his eyes earlier tonight, but also what my dad had told me about him losing it with the fish buyer. Anyone who could clock a grocer with a lead weight could just as easily have walloped old Gino on the head, right?

But what about Frank? I'd witnessed him heave a rock-hard bocce ball at a group of old men for no reason other than their laughter at his errant throw. Could he have been equally angry at something Gino had said or done and retaliated in a similar manner? He could have used a bocce ball, but it could also have been some other blunt object lying close at hand. Something like an oar from my father's Boston Whaler. And that would explain why Gino's cap had fallen into the boat.

Well, I thought as I made my way through the Solari's dining room toward the back of the house, *if that's the case, hopefully they'll find some prints—other than Dad's—on the oars.*

It wasn't even eight o'clock, but just five tables remained and they'd all been served their entrées. *A slow night. Good.* That meant Dad would be able to get to bed early as well. We both needed a full night's sleep in preparation for our big day tomorrow.

I found him in the office, studying a handwritten sheet of paper. "Oh, hi, hon," he said, looking up when I came through the door. "I thought you'd gone. I wanted to talk to you about tomorrow."

"Sorry. I just went outside for a bit to get some air."

"Yeah," he said with a laugh, "it is a bit funky in here from all that cabbage you boiled. Here." He handed the paper to me. "You wanna sit down for a sec and decide who's going to do what so we don't have to figure it all out tomorrow morning?"

"Sure, no problem."

I pulled a folding chair up next to Dad, and the two of us conferred about setup, beverages, food prep, and logistics for the pre-dinner appetizers in the restaurant and the sit-down meal in the tent. After we'd finished, he headed back to the kitchen and I went in search of Giulia to make sure our head waitress was in on the game plan.

That done, I plopped down once more in the Solari's office to check my phone. Nothing urgent, thank goodness, since all I wanted to do right now was go home, play with Buster while I had a soothing nightcap, and then fall into bed.

I hoisted myself out of the chair with a grunt and made my way back to the kitchen, where Dad was helping Emilio with the final cleanup. Slipping behind my father as he pulled plastic wrap over a container of left-over tarragon-cream sauce, I planted a kiss on his cheek. "See you tomorrow morning," I said, then headed out the back door, the screen slamming behind me.

The sun had been down for a while, but off to the west the sky still glowed a violet and cobalt blue where it met the Pacific Ocean. Pulling my jacket closer around me, I walked across the now-empty bocce court to the railing and inhaled deeply. After the closeness of the Solari's kitchen, the cool, salt-sea air was a welcome relief.

Strains of laughter and seventies rock music escaped from the restaurant bar two doors down, and I tried to make out the song. Bob Seger, maybe? It sounded a little like "Night Moves," but the slap of water against the wharf piers was too loud for me to tell for sure.

I tilted my head back and gazed upward. Dark clouds raced across the sky, and between them a host of stars gleamed in the moonless night. *Please, please let it not rain tomorrow.* Yes, we did have the tent, but it would still be a bummer of mammoth proportions if we had to transport all that food from the restaurant kitchen to the tent in a downpour.

Leaning forward again, arms crossed on the railing, I stared out across the inky inlet toward West Cliff Drive. *Okay, I really should get myself home and to bed*, I thought, and stood up. But as I pushed back from the railing, a shadow fell on its wooden frame. I had just enough time to register that someone must have come between me and the security light attached to the back wall of Solari's before I felt a sharp blow to the back of my head.

I crumpled, falling limply across the railing. Too dazed to pick myself up, I drew a slow, shallow breath and tried to turn my head to see my assailant. But before I could even open my eyes, I was lifted up by my legs.

It didn't take much. Once I was about a foot off the ground, the weight of my upper body did the rest of the work and I slid over the side of the railing. Down I plunged.

Into the cold, black water below.

TWENTY-FOUR

THEY SAY THAT profound and insightful images can flash through your brain in times of great danger or stress—key memories or visions of a future now in peril. Which is a pretty accurate description of my first thought as I sank into the murky depths: *I'm going to pass out and drown, and no one will ever know what became of me.*

But the very next one was, *Ohmygod, this water is freakin' cold!*

It was the temperature of the ocean that likely saved me. Its iciness snapped me out of my daze, prompting me to stop my tumble and swim for the surface as fast as I could. I popped up out of the water and gasped for breath, only to be immediately slammed by the surge against one of the piers.

Ignoring the throbbing in both my head and my shoulder, I pushed off from the wooden piling and coughed up the salt water in my throat. Back up on the wharf, I could make out the dark, backlit shape of a man leaning over the railing, peering downward. As soon as he spotted me, he raised his right arm as if about to throw something, then lowered it again.

I knew I should try to swim away, but the surge kept sweeping me back toward the wharf, knocking me against its mussel- and barnacle-encrusted piers. Doing my best to protect my head and sore shoulder, I kept pushing off from the pilings with my hands, which were now cut and bleeding from the sharp shells, and every time I came up to breathe I got a mouthful of seawater along with air.

Panic began to set in. I was achy, freezing, exhausted, and terrified I was going to be knocked unconscious by bashing my head against one of the wooden piers. A vision of my drowned body lying tangled in a pile of kelp like Gino's flashed through my mind, and I started to scream.

"Help! Help me, *please*! I'm down here in the water!"

But my feeble cry was swept away by the wind and drowned out by the churning water crashing against the wooden piers.

Then it began to rain. Hard.

And that's when my emotion changed from fear to fury. *You can do this, Sal. You're a strong swimmer. You have to get out of this and nail that scumbag. Just think.*

I realized that in my panic I'd been doing it all wrong. This wasn't technically a rip current, but the same rules applied. The first thing was to remain calm and not struggle. Well, I'd failed that one already. But the second rule was not to swim directly against the current or you'll just tire yourself out. You have to go at an angle.

Since the surge seemed to be coming from the direction of Cowell's Beach, I needed to swim parallel to the shore, or even out to sea, to get free from the current that was slamming me against the wharf. Only then should I head back inland.

Pushing off from the sharp pilings one more time, I summoned all my strength, calling up memories of those summers I'd spent as a junior lifeguard in this exact same spot. After about forty strokes I stopped and treaded water, the rain coursing down my face. *Was I being swept back toward the wharf?* No, I could tell by focusing on the distant lights of the Dream Inn that I was holding steady. All I had to do now was make it to the beach. I could do that easy, right? I must have swum it a dozen times as a teenager.

Less frantically now, I headed for shore. I could tell from where I was along the length of the wharf that I was making progress, but it was slow going. Every few minutes I'd stop and tread water again to catch my breath and then continue on.

After what seemed like at least a half hour but was probably only fifteen minutes, my feet touched bottom and I dragged myself onto the beach and dropped to the sand. As I lay there in the rain, I had the ironic thought that in the end, here I was indeed washed up on the shore just like poor old Gino. *Well, not just like him, thank God.*

I started to chuckle softly, in that way people who've narrowly escaped a scary situation have a tendency to do. It's really more delayed hysteria than it is humor.

But my smile vanished as I saw a tall man in dark clothing running across the sand toward me. It had to be my assailant, coming to finish me off. I pulled myself to a sitting position, knowing there was no way I could outrun anyone right now. This was it.

When he approached, I raised my arms in front of my face instinctually, as if that could protect me from his attack. The man stopped before me, breathing heavily, then dropped to his knees. I closed my eyes, waiting for the inevitable.

"Are you all right?" he asked. "I saw you coming out of the water and wondered what—" And then he let out a gasp. "Ohmygod, you've got blood all over the back of your head! I gotta call nine-one-one!"

As he spoke to the person at the call center, I fell back onto the sand. This time I laughed out loud.

I WASN'T LAUGHING two hours later as I lay on a gurney in the ER. It was a busy Friday night and all the rooms were full, so my bed had been rolled into a corner of the hallway till one opened up. My head hurt like hell— the meds they'd finally given me hadn't fully kicked in—and even though I had three thermal blankets over me, my teeth were chattering and I felt as if I'd never be warm again.

They'd cleaned and patched up my head. It was merely a surface wound, the doctor had said, and only looked bad because of all the blood vessels near the surface of the scalp. I'd been lucky that the blow had apparently glanced off the side, but they still wanted me to stay the night for observation.

Which was fine by me. Maybe I could stay here indefinitely, or at least until they caught whoever had come after me. Since he'd failed the first time, it seemed likely he'd be back soon to try to finish the job. *Best not to think of that right now.*

"You look like the Invisible Man," Eric said, nodding toward the white cloth bandages wrapped snugly about my cut-up hands.

When the EMT had asked during the ambulance ride if there was anyone I'd like him to call, Eric had been the first person I'd thought of. Eric had wanted to call my dad, too, but I'd told him that since it looked as if I was going to be fine, I wanted to let Dad get a good night's sleep. No reason for both of us to be useless tomorrow.

Because I clearly am going to be little help, I thought, staring glumly at the bulky bandages. "Too bad I can't turn invisible," I replied, "and just disappear for the next few days."

Eric checked his phone, then stowed it back away. "I called the cops," he said, "and also left a separate message for Detective Vargas. I was just looking to see if he'd gotten back to me."

"Yeah, the EMT said the nine-one-one center also contacted the police. I'm sure I'll be getting a visit from one of them sometime tonight."

"No doubt." Eric leaned back in the plastic chair he'd dragged in from the waiting room, shoved both hands into the pocket of his Santa Cruz Skateboards hoodie, and eyed me solemnly.

"No need for the funereal look," I said. "I'm fine. At least physically, anyway. I gotta say, it does kinda freak me out that the creep is still out there."

"I can imagine." If anything, Eric's expression had now become even more somber. "You haven't named anybody, so I'm guessing you don't know who did it?"

I shook my head and immediately regretted the action. "No, the guy was backlit, so all I saw was that he had on dark clothes and was fairly tall."

"Not much to go on," Eric observed, unhelpfully.

"I know. The only other thing I can tell you is that whatever he hit me with was hard, though thank God he didn't connect well. I saw something in his hand after I was in the water, but I couldn't tell what it was."

"How big? Like a bat? 'Cause that's what the cops are thinking might have been used on Gino."

"No, it was small and compact. More like a rock. Or a bocce ball." I told Eric about the guys who'd been packing up their gear after a game out in the same spot just fifteen minutes before I'd been hit on the head. "So one of them could still have been hanging around and, when he saw me, realized he had the perfect opportunity to get me out of the picture."

"You thinking of anyone in particular?" Eric asked.

"I am, but I have no proof. And no great motive, either." I told him my suspicions about Frank, the old man with the temper we'd seen playing bocce the week before, and how he and Angelo had overheard the two of us talking on the phone that morning. "I chatted with Frank afterward a little bit, and when I asked about Gino, he got all serious."

I shifted in my bed, but it was hard to do without using my hands as support. Eric got up and helped me adjust the pillows behind my back.

"Thanks. It sucks being so helpless. So, anyway, I'm thinking it's possible that Frank was the old man Sean saw arguing with Gino the night he disappeared. And if he was the one who killed him, maybe he got spooked when he heard me telling you about going to the police. He was one of the guys I saw at the bocce court tonight, so I know he was at the scene, as they say."

"Maybe." Eric returned to his plastic chair and tipped back on its back legs. "So what about that Bobby guy? Didn't you think last week that it might have been him who killed Gino?"

"Yeah, but once I found out he wasn't going to inherit Gino's boat, and then saw how upset he seemed by his death, he didn't seem too likely as a suspect. And I'm not sure why he'd want to get rid of me, anyway. Especially since I've just hired him to help with that big tent. He sure won't get paid on Sunday if it turns out he's trying to off his boss."

My chuckle was only halfhearted, though, since when I really thought about it, I had no more evidence supporting Frank as the culprit than I did Bobby. And unlike the old bocce player, Bobby at least had had a close relationship with Gino. And, I realized with a twinge in my stomach, he'd also been there this morning when I'd talked on the phone to Eric. *Could Bobby have overheard our conversation?*

Eric interrupted my fretting. "You said it was a man who knocked you on the head and pushed you over the side, but is there any way it could it have been a woman?"

"Anastasia?" I filled in. "Huh. That hadn't occurred to me. I just assumed it was a guy 'cause of their build. And also, I saw her drive away about a half hour before it happened. She'd had dinner at Solari's with Angelo tonight. But I suppose she could have come back later and then put on a big jacket to disguise herself. And she is tall, actually…"

A sharp cry from one of the rooms down the hall made us both jump. Almost immediately it grew into continuous shrieking, interrupted by the occasional stream of shouted obscenities. A med tech in blue scrubs ran into the room and the screaming subsided.

"So you finally met the mysterious Anastasia?" Eric asked once the noise had come down to a hoarse moaning.

"Yeah. And it looks like she is legit, after all." I told him the real name of the newspaper she was writing for and how she'd had dinner with Angelo and Gino to interview them for her article. "But we were right about one thing. Gino *was* hot for her. She said he came on to her after dinner and she had to shove him away." I frowned in distaste. "Why do guys do that, anyway? You know, just all of a sudden start kissing you without any advance warning."

Eric didn't answer. I guess he figured he wasn't responsible for the actions of his entire sex.

"Anyway," I went on, "I suppose she could have been lying when she said she left him alone after that. Oh, and get this: she also told me about someone hiding and watching when Gino came on to her. But maybe it's all totally a lie. Maybe she was so pissed off at him for slobbering all over her like that that she shoved him into the water."

"But why, then, would she even tell you about him coming on to her? It gives her a motive for his death."

I shrugged, which brought a flash of pain to my shoulder. It appeared I'd have to cease all nonverbal communication until I healed some. "I don't know. But I do know that it did happen, because that guy who wrote the letter to the paper, Marvin? He told me he and his wife saw Gino kissing some woman after dinner. So maybe Anastasia knew that people had seen them and that's why she couldn't hide that fact."

"You think she'd be strong enough to push him over the side of the wharf?" Eric asked.

"Well, he had been acting pretty out of it. She said she'd had to help hold him up when they were walking and stuff. And she seemed like a strong gal. So, yeah, she probably could have lifted him over the side without too much trouble."

"And done the same to you, too?" Eric asked.

I frowned. "I guess so. But why?"

"How about because you've been poking your nose into Gino's death? You did tell me you asked her about what happened that night. Maybe she thinks you're getting too close to the truth."

Neither of us spoke. I watched a paramedic wheel another casualty on a gurney into the hallway while Eric checked his messages again. If my phone's circuits hadn't been completely fried by the plunge into the ocean, I'd have done the same.

"Still no answer from Vargas," he said, peering at the screen.

"Maybe he has a life," I said. "It is Friday night. He's probably out with his wife or girlfriend doing something fun."

Eric slipped the phone back into his jeans pocket. "So is that everyone?" he asked. "Are there any other people you think could have attacked you tonight?"

There was one more, but I hated the thought of it. "Angelo," I said softly.

"Really? Why him?"

"It's partly 'cause of this weird look he gave when Anastasia was talking about Gino coming on to her, and when she mentioned she saw someone watching them. All of a sudden I got this feeling that maybe the guy watching them had been Angelo." I shivered and snuggled down further under the covers.

"It's obvious that he's totally into her," I said after a bit. "So maybe he got super jealous seeing them kissing. Maybe he didn't realize Anastasia had rejected Gino's advances. And I know that Angelo and Gino had already had a falling out, because Angelo told me so. This could have been like the last straw for him—the one that sent him over the edge, if you'll pardon the mixed metaphor."

"And then he went after you because...?"

"Well, I know he was pretty despondent tonight, so maybe he figured he had nothing to lose." I told Eric about Anastasia turning away from his kiss and how he'd been laughed at by Frank. "And I just found out the other day that Angelo also has quite the temper. My dad told me that years ago he threw a guy off a fishing boat for making fun of him, and that he also once went at a fish buyer with a big ol' lead weight."

I chewed my lip—at least that was one motion that didn't hurt. "Maybe he was upset because Anastasia had told me what happened with her and Gino." And then I had a thought.

"Oh, Jesus," I said, turning to Eric. "I told Angelo and Anastasia at dinner tonight that I was going to tell the police everything she'd said."

"So maybe Angelo wanted to get to you first."

TWENTY-FIVE

I WAS RELEASED from the hospital at eight thirty the next morning. It would have been earlier if the release hadn't coincided with the nurses' shift change, which meant it took over an hour to locate someone to come sign me out.

The SCPD detective on duty had shown up to take my statement soon after Eric left and had assured me they would do their best to apprehend the suspect. But we both knew the assertion was pretty much meaningless, since they had no way of knowing who the suspect even was. Then, at around one am, I'd finally been moved upstairs to a real room, but since I was thereafter awakened once an hour to have my vitals checked, I didn't get a whole lot of sleep. Not that I could have slept much in any case: every time I started to drift off, I found myself struggling for breath, as if once more fighting the ocean surge that threatened to pull me under water.

Eric came to pick me up, bringing a clean—and dry—set of clothes. Groggy from the drugs and lack of sleep, my head throbbed and my shoulder and hands ached. Nevertheless, I told him to take me straight to Solari's. "I promised Dad I'd be there at nine, when all the stuff gets delivered."

"Uh, there's something I need to tell you," Eric said as we merged onto Highway 1 north. "I called your fa-

ther last night as soon as I left the hospital to let him
know what had happened. But I made him promise not
to come down to the hospital to visit. I know Mario well
enough to know he would have been mad as hell not to
have found out till this morning."

"Yeah, you're right," I said. "I wasn't looking forward to telling him anyway, so thanks."

Traffic was light on this Saturday morning, but Eric
had to slow as we approached the Fishhook, where the
freeway makes almost a three-sixty-degree turn, and I
held onto the handhold as best I could to keep my sore
shoulder from being pressed against his body.

"How's Buster?" I asked once the road had straightened out and we were headed toward town. Eric had
agreed to spend last night at my house to look after
the dog.

"He's fine," Eric said. "Though he did think it a
little odd that it was me in your bed last night instead
of you. But once I let him under the covers to snuggle
with me, he seemed totally cool with it all. I got up early
and took him for a long run, by the way, since I figured
he wouldn't be getting much attention today. He was
crashed out on the sofa, snoring, when I left the house."

"I'll go home later, after I make sure everything's
been delivered for tonight, and hang out with him
for a while. But thanks so much for doing that. I owe
you one." I leaned over and kissed Eric on the cheek,
prompting a goofy smile.

We didn't speak for a few minutes, Eric humming
a spirited bass line from some piece I didn't recognize
and me gazing out the window, wondering if my show
of affection had given him the wrong idea. I got my answer almost immediately.

"You know," Eric said, glancing my way, then returning his attention to the VW van we were following down Chestnut Street. "I've been thinking about us…"

He trailed off, no doubt hoping for some sort of encouragement from me. But I didn't respond, keeping my gaze fixed on the brightly colored dancing-bear stickers covering the van's rear window.

"It's just that seeing you last night like that," he went on, "so anxious and scared an' all after what happened, it made me really think about how much you mean to me. That maybe we should try it again, us—"

"No, please. Don't," I said softly, willing the tears in my eyes to stay put. "I just can't. Not right now."

Eric nodded. "I get it. Now was a bad time to bring it up. Sorry." He stared straight ahead, jaw set, hands gripping the wheel.

We drove on in uncomfortable silence, and as we approached the entrance to the wharf I became aware of the weather for the first time today. Puffy white clouds floated in a pale blue sky and people were in shirtsleeves, so it had to be warm out.

"Ohmygod, I am *so* glad it's not raining today," I said, hoping to lighten the mood. "At least one thing's going my way."

"Yep," was all Eric had to say.

We bumped down to the end of the wharf and pulled up at Solari's next to a large truck with "June's Party Rentals" printed in blue letters on the sides and back. "Hey, and something else to be grateful for," I said. "The delivery's on time."

I opened the door, then turned to face Eric. "Thanks again," I said, touching him on the arm. "Really. For everything. I'll see you tonight. Oh, and be sure to take good notes for me today at class, okay?"

I'd originally hoped to fit our plein air painting class between this morning's setup and tonight's dinner, but that wasn't going to happen now. Not that I'd have been able to paint or take notes with these bandages on, in any case.

"Will do," Eric said, watching as I climbed gingerly out of his Lexus. "You sure you're okay to work today?"

"No, but I don't see as I have much of a choice."

What had been a slight frown on his face now became a scowl.

"Don't get all bent out of shape," I said. "I'm mostly just going to be directing people where to put stuff, and I promise I won't overdo it." Slamming the door, I waved good-bye as he turned around and made his way back down the wharf.

I knew I'd probably hurt Eric's feelings. It had to have taken a lot of guts for him to say what he did, and then to be shut down like that when he'd allowed himself to be so vulnerable must have been horrible. But I simply wasn't ready to make the kind of decision he wanted. And although I'd used the excuse of my attack last night to put him off, that was all it was. An excuse. Because I wasn't sure I'd ever want to change the way things were now. It seemed like the perfect situation—having him as a best pal without the entanglement and heartache that came with being a "couple."

But truly, I think my biggest fear was that if we did go back to our old relationship and it were to once again fail, we'd risk losing it all. And I couldn't even fathom what my life would be without Eric as a friend.

Once his Lexus was out of sight, I headed around the side of the restaurant to the back of the building.

Dad was out by the tent, going over the invoice with one of the delivery guys. When he saw me come around the corner, he raced over and started to give me a bear hug, but then pulled back.

"It's okay," I said. "I'm not that beat up. Just go easy on the left shoulder."

He took me again in his arms, more gently this time. "I'm so sorry, *bambina*. I was worried about you all last night. Are you sure you're well enough to be here?"

"That's why I didn't want to tell you till this morning," I said, releasing myself from the embrace. "I knew it would keep you up. But really, I'm fine. They wouldn't have let me out of the hospital if they didn't think I was okay. Here, let me deal with the delivery." I reached for the invoice, and for the first time Dad noticed my bandages.

"Oh my lord," he exclaimed. "What happened to your hands?"

"Just some cuts I got from the barnacles on the piers. They aren't all that bad, but the doctor was worried about infection 'cause of the bacteria the barnacles can carry. So I have to keep them bandaged for a few days."

Dad's face was all scrunched up and I was afraid he was going to cry. "Look," I said, "why don't you go inside and get started in the kitchen. Once I confirm that all the stuff's been delivered and make sure everyone's clear about how it needs to be set up, I'll go home and rest for a while, okay?"

"But the man who did it is still out there," Dad said. "I'm not sure it's safe for you to be—"

"*Babbo*," I said, "no one's going to attack me in broad

daylight with all these people around." I didn't mention that some of the people who tended to hang out around here were in fact on the top of my suspect list. But if I did see any of them skulking about, I'd be sure to be on my guard.

This seemed to appease him. With a squeeze to my good shoulder, he headed into the restaurant. The delivery guy had left while Dad and I and were talking but now reappeared with another man, the two of them rolling a cart loaded down with large round tables.

"Those go inside the tent," I said. Sean and Emilio came out the back door at this moment, no doubt sent by my dad, and I directed them to start setting up the tables, as well as the folding chairs once they were rolled out, too.

I was reviewing the invoice, checking it against my original order, when I heard someone call out my name. I looked up from the list, a bandaged finger marking the spot at which I'd stopped ("140 dessert forks"). "Ah, Detective Vargas. I was hoping to see you this morning."

"Is there somewhere private we can talk?" he asked.

"Sure." I led him inside. Passing my father in the hallway, I raised my eyebrows as if to say, "See? No need to worry about me; I have a police escort." Dad didn't appear terribly amused, however. The sight of the detective must have made him a little leery.

Once in the cramped office, Vargas nodded for me to sit at the desk and he took the folding chair. "You're a hard woman to get hold of," he said. "I must have left a dozen messages on your phone since last night."

"Yeah, well, my phone isn't working so hot right now. That little ocean swim I took last night wasn't all that great for its innards."

"Ah, right." The detective smiled. "Good point. Well, anyway, I'm sorry I wasn't able to come down to the hospital to talk to you, but I was tied up with another case. Is now a good time for us to chat?"

"Well, we're hosting a hundred and forty guests tonight for that sister-cities dinner and there's still a ton to do. But I can certainly give you a few minutes."

"Great." Vargas pulled a notepad from his pocket and clicked open his pen. "I know you already told this all to Detective Collins, but I'd love to hear it again for myself. Why don't you start by telling me what exactly happened last night."

"Okay." I recounted how I'd been standing out behind the restaurant looking at the ocean when someone had come up from behind, hit me on the head with a hard object, and then lifted me up over the railing and shoved me into the water. "Just like what happened to Gino Barbieri," I said.

"Did you get a look at who it was?"

"No. The person was backlit so I couldn't see their face. But he was fairly tall, and strong enough to lift me up."

"So you know it was a man?" Vargas asked, looking up from his pad.

"Not necessarily. It could have been a tall woman, I suppose."

He jotted down some more notes. "Okay, and is there anyone you have reason to suspect might be the one who attacked you?"

"Well, as I mentioned before, I figure whoever did this to me probably did the same thing to Gino. You know, same MO, as they say in cop shows."

The detective managed not to roll his eyes, but I could tell he wanted to.

"And I do have a few people in mind who might have had reason to get rid of Gino, but I can't say any of the motives I've come up with are all that strong. But hey, on the bright side, at least this should take my father off the suspect list, right? I mean, he wouldn't push me off the wharf—not when he needs me to help out at that big dinner tonight."

My attempt at levity was met with a thin smile. "How 'bout you tell me about these suspects and motives you've come up with," he said.

"All right, I have several. Four, actually, if you include Bobby." I explained why I'd originally suspected Bobby, and then told him about the bocce player Frank, and about Angelo, and the reasons they might have had for at least fighting with Gino even if they hadn't intended to kill him. Then I recounted what I knew about Anastasia, and how Gino had come on to her after dinner the night he disappeared.

"And you said she saw someone who'd been watching when this happened?" Vargas asked when he'd finished writing everything down.

"Uh-huh. She said they were hiding behind that kiosk out there, the one with the information about the Italian fishing fleet, but that she just hurried past because seeing him creeped her out."

"We've already spoken with Bobby and Angelo, but I guess I'm going to have to talk to…" He consulted his notes. "…Frank and Anastasia as well." Tapping his pen on his pad, he stared absently at the cycling poster on the wall above me, then shook his head. "Seems like lots of people had issues with old Gino."

"I know. But if he really did have copper poisoning," I said, "it makes sense. He could have gotten so crazy that he just ended up pissing them all off." And then I chuckled. "Who knows, maybe it's just like *Murder on the Orient Express*. Maybe they all did it together."

My laughter died, however, as I took in the detective's grave expression. Because, much as I tried to pretend everything was fine, he was right. It was not fine. Whoever had killed Gino—and had tried to do the same to me—was still out there.

ONCE I'D CONFIRMED that all the tables, chairs, plates, flatware, tablecloths, napkins, steam tables and trays, serving utensils, and—perhaps most important—the porta-potties, had been delivered, I headed home to rest for a few hours. But not before stopping to buy a replacement for my waterlogged cell phone. No way could I make it through another day without one.

It was now almost noon, and I had to be back at around three to help my dad with the last-minute cooking. Though how much help I'd be with these bandages on was a big question. But at worst I'd be able to direct the new prep cook, Joe, on what to do.

Solari's was closed to the public today, thank goodness, so the kitchen would be free all day for the big dinner. When I'd gone inside to say good-bye to my dad, the counters had been covered with platters upon which Joe was arranging salami, sliced cheeses, peperoncini, and olives, as well as sheets of fugassa ready to be topped with pesto, and cheese and onions.

Buster greeted me at my front door and was so excited he almost knocked me over. "Settle down," I said, kneeling to let him give my face a thorough washing.

"I don't need any more bruises right now." But his agitation was understandable; this was the first time since I'd adopted him the previous spring that he'd ever spent a night without me.

After taking a walk around the neighborhood so Buster could leave his calling card at all his usual spots, the two of us crawled into bed for a snuggle and a nap. I lay on my side in the shape of a C and the dog curled up in a tight ball against my belly. He immediately closed his eyes, and within two minutes I could hear his regular breathing. Staring at the photo of my Aunt Letta I'd hung on the wall next to the bed, I willed myself to follow suit. I'd need some more REM sleep before tonight if I didn't want to be a complete zombie.

But exhausted as I was, my body refused to relax. I rolled onto my back and the dog in turn stretched out full length, making sure he had as much contact with me as possible. Maybe if I tried a breathing exercise, that would help. *In...out...in...out...*

But all that did was take me once more back to last night and the panic I'd felt gasping for air in the rough water, trying to escape the violent surge that had kept throwing me against the barnacle-encrusted pilings.

Great. Now I was *truly* awake.

It wasn't surprising, though. How could I possibly sleep with so much to worry about? Not only was some crazy man—or woman—lurking out there who clearly wanted to kill me, but I had to orchestrate a five-course dinner tonight for a hundred and forty people, including a bunch of VIPs from Italy and the City of Santa Cruz, with a welt on my head, an aching shoulder, and hands so covered in bandages that I could barely hold on to a spatula.

This last reflection sent my thoughts racing to Gauguin. *Oh, God... I'm scheduled to work the hot line there tomorrow night.* No way could I do that now. Javier was going to freak out. With this on top of everything else, I wouldn't be surprised if he decided to simply throw in the side towel as soon as he heard. I'd be lucky if I even had a head chef next week.

Rolling once more onto my side, I started to cry. The tears fell slowly at first, but the more I thought about Javier quitting, the faster they came, until I was sobbing uncontrollably. Why couldn't he be happy at Gauguin? What was so important about being the owner of a restaurant?

My sobs ceased as I had a realization. And what was so important about me being the sole owner of Gauguin? It wasn't, was the answer. Sitting up, I wiped my eyes. Yes, that was the obvious solution: Why not offer to sell half the restaurant to Javier?

But the question was, would he even want to be co-owner with me?

TWENTY-SIX

FOUR HOURS LATER I was standing at the range top in the Solari's kitchen tending pots of Nonna's Sunday gravy (which we were calling "Braised Beef and Pork in Red Sauce" for tonight) and chicken cacciatore. Though my bandaged hands had proved useless for most chores, I was able to grip a large spoon well enough to keep the food from sticking to the bottom as it came up to a simmer.

Once they were heated through, I directed Sean to transfer the two entrées from their enormous pots into hotel pans and take them out to the steam tables we had set up in the back corner of the tent.

Dad was at the stove whipping up the sauce for the tagliarini with brown butter, sage, and porcini mushrooms while Emilio was sorting through the bags of mussels we'd procured from Stagnaro Bros. for the spaghetti dish. The stuffed cabbage and fried polenta were now in the oven, the spinach salad with orange, fennel, and black olives was all prepped and chilling in the walk-in fridge, and the zucchini spears were sizzling in giant pans on the stove.

Man, does it smell good in here!

Satisfied that all seemed in order and that I was no longer needed in the kitchen, I headed out to the tent to make sure the tables were properly set and the beverage stations stocked and ready and that the wait staff all knew their jobs. We'd hired several extra servers for the night and, since they all had banquet experience, I was relying on them to set the example for our regular gals, who'd never before had to deal with a crowd of this size. After giving the front-of-house staff some last-minute instructions (such as, don't do any serving or clearing of dishes while any of the VIPs are making speeches), I locked myself in the tiny office to change into my party clothes. I'd decided on black slacks and a burgundy-colored silk blouse that would hide any red sauce I happened to spill down my front during the evening.

The event was scheduled to start at five o'clock. Since I'd been designated the official greeter, I walked back through the dining room a few minutes before the hour and unlocked the front door. But as soon as I stepped outside, my heart sank.

At least twenty people were swarming around the sidewalk in front of the restaurant, and it was obvious that they were not eager, early guests for the sister-cities dinner. Not only was their attire far more casual than the evening wear I expected most attendants to wear, but many of them were bearing familiar placards: "HAPPY INDIGENOUS PEOPLE'S DAY" and "SOLARI'S SUPPORTS IMPERIALISM."

Oh, no. Since they hadn't been here last night or at all during the day today, I'd allowed myself to hope that the protesters had given up their mission. Clearly, they'd just been saving themselves for the big night.

When they saw me emerge from the restaurant, the crowd began to chant: "No to Columbus Day!" Closing the door behind me, I approached the man I'd talked to before.

"I see you're back," I said, forcing a smile. "And you've brought reinforcements."

"You didn't think we'd miss the main event, did you?"

"Of course not. But I do hope you'll continue to be respectful of our guests and not block access to the restaurant. As it is now, it's kind of hard to get past you all."

Right as I said this, the first guests arrived—a couple of city council members I knew and behind them my *nonna*, who was being escorted by a much younger woman from church. Threading her way through the crowd with a scowl, Nonna batted with her cane at a young, scrawny guy with stringy blond hair. "*Vai via!*" she snapped, which is probably best translated in this context as "Get lost, punk!"

That did the trick. In the face of my formidable eighty-seven-year-old grandmother, the bunch melted back like a stick of butter sliced in two with a hot knife. They watched until Nonna disappeared into the restaurant and only then took up their chant once again. But at least, I was glad to see, they remained where they were, leaving a wide corridor between what was now two separate groups.

"Thanks," I said to my guy, then went to stand next to the front door, hoping my welcoming smile would alleviate any nervousness our guests might feel on having to pass through a gauntlet of shouting agitators.

By five thirty, almost a hundred people had arrived and were milling about the Solari's dining room, whose tables had all been pushed up against the walls to make room for the crowd. But we were still waiting on the Italian contingency. My dad had been out to check three times already, and even I was starting to glance at my watch every couple of minutes. *No way could they have forgotten, right?* The dinner was in their honor, after all.

I peeked through the door into the dining room, where folks were standing in groups, sipping from glasses of Prosecco and nibbling olives and rolls of thinly sliced dry Genovese salami.

As I watched, Stefano, Bobby's father, helped himself to three slices of cheese and four chunks of Mortadella from the tray offered by Cathy. I half expected him to wrap them up in a cocktail napkin and stuff the booty into his jacket pocket, but instead he ate the pieces one by one and then washed it all down with a healthy slug of sparkling wine.

And then I noticed the threesome behind Stefano, back by the picture window: Angelo and Anastasia were chatting with Frank. The sight of them made me flinch, even though it made total sense that they'd be here tonight. I tried to envision their figures superimposed over the backlit shape of the person who'd attacked me, but it was no good. Any of the three—as well as any number of others in the dining room right now— could have been the one looking down at me from the wharf last night.

Shaking off this image and the feeling of dread it instilled in me, I turned back to the crowd of protesters. Compared to whoever had bashed me on the head and shoved me into the icy water, these people now seemed loving and warm, and I smiled at a woman near the front of the group. My friendliness must have taken her by surprise, because she broke off her rendition of a rude song about Christopher Columbus to flash a shy smile back at me.

Just then, a group of about a six people came striding through the corridor between the protesters, laughing and jabbering loudly in Italian. *Finally*. The guest of honor had arrived.

"*Buona sera, signora*," I said to the woman I recognized from the photo in today's newspaper as being the mayor of Sestri Levante. "*Benvenuto al ristorante Solari. Io sono Sally Solari.*"

"*Ah, molto piacere!*" She leaned over to plant a pair of *baci* on my cheeks and I did the same to hers.

"Okay, that's pretty much the extent of my Italian," I said with a laugh, "so I sure hope you speak a little English."

"Indeed I do. And it has been improving these past days that I have been spending in your beautiful town. Here, please won't you meet my compatriots?" She turned to the other dignitaries by her side, but before any introductions could be made, one of the protesters shoved his way between us. It was the guy with stringy hair that Nonna had whacked with her cane.

Leaning down so his angry face was just inches from the mayor's, he started shouting: "You're so proud of your countryman, but don't you realize he's just a symbol of imperialism and the subjugation of the Third World?"

Without thinking, I took hold of the man from behind to pull him back, which immediately triggered a throbbing in both hands as well as a searing pain in my left shoulder. "You need to cool down," I said, quickly letting go. "You're getting way too close."

The mayor—who seemed not to have noticed either my bandages or the spasm that had passed across my face as I'd grabbed hold of her aggressor—waved a hand and laughed. "It's okay," she said. "I am used to things like this. We have plenty of the protests and the strikes in Italy as well." Turning to the man, her face became serious. "And I just want you to know that, as an active socialist from many years, I am very aware of the issue of *imperialismo* and of the part my country has played in this problem over the course of history. And I, for one, do not consider Cristoforo Colombo to be a great hero or a symbol of Italy. So you can save your lectures for somebody else, yes?"

I would have loved a photo of the protester's dumbfounded expression. Mumbling an incoherent apology, he shrank back into the crowd. "Let us go inside, shall we?" the mayor said, gracing him with one last withering smile.

As soon as we stepped into the dining room, our group was surrounded by members of the Santa Cruz sister-cities committee, who promptly whisked the mayor and her fellow Ligurians off to meet the various Santa Cruz dignitaries in attendance at the event.

I left them to it and went in search of my father. *Should I tell him what the mayor said about Christopher Columbus? Nah*, I decided. I was pretty sure he'd already come to the conclusion that I'd been right about the whole thing. No need to twist the knife.

Dad was in the far corner of the dining room, surrounded by a gaggle of people. He'd changed from his chef's clothes into dark brown slacks, a beige jacket, a pale blue dress shirt, and a red tie. No one would ever accuse him of being a style maven. The group listening to him talk consisted of several city council members and a couple of guys I recognized from the DA's office. Which reminded me: Where the heck was Eric? It was now a quarter to six and the meal was supposed to start in fifteen minutes. Even though punctuality was not his strong suit, he was rarely late for the food portion of events. Was he still upset with me about this morning?

As I scanned the crowd in search of his blond head, I spotted Bobby with his father. Stefano was still scarfing down antipasto and was chewing and nodding as his son spoke animatedly, waving his hands for emphasis. The dad had a physique similar to his son's, but if this was the way he always ate, how the heck did Stefano maintain his slender build?

I wondered about Bobby's presence. He'd told me his parents were coming tonight, but I hadn't seen his mother anywhere. She must have bagged out and he'd come in her place. At a hundred dollars a pop, you wouldn't want to waste a ticket.

Spying Eric finally wandering into the room, I left off musing about Bobby and his father and made my way toward him.

"You look spiffy," I said. "Like you're dressed for a trial."

"Yeah, well, I figured suit and tie was kinda de rigueur for meeting a bunch of foreign mucky-mucks. Not that I've actually met any of them yet."

"Well, hey, I can arrange that if you want. So how was class this afternoon?"

"Good. We went up to Wilder Ranch and painted the old buildings and the goats and horses and stuff."

"Did you take notes for me like I asked?" The sudden slump of his shoulders answered my question. "You forgot."

"Yeah. Sorry. But I can tell you Omar's message of the day: 'Forget what you know.' He kept going on and on about how our preconceived ideas limit our ability to see as an artist. Like, even though we all knew that the big barn there at the ranch is painted white, it didn't look white in the bright afternoon sun. It had a lot of yellow and blue in it, too."

"I like that. Forget what you know. Easier said than done for us lawyer types, though. Oh, hey, there are the Italians," I said. "C'mon and I'll introduce you."

Before we could make our way through the packed crowd over to them, however, my dad clapped his hands and quieted everyone down. "If everybody would please make their way outside to the back of the restaurant where the tent is and then find your seats, we're going to get started with the dinner in a little bit."

"Good," Eric said. "I'm starved."

"Well, you might want to snag some of the antipasto then, if there's any left, because I happen to know the speeches are going to take a while."

"Oh, great," Eric said. "Any chance I could just hang out in here until they're over?"

"No way, José." I punctuated my response with a jab to his ribs with my elbow. "Why don't you go sit with your DA friends, 'cause I have to go direct the dinner service and make sure everyone gets their food on time and that we don't run out of stuffed cabbage for the vegetarians."

"Like there'll be any vegetarians here tonight," Eric said with a snort.

"Hey, you never know. This is Santa Cruz."

I made my way through the crowd toward the kitchen like a salmon swimming upstream against all the hungry people making their way outside, then down the hall and out the back door to the big tent. Several dozen guests were already inside, wandering around trying to decide at which of the round tables to sit.

The sun was now low enough that the decorative lights we'd strung inside the tent were making a difference, and the draped pattern my dad had decided on imparted a festive atmosphere to the place—kind of like the twinkling fairy lights you'd see in one of those summer gardens in Italy. Which I guess was the whole idea.

Entering the tent, I turned the corner and almost ran smack into Detective Vargas. He held out his arms to keep us from colliding.

"Oh. Sorry," I said. "I didn't expect anyone to be standing there."

"Obviously." You couldn't tell it from his set mouth, but his eyes were definitely laughing.

"Are you here to eat or are you working?"

"Both," he said. "The chief had two extra tickets, which he kindly gave to me." Vargas nodded toward a petite woman with short blonde hair—his wife? girlfriend?—who was talking with the SCPD chief of police and a woman I figured must be the chief's wife.

"And I have to say," the detective went on, "I am looking forward to a good Italian meal. Though I'll have to forgo the wine that accompanies it. Gotta be on my toes tonight."

"What? You worried there might be another murder committed here during the dinner?" I asked with a chuckle.

But he didn't join in my laughter.

"Yeah," I conceded. "I guess it's not all that funny."

TWENTY-SEVEN

ERIC'S DESIRE TO avoid the speeches proved to be well founded.

My dad and I had wanted to spread them out over the night, having a couple before dinner, a few more while everyone ate, and then finishing off with the final presentation of the official "Proclamation" over the dessert course. But this idea had been nixed by the sister-cities committee, who were afraid that once the meal commenced it would be difficult to get folks to quiet down enough to hear what was being said. Their one concession had been to hold off the presentation of the Proclamation until right before dessert.

They were probably right, but the end result was thirty minutes of bureaucrats droning on and on about "what an honor it is" to either host or be hosted during the Italians' visit to our fair city, depending on who was giving the speech. And since I'd instructed the wait staff to hold off serving and clearing during the speeches, empty wine carafes were not being replenished, something that would have at least helped alleviate the boredom.

Standing at the back of the tent waiting for the last speech to end, I scanned the tables, looking for the people I suspected might have shoved me—and Gino—off the wharf into the ocean. Angelo and Anastasia were sitting next to each other at a table not too far from where I was standing, and it was obvious neither was the least bit interested in the city council member's gushing declaration of her love for Italian culture. Angelo had eyes only for his young escort, but she seemed far more focused on the cuticle of her nail than on the older fisherman by her side.

So what is she doing here with him, then? How much material does she need for her newspaper article?

With a shake of the head, I turned to search the other side of the tent and spotted Detective Vargas sitting with his date, the chief and his wife, and the district attorney contingency, Eric included. With the exception of Vargas, whose eyes were darting rapidly about the tent, the rest of the table seemed focused on the speaker—though a couple of the DAs looked as if they might be about to nod off. The detective glanced my way, and when he caught me watching him, inclined his head toward the table in front of his.

Frank was there, sitting with several folks I recognized as other bocce players. Though most of them were smiling at the city council member's remarks, Frank was staring across the room, a scowl accenting the furrows of his craggy face. From what I knew of the man, this wasn't especially surprising, but I did wonder what had piqued his ire at this particular time. I followed his gaze to try to ascertain what held his attention.

Could it be Angelo or Anastasia? It sure seemed as if that was where he was looking. But why would he be angry at either of them? They'd seemed perfectly jovial together when I'd seen the three of them during the antipasto course.

And then I noticed the table behind Angelo and Anastasia, at least from Frank's perspective. Bobby sat there with his dad, Stefano. *Could Frank be watching one of them?* I studied the father and son. Bobby was helping himself to the last of the red wine in the table's carafe and Stefano was facing the podium, listening as the speaker began to wrap up her comments.

"And so, in conclusion, I'd like to thank the sister-cities committee, Solari's restaurant, and most especially, all of you who made the long journey here to Santa Cruz from Sestri Levante."

Finally. I was about to turn and head outside to alert the wait staff that dinner service could commence when I noticed a commotion at Bobby and Stefano's table. Several people had jumped up and were now blotting at a spill with their red cloth napkins. *Damn.* Someone must have knocked over a glass. Grabbing several bar towels from the bus station we'd set up near the exit, I darted over to the table and assisted with the cleanup—though with my bandaged hands I wasn't a whole lot of help.

It was red wine, but luckily the liquid seemed to have stayed on the table. "How can you be so clumsy?" Stefano shouted at Bobby, who was staring at the spill with a slack mouth and unfocused eyes.

"It's okay," I said. "No one got any wine on their clothes, and we'll get this cleaned up in a jiffy." Giulia and one of the temp servers had already arrived with a clean tablecloth, and the two of them had the table reset in a matter of seconds. While everyone got reseated, Giulia fetched more wine to replace the empty carafes at their table.

"See? Just like new," I said in a sprightly voice.

But Bobby just continued to stand there, making no move to sit back down. After a moment he shook his head and wandered off, mumbling something about using the restroom.

Stefano saw me watching his son and shrugged. "I guess maybe he's had a bit too much wine on an empty stomach. I told him he needed to eat some of the anti-pasto, but he said he wasn't hungry." *Well, that's one difference between father and son.*

Other than that mishap, the dinner service went with-out hiccup. Bobby returned to his table a few minutes later, and I was happy to observe he did not refill his wine glass. The noise level rose as folks ate and drank their way through the salad, pasta, and main courses, and before long it sounded like a raucous party in the big tent.

Halfway through the entrée, I was heading for the back door of the restaurant to call for another tray of cabbage rolls when I spied two people slip out of the tent and cross the courtyard. I peered at the familiar figures: it was Angelo and Anastasia. Following behind as the pair made their way around the side of the build-ing, I watched them cross the street and climb down the stairs on the Boardwalk side of the wharf to the lower-level boat launch area.

Now what could they be up to? And then I heard the harsh barking of the sea lions and realized he must be taking her down to where you could see the marine mammals up close as they lazed on the wooden cross-beam supports below. But what if he had something else in mind? Like getting back at Anastasia for her rebuff the previous night?

The cabbage rolls could wait.

I had just started after them when someone called out my name. It was Emilio, standing at the back door to the restaurant.

"You got a sec?" the cook asked.

"Uh, what is it?" I asked with a glance toward the boat launch stairs. "I'm kind of in the middle of something."

"I just need to know where everyone's at out there. You gonna need any more of the mains, or can we start putting stuff away?"

I crossed to the door and poked my head into the dish room. Sean and Joe were taking a break, leaning against the counter and sipping from tall glasses of Coke. It had been a hectic two hours, but now that the main course was being served, their work for the night was basically done.

"We're good on everything, except there seems to have been a run on the cabbage rolls. I was actually just coming out to get some more. Are there any left?"

"One more tray. Joe, you wanna grab it and take it out to the steam tables?"

"Will do." The prep cook set down his soda and headed for the kitchen. Grabbing a pair of dry side towels, he removed the tray of cabbage rolls from the warm oven. I held the screen door open and he stepped outside. He'd taken just a few steps toward the tent when the sound of someone shouting rose above the clamor of the dinner guests.

"I guess someone in there must have had a bit too much to drink," Joe said with a laugh.

"I don't think that came from inside the tent." But he didn't appear to hear and continued across the courtyard with his hot tray.

I stopped to listen, turning my head different ways to try to discern which direction the shouting was coming from. Definitely not inside the tent, or the restaurant either. It was farther away. I jogged around the side of the building, at which point the sound became much louder. It was coming from the other side of the wharf. *Where Angelo and Anastasia went.*

Running full tilt now, I darted across the street and through the parking lot and leaned over the railing that ran along the far side of the wharf. A figure was thrashing about in the ocean, but the foul language streaming from his mouth conveyed anger more than fear. *I know that voice*, I thought, and squinted into the blue-black water. The setting sun had almost reached the horizon, and as its last golden rays illuminated the face of the man below me, I saw that I was right.

"Bobby!" I shouted. "What the hell happened?"

He stopped his swearing and looked up at me, then splashed his way toward the landing on the lower level. "She *pushed* me in!" he shrieked as I descended the stairway. Only then did I notice that Angelo and Anastasia were still down on the boat launch. The old fisherman was clutching the young woman's arms from behind.

"You even *look* at me, I swear I'll knock you in again!" Anastasia hollered as Bobby dragged his dripping body up onto the wooden boards. He didn't seem like someone about to make any kind of move on her. He looked more like he was about to cry.

I was standing there gaping at the scene, trying to figure out what had just happened, when a deep voice boomed out from above. "Don't any of you move!"

Detective Vargas trotted down the stairs, his left hand holding the phone he was speaking into and the right hidden under the flap of his suit jacket, ready to draw his firearm if need be. Behind him, a half dozen people crowded around the top of the stairway, gawking at the scene below.

"Okay, what's going on here?" the detective asked, slipping the phone into his pocket but keeping his right hand where it was.

"It was *her*!" Bobby said, and pointed a wet finger at Anastasia. "She slugged me and then pushed me in the water!"

"Which he deserved," she retorted. "The scumbag grabbed me someplace he shouldn't have." Angelo was nodding vigorous agreement to this statement.

"I saw what happened," a new voice called out.

Vargas turned toward the man who'd spoken—one of the gawkers at the top of the stairway. "And what exactly did you see?" he asked.

"The two of them," the man indicated Anastasia and Angelo, "and that guy who was in the water were talking, when all of a sudden without warning she just goes for the dude. Punches him in the face and then shoves him over the side."

"You didn't see him grab her first?"

The man shook his head. "I didn't see anything like that."

"But Bobby was standing behind her," Angelo protested. "So that man couldn't have seen how he grabbed hold of her…front."

"Okay, look." Vargas finally lowered his right hand, then reached into his jacket pocket. "I'm afraid I'm going to have to take you into custody," he said, pulling out a pair of handcuffs.

"What?" both Angelo and Anastasia cried out in unison.

"I'm sorry, ma'am," the detective said. "But you've admitted to striking Bobby and then knocking him into the water, and now we have a witness who says the battery was unprovoked. If the evidence proves otherwise, you'll be released right away, I assure you." He moved toward Anastasia, but Angelo stepped between them.

"No way, you can't be serious," the fisherman said. "She didn't do anything—" At the howl of an approaching siren, he stopped. A moment later the police cruiser pulled up above, its red flashing lights imparting a bizarre disco feel to the now dimly lit boat launch area.

An officer jumped out of the car, pushed through the crowd above—which was growing by the second as more and more folks hurried over to see what the commotion was—and took the stairs two at a time, coming to a stop at the detective's side.

Vargas and the cop spoke briefly in low voices, after which the police officer nodded to Anastasia. Jaw clenched, she turned around and placed her hands behind her back, allowing him to click on the cuffs. The cop then led her by the arm up the stairs and helped her into the squad car. Angelo stared after them as the car pulled away. After a moment, he frowned and shook his head, then slowly mounted the stairs to the wharf's upper level.

The crowd above dispersed quickly once the police car had driven off, leaving the detective and me alone with Bobby. Vargas turned to the soggy figure, who was still slouched over near the edge of the wooden deck. "Why don't you tell me what happened, Bobby?"

He raised his head, mumbled something neither of us could understand, then dropped it back down again.

"What's that?" The detective moved several steps closer.

"I dunno," Bobby said in a slurred voice. It was clear he was still feeling the effects of that earlier wine. "I came down here to get some air, to sit a while and just check out the Boardwalk...and then *they* came down here, too." He pointed to the spot where Angelo and Anastasia had been standing earlier. "So we start talking and next thing I know, she *shoves me in the water.*" This last bit came out almost as a wail, after which he lowered his head once more and began to cry in big, heaving sobs.

Vargas and I watched him for a moment, and then I asked in a low voice, "You think Anastasia might be the one who attacked me and Gino?"

"I think it's possible. From what you told me this morning, she was the last known person to see Gino alive, at which time she admits he made unwanted advances upon her. She could have easily knocked him into the water in retaliation for that. And we now know she's perfectly comfortable pushing people over the side of the wharf," he added. "I'd been planning on having a chat with her tonight once everyone finished eating, but now, who knows? Maybe she'll say something helpful while we have her in custody for this Bobby thing."

Bobby stood up slowly and came toward us. The sobs had subsided, but tears were still flowing down his cheeks. "Gotta go to the shop and change outta these clothes," he mumbled.

We watched him make his way unsteadily up the stairway and then head toward his father's store. "What about him?" I asked as Vargas followed him up the stairs. "You don't think it could be Bobby who attacked Gino and me?"

He snorted. "C'mon. Just *look* at the guy. He's pathetic."

TWENTY-EIGHT

I WANTED TO follow Bobby to his dad's gift shop but
knew Vargas would frown on such activity. So instead, I
accompanied the detective back to the dinner. The boat
launch where the ruckus had occurred was on the other
side of the wharf, out of sight of anyone in the big tent
behind Solari's, and it didn't appear that those in attendance had even heard the squad car's siren as it arrived.
But given the noise level at the dinner right now, this
wasn't surprising.

"So, what brought you down there to the landing?"
I shouted over the roar as we rounded the corner of the
restaurant.

"You did," he said.

"Me?"

Vargas grinned. "Well, you among all the others.
First Bobby left, and then a few minutes later I saw
Angelo and Anastasia sneak out, too. That was one too
many suspects for me not to check out what was going
on, and then once outside I saw you take off across the
street, so I followed."

"Ah, got it," I said. "So you're not going back to the
station now to interview Anastasia?"

"Nah. I think it's best we let her stew for a while first.
I'm gonna hang out here till the dinner's over to make
sure there's no more fires to put out, and then I'll head
on down to talk to her."

The detective stopped at the entrance to the tent and looked around. The Santa Cruz mayor had stepped up to the podium and quieted everyone down and was reading from a document he held in his hand:

"Whereas the City of Santa Cruz wishes to acknowledge its shared history with its sister city, Sestri Levante, and the debt it owes such city as a result of its citizens who first came to settle in Santa Cruz almost a century and a half ago; and whereas the two municipalities wish to acknowledge our shared appreciation of the arts and culture…"

"Do you see Angelo?" Vargas said, leaning over to speak into my ear.

I scanned the diners, who—from the glazed expressions most wore—were clearly more interested in their panettone and hazelnut gelato than the text of the mayor's Proclamation. "No, I don't see him anywhere," I answered after checking out all fourteen tables. "The place he was sitting at before is empty. I guess he must have left."

"Huh," the detective said, and strode inside. I watched him skirt the canvas walls at the back of the tent, his dark eyes searching for the fisherman. Now was my chance. Slipping back outside, I made my way along the side of the Solari's building and then down the sidewalk toward Stefano's gift shop.

The lights were all off inside except for one at the far back of the store. I tried the front door. *Unlocked.* Turning the handle and opening the door as quietly as I could, I stepped inside and softly closed the door behind me.

A sound was coming from the back room. Someone talking. I waited for my eyes to adjust to the dim light and then crept forward, doing my best not to knock into all the postcard racks and stands of knickknacks bearing images of surfers and redwood trees and the famous Santa Cruz roller coaster.

Once closer, I could tell that it was Bobby talking to himself. "I'm sorry, I'm sorry, I'm sorry," he was saying, though it came out as more of a moan than normal speech.

Sorry for what? Coming on to Anastasia, like she said?

He broke off speaking and started to sob once more. But after a minute the sobs ceased and all I could hear was panting, as if he'd been engaged in some kind of vigorous exercise, accompanied by the sound of rhythmic creaking. Listening to his rapid breaths, I stood frozen in place behind a rack of fishing lures wrapped in tiny plastic bags.

What on earth was going on with the man? He wasn't acting like someone who was merely drunk. Could he be having some sort of allergic reaction to the liquor? I knew he'd had a lot of wine tonight, but...

And then I stopped myself. *What exactly did I know?* That Stefano had said that perhaps his son had had a bit too much to drink, and that Bobby had seemed drunk when he knocked over his wine glass.

But as I thought this, my painting teacher's voice came into my head: "Forget what you know. Your preconceived thoughts limit your ability to truly see."

So what, then, did I *see*? I risked a peek around the door. Bobby was slumped over on a plastic chair, still in his wet clothes, rocking rapidly back and forth. He had his back to me, so I took a few steps closer. What was that in his hands? A piece of paper. No, a photograph.

Standing as tall as I could, I craned my neck to see

if I could make out the image he was staring at. And then I quickly stepped back, suppressing the intake of breath that threatened to betray my presence.

It was a photo of Bobby and Gino, standing at the prow of Gino's boat with their arms about each other's shoulders.

The sound of a scraping chair caused me to back off even farther. But no, he hadn't stood up. I could now hear the rapid tapping of feet on the hardwood floor along with the creaking of the plastic chair, and he was back to his panting again.

Would simply being drunk cause this behavior? I didn't think so. But something was certainly wrong with the man. And his behavior had been a little odd for a while, now that I really stopped to consider it. I thought back to the various times I'd seen Bobby over the past two weeks. How he'd seemed agitated and then depressed that day in Gino's house; how he'd complained of lack of sleep when I saw him in front of Solari's; how anxious he'd seemed of late, always tapping his feet; and the mood swings and crying I'd seen today.

All symptoms of copper toxicity, weren't they?

I retreated to the corner of the store where the light from my new phone couldn't be seen by Bobby in the back room. Pulling up the website I'd bookmarked before, I read through the list of copper poisoning symptoms once again: anxiety, depression and hypersensitivity, hyperactivity, insomnia, mind racing, and mood swings. And one I hadn't paid attention to when I'd been focusing on Gino as the one with copper poisoning: dermatosis. Which would explain what had looked like acne on Bobby's face that day at Gino's house.

That had to be the answer.

But why would Bobby have gotten copper poisoning? Maybe he'd been eating the red sauce Gino had made in those copper pots, too. But then I remembered that he'd said he didn't eat Gino's cooking much, and that's why he'd kept those burritos in his freezer. So what else had copper in it?

I punched in a query about the causes of copper poisoning and got the same ones I'd read before: drinking water, copper cookware, birth control devices…nothing that seemed particularly applicable here. But then my eye was caught by a note at the very bottom of the article: "Copper has been found to be toxic to bacteria and algae and is thus commonly used as an algicide, such as in the copper-based paint used as a marine antifouling agent."

Of course. My dad had used that antifouling paint and was always fanatical about wearing a special mask when applying it. I thought back to the gleaming, black paint I'd seen on the hull of Gino's boat the afternoon I'd talked to Bobby at the old fisherman's house, and then remembered the black splotches I'd seen on his clothes that same day. He and Gino must both have been painting the boat with that antifouling paint, and if they hadn't worn a protective mask…

An image came to me of Gino and Bobby, both of them anxious and paranoid from copper poisoning, arguing behind Solari's the night Gino disappeared. Then when Gino pushes it a little too far and says something truly hurtful, Bobby loses control and goes for the old man.

But later, Bobby is "sorry"…

Shoving my phone into my slacks pocket, I emerged

from my corner and crept toward the front door. I had to tell Vargas about this.

Bobby was now talking to himself again, but I couldn't tell what he was saying. I tried to make no sound as I made my way through the dark shop, and was doing a great job of it until the sleeve of my silk blouse caught on a metal piece that was sticking out from one of the postcard racks. The stand teetered, but I was able to catch and right it before the metal frame went crashing to the floor.

Thank God. I steadied the rack with both hands and was about to turn back toward the front door when an entire stack of postcards that had slipped to the edge of their holder fell with a clatter to the floor.

The muttering in the back room ceased. *Oh, shit.* I needed to find a place to hide—fast. Dropping to my hands and knees, I crawled toward the edge of the shop. A display had been set up advertising the big surf contest coming to town next week, and I crouched behind the large cardboard poster depicting a young man in a bright blue wetsuit carving up a glassy wave.

Bobby appeared in the doorway, his tall body a silhouette framed by the light coming from behind him. *This could be bad.* Ducking back down, I pulled my phone out once more. I didn't have Vargas's number so instead I texted Eric, who was likely still sitting at the detective's table, chowing down on panettone and hazelnut gelato. "Help! Come rt now to stefanos gift shop!" I typed and sent, then dropped to my knees and peeked around the sign to check on Bobby's movements.

He had taken several steps into the room and was cocking his head, listening for further noises. After a moment he spoke: "Who's there?"

No way was I going to answer.

He continued to stare out into the dark room and I held my breath, praying he'd decide it was nothing and go back into the storeroom.

I didn't want to make any move, but I'd begun to experience a shooting pain in my right knee, and after another agonizing minute I had no choice but to change positions. Placing my hands on the floor to steady myself, I moved from my kneeling stance to a squat. As I did so, however, my bandaged hand bumped against the surf poster. It wasn't a loud noise but certainly enough to tell Bobby my location. And I was a sitting—or rather, squatting—duck, backed up against the wall as I was.

Footsteps were coming my way. *Think fast, Sal.*

"I know what happened, Bobby," I said, trying to disguise my voice by pitching it lower than normal. "I understand."

The footsteps stopped. "No one could ever understand."

"But I do. I know how much you loved him, and how hard it must have been to hear him say those things to you."

Bobby made no answer to this, and I was afraid he was going to simply reach in and grab me from behind the surfing display. But several beats passed with nothing except the sound of his heavy breathing. And then I heard a muffled *thud*. I risked a quick peek around the poster. Bobby had slumped to the floor and was staring my direction but was making no move toward me.

"It's okay," I encouraged, still watching him from behind the poster. "I know you didn't mean to hurt him."

He was nodding now, and it sounded as if he'd started to cry again. "I'm so sorry," he said. "I just got so mad when I saw the two of them like that. I couldn't help it. All I wanted was for him to tell me I was still important to him, that he hadn't switched from liking me best to her." Bobby's voice caught, and he broke off.

I wasn't sure if he was going to say anything further when he almost whispered, "But Gino just laughed at me when I told him that. Said I sounded like some kind of sissy."

"That must have been awful," I said, shifting my position once more.

Bobby nodded. "He didn't get it at all. But he was like my dad. Better than a dad, 'cause he treated me like a real pal."

"But then, that night by the bocce court, when he was being so cruel," I prompted him. "You just couldn't help it…"

"I didn't mean to do it! But he kept fighting back, and he was laughing at me. So I hit him. And pushed him over the side." More sobs, followed by harsh panting.

A car pulled up outside at this moment, and its headlights streamed through the shop windows, momentarily blinding me.

And, I realized with a gasp, illuminating my face for all the world to see.

The car lights shut off and Bobby jumped to his feet, as if brought back to life by the realization that it was me he was talking to.

A second later he was coming at me, arms outstretched and fury in his eyes.

TWENTY-NINE

Rɪɢʜт ʙᴇꜰᴏʀᴇ ʜᴇ reached me, our gazes met, and in one of those time-slows-down moments, I noticed again the patch of acne on his face—like that of a teenager with raging hormones.

Bobby made a grab for my neck, and when I ducked, his momentum made him fall on top of me instead. Without thinking, I tried to take hold of his arms, but my bandaged hands proved useless as anything other than padded boxing gloves. He was panting hard now and hissing into my ear. "*You!* I knew you were bad when you said that stuff on the phone about telling the police about me."

Huh? Rolling over on my side, I tried to wriggle free from his grip around my waist, but he was too strong for me to escape. *What was he going on about?* And then I remembered the phone conversation I'd had yesterday morning with Eric—boy, did that seem like a long time ago. So Bobby *had* heard me.

"Too bad you didn't drown, too," he growled. "How come Gino had to die and not you?" At this point he momentarily relaxed his grip, allowing me to roll once more onto my back. And as I rolled, I aimed a sharp kick with my knee to his middle region.

"Aiee!"

Success. Collapsing onto his side, Bobby released me to grab hold of his crotch. I scooted out from underneath

the whimpering man and was about to sit up when another form came hurtling down on top of Bobby.

"Don't move a muscle," the deep voice commanded.

Detective Vargas.

Another shape hovered overhead, peering down at
me.

"Eric," I said. "You got my text."

"Text?" he deadpanned. "I didn't see any text. We
just thought we'd do a little after-hours shopping is all.
And hey, it looks like we ended up with the perfect gift
to take home."

Vargas was giving Bobby his Miranda warning as
he snapped a pair of cuffs on the still prostrate figure.

"How long have you been here?" I asked Eric.

"Long enough to hear plenty to put him away for a
long while."

"So, what? You were just standing there, waiting,
while a madman was trying to throttle me?"

"Well, you were doing such a good job of getting
him to talk, it seemed a shame to interrupt. And we did
come to your rescue as soon as—"

"As soon as he was out of commission and it was no
longer needed," I finished.

Eric held out a hand to help me stand, but I waved
him off. Not only do I dislike being treated as helpless,
but I couldn't have grabbed hold of him in any case—
not with the bulky bandages on my hands. Using my
knuckles to push off from the floor like some kind of
clumsy ape, I made it to my feet. "So now what?" I
asked.

"Now Vargas takes Bobby down to the jail and I get
you back to the dinner for a stiff glass of limoncello."

"Sounds awesome. Too bad it's not on the menu tonight."

"Well, that hasn't kept Mario from passing bottles of the stuff around to all the folks who are still there," Eric said, taking me by the arm. "C'mon, leave the detective to his business, and let's you and I go have us a well-deserved drink."

"I'm not sure how much you deserve one," I said with a last glance at Vargas and Bobby. "But I'm pretty sure I do."

EARLY SUNDAY MORNING the storm returned with a vengeance. But I didn't care. It could pour torrents for the next week straight, I thought as I lay snuggled in bed with Buster stretched out beside me. We'd made it through the big sister-cities dinner without the tent collapsing under a pool of water, and I wasn't going to be able to grip my bike handlebars for several days. So for now, let it rain.

I hadn't gotten home till almost twelve the night before. Eric and I had drunk our limoncello—several each, actually—and after he left I'd stayed at the restaurant a while to hang out with my dad. With my hands bandaged as they were, I couldn't do much to assist with the cleanup, but I'd kept him company as he and the other kitchen staff wrapped up containers of Sunday gravy and cabbage rolls, decanted half-filled bottles of wine into larger ones to save for cooking, and scrubbed and wiped down the range top.

Dad and Emilio had been oblivious to the two arrests made during the dinner, so I gave them a detailed account of Anastasia shoving Bobby in the water and then Bobby's manic behavior afterward at his father's shop. "So I think Bobby probably did grab Anastasia down on the boat landing," I said, "given the way he was acting later. Just like she and Angelo said."

"But do you think it was her who knocked Gino into the water, or Bobby?" Dad asked.

"Bobby admitted that he hit him and then shoved him over the side. And it's clear now that Bobby was also the guy Anastasia saw that night out by the *Marcella*, right after Gino came on to her. Bobby sounded pretty upset with Gino—jealous of him, or of his attentions to her, anyway. And that was clearly the reason the two of them fought that night. But the whole thing is pretty strange."

"Well, at least I'm out of the picture as a suspect now," Dad said, then hoisted a hotel pan full of chicken cacciatore and headed for the walk-in.

As I lolled about in bed the next morning, listening to the redwood window frame rattle in the wind and rain, I considered what my dad had said. He was obviously no longer a suspect—no doubt they'd dropped him as soon as I'd been knocked into the ocean—but I did still wonder how Gino's cap might have ended up in his boat.

Closing my eyes, I envisioned the scene that night by the old Monterey clipper: Bobby hiding behind the kiosk waiting for Anastasia to pass by, then creeping up toward Gino. And Dad's skiff was near the back of Solari's, not twenty feet from where Anastasia had said she and Gino had been standing.

Bobby must have confronted Gino, after which they argued. That had to have been when Sean looked out back and saw what he thought was an old man arguing with Gino. But in the dark, with his thin, slouching figure, I could see how Sean could have assumed

Bobby was one of the old guys who hung out back there by the bocce court.

Then there must have been a struggle. Bobby had said that Gino had been fighting back. And if that had happened over by Dad's Boston Whaler, the cap could easily have fallen off and landed inside. And then they ended up at the wharf railing, at which point Bobby hit the old fisherman and then pushed him over the side to drown.

I was interrupted in my musings by my cell going off. Reaching over the snoring Buster, I grabbed it from the bedside table. "Hey, Eric. What's up?"

"I just got off the phone with Vargas. He wants you to stop by the station when you have the chance to make a full statement."

So Eric was going to be all business this morning. No "How ya doin', babe," or any of his usual affectionate banter. I must have scared him out of that. Which was a good thing…wasn't it?

"No problem," I said. "I was planning on doing just that as soon as I had some coffee."

"Good. Anyway, since I was there last night and assisted with the arrest, he's keeping me in the loop about what's going on with Bobby."

"And?"

"And it appears that even after he was Mirandized, he kept on blabbering the whole way down to the jail. And boy, oh boy, did he confess."

I sat up, startling Buster out of a dream that, from the way his paws and nose had been twitching, involved chasing a small, furry critter. "What did he say?"

"Basically the same things we heard him say at his dad's shop, but with more detail. That while they were arguing he'd picked up an oar he found in a boat just to scare Gino, but when he kept laughing at him, Bobby whacked him with it and shoved him over the side. And then when he saw Gino floating there in the water looking like he was dead, I guess he freaked out and ran away."

Just as I'd been envisioning.

"And he also mentioned you," Eric added.

"Me? What did he say?"

"That you deserved what you got, which was apparently a blow to the head with a bocce ball that someone had left lying around. He said you were a busybody—though he included a not-very-nice modifier with the phrase—and that you were always looking at him funny. Is that true? Were you looking at him funny?"

"I don't think so. I mean, I guess I did sometimes look at him maybe a little more intently than normal. 'Cause he's seemed kind of off of late. And he's had a case of acne, which is pretty unusual for someone his age."

"Weird," he agreed.

"Yeah, but it is one of the symptoms of copper toxicity. As are paranoia and acting strange in other ways. So did you tell Vargas about my theory—that he got poisoned from sanding and painting Gino's boat without proper protection—you know, wearing gloves and a mask and stuff?"

"I did, and he's going to have tests run on Bobby." Eric chuckled.

"What?"

"Vargas told me to tell you you might just make a good detective after all if you ever decide to change careers."

KRIS AND BRANDON were setting out the *mise en place* inserts for the hot line when I walked into the Gauguin kitchen at four o'clock that afternoon. Our old cook, Reuben—who'd left the previous July to head up the kitchen at another restaurant—was at the Wolf range, stirring a sauce pot. He'd agreed to come in tonight as a favor to me since his new place was closed on Sundays.

"Ohmygod, what happened to your hands?" Kris exclaimed.

"It's not as bad as it looks," I said, waving off her horrified expression. "I cut them up on some barnacles while, uh…swimming, is all." They'd no doubt learn the truth before long, but I didn't really feel like talking about my ocean ordeal right this minute. "Is Javier up in the office?"

"Yeah," the line cook said. "But he's in a bit of a sour mood today. He came in about fifteen minutes ago and headed straight upstairs without even saying hello."

Uh-oh. That didn't sound good.

I found Javier standing at the office window, staring down at the neighbor's backyard. I came to stand next to him, but he barely acknowledged my presence. The apple and plum trees had begun to shed their foliage, which was now scattered about the lawn in a brown-and-orange carpet. As we watched, a gust of wind swept up a pile of leaves and swirled them around in a miniature tornado.

"Okay, what's wrong?" I said after the whirlwind had died down. "You still mad at me?"

"Mad at you?" Javier frowned, as if he didn't understand the question. "Oh, right," he said. "That. No, I'm not mad at you." With a sigh, he turned from the window and sat heavily on the desk chair. Then, noticing my bandages for the first time, he looked up. "What the hell happened to your hands?"

I gave him the truthful but abbreviated version of my run-in with Bobby, then told him about Bobby's bizarre behavior and arrest the night before. "So, anyway, it looks like I won't be back on the Gauguin hot line for a few days at least," I said, displaying the thick wrappings about my hands. "Any chance Natalie could work a few more nights this week?"

This prompted yet another sigh, even louder than the first.

My gut tightened. He *was* still mad at me. And for good reason, too. "Oh, God, Javier, I am so sorry. I know I've been completely useless lately, but this time there truly was nothing I could have done to prevent—"

He held out his hand. "No, stop. It's just... I've realized that it's not going to work."

I was about to protest that we *could* make it work, that we simply needed to talk things through, when he turned to face me. The utter devastation in his eyes told me it wasn't us he was talking about.

"It's Natalie," I said, and he nodded. "You two had a fight."

"Worse than a fight," he said, slumping over onto the desk. "If it was just that, it would be easy. We could talk it over and then kiss and make up and everything would be fine. But this... I don't know."

I took a seat in the green wing chair across from him. "What happened, Javier?"

He clenched and then released his jaw a few times before answering. "As soon as we started working together in the kitchen that first night here, Thursday, I knew right away it wasn't going to work. She has a totally different style from me. She's completely disorganized, doesn't plan anything in advance."

Javier sat up and shook his head. His eyes now betrayed frustration as well as sadness. "Like—and this is just one example—I'd asked her to check how many reservations we had and then prep enough of the sides for that amount, but she just totally spaced it out, and then we were slammed all night long as soon as the rush started." Picking up the wooden tiki, he stared glumly at its carved features. "It ended up driving me crazy working with her those three nights."

"Okay, look," I said. "So we'll find somebody else to work for me the next few days. You and Natalie got along fine before you worked together, so as long as you don't do that again, I'm sure everything will be—" And then I stopped.

Of course. That was why he was in such anguish. His dream of opening his own restaurant with her had been abruptly deflated, like a chocolate soufflé yanked violently from the oven before it had time to set.

Our eyes met. "Right," he said. "There's no way we could open a restaurant together. It would never work. We both realize that now." Letting out a long stream of air, he set the tiki back down on the desk. "So I guess you're in luck. Since there's no way I can afford to buy a restaurant on my own, it looks like I'll be staying here for a while after all."

"Maybe there's someone else who'd like to go in on a restaurant with you," I said.

Javier started to laugh, but he stopped when he saw the serious look in my eye. I reached out and laid my bandaged hand over his.

"Any chance you'd like to become co-owner of a

little French-Polynesian place here in town? 'Cause I hear tell the owner is looking for a partner to buy out half her interest, and I think you might be exactly the person she's looking for."

"She's looking for an equal partner? Fifty-fifty, with an equal say in how the business is run?"

"Yep. And I have it on good authority that she's especially interested in someone who wants to spread his creative wings and have full say over creating some exciting new dishes for the menu."

Javier grinned. "Sounds like the perfect partner to me."

THIRTY

SHAFTS OF SUNLIGHT streamed through the towering red-woods, the beams casting bright spots on our class as if we were being lit by some celestial control booth above. The dozen painters were scattered evenly about the concrete piazza, stepping back from their easels to gaze out at the golden hills and the Monterey Bay below, then moving back in to dab blobs of burnt umber and turquoise onto their paper.

We'd come up to the university for our last plein air class, and Omar was in high spirits this afternoon. "You all have progressed *so* far in so little time," he said, moving from student to student to check out our work. "Not a month ago, some of you barely even understood the concept of negative space, but now? Every single one of these paintings shows a strong sense of technique. And they're full of vitality and emotion as well."

I stared at my landscape, wondering if the oak-dotted meadows with the expanse of bay in the distance did in fact show emotion, or if the piece was simply amateurish. My bandages had come off a few days ago and the doctor had said my hands were healing nicely, but they still felt clumsy and stiff.

Eric wandered over and studied the painting along with me. "I like the composition," he said after a bit. "The way the tables and chairs in the foreground are cut off at the edge, framing the picture in an unexpected way. It's very photographic. Kind of like Degas."

He continued to stand there, eyes directed toward my easel but slightly glazed as if not really focusing on the painting. I had a feeling I knew what was on his mind.

"You know," I said, "we never did talk about what you said in the car that morning I was released from the hospital."

Eric turned my way but didn't speak.

"I was meaning to bring it up sooner, but with all that happened that night at the dinner and then, well, I haven't seen you since…"

"It's okay," he said.

"No, it's not okay. We need to talk. But not with all these people around." I set down my paintbrush and led Eric to the low cement wall dividing the piazza from a large grassy area where several barefoot students in cargo shorts were tossing a Frisbee back and forth.

We sat with our backs to the class, facing the glorious panorama of redwoods, live oak meadows, and the ocean far below. "Anyway," I said, "I've been thinking a lot about what you said, and why it's so hard for me to talk about it."

"Well," Eric replied with a chuckle, "it's not as if you've ever been much thrilled to talk about your feelings."

"True." I watched as one of the Frisbee players made a leaping catch, nearly landing on a young woman who'd lain down nearby with a fat textbook. The man leaned over to apologize, prompting a flirtatious laugh from the other. Once the game had recommenced and she'd gone back to her book, they continued to cast shy glances each other's way.

Eric and I hadn't been much older than these two students when we'd first met. *Could we possibly have seemed so young and naïve in the early days of our courtship?*

I turned back to face him. "You have to know how much I care about you."

"I guess. But what exactly does that mean?"

"It means I'm terrified of risking what we have right now if we try to push it further and go back to where we were before. Because we both know how that ended."

Eric laid a hand on mine. "What's the worst thing that could happen? If we can't make it work this time, it'll be just like it is now again."

But I wasn't convinced. I wasn't sure either of us could survive a second breakup and simply go back to being friends once more. Especially Eric.

I stared out at the sparkling water. Across the bay, the rugged Santa Lucia range rose above Monterey and Pacific Grove to the south. Eric and I had once gone backpacking in those mountains during our law school years. The best part of the hot and dusty hike had been the meal we'd stopped for afterward in Big Sur. We'd vowed, over fat burgers and frosty pints of beer, to never put each other in such misery again.

Did this count? Was I making him miserable? Was I making *myself* miserable?

"How soon do I need to decide?" I asked.

"Certainly not right now," Eric answered, relief in his voice. "Or tomorrow, or even next month. All I'm asking is that you leave yourself open to the possibility."

"Okay, I can agree to that." I stood up and took his hand. "C'mon, let's go paint."

* * * * *

SPINACH SALAD WITH ORANGE, FENNEL, AND BLACK OLIVES (SOLARI'S)

(SERVES 6)

This is the salad my dad, Mario, came up with for the big sister-cities dinner that Solari's hosted for the visiting dignitaries from Sestri Levante. The combination of the sweet oranges, crunchy fennel, and salty olives makes for a zesty palate cleanser. And because the salad can be prepared in advance and then tossed at the last minute, it's a terrific side dish for a dinner party of any size, from four to forty guests.

Use only the bulb of the fennel, and core and quarter it before slicing. For the oranges, make sure to remove most of their white pith, as it can be bitter. You can squeeze the two teaspoons of juice needed for the dressing from one of the oranges before cutting it up.

The dressing can be made a day ahead and kept in the fridge; just be sure to take it out at least a half hour before service, and give it a good stir before using.

Ingredients

For the Dressing:
2 teaspoons Dijon-style mustard
¼ teaspoon ground black pepper

½ *teaspoon sugar*
1 teaspoon balsamic vinegar
3 tablespoons olive oil (preferably extra virgin)
2 teaspoons orange juice
For the Salad:
2 cups navel oranges, peeled and cut into bite-sized
chunks (about 3 large oranges)
2 cups fennel, thinly sliced
1 cup sliced, pitted Greek-style black olives
6 cups baby spinach
salt and pepper

Directions

Mix the mustard, pepper, sugar, and vinegar together in a bowl until smooth and the sugar has dissolved. Slowly drizzle the olive oil into the bowl, using a wire whisk to incorporate it into the other ingredients. (Don't beat it too hard, or the oil can become bitter.) Once smooth, finish by whisking in the orange juice. Add more juice or a little water if needed to thin to your desired consistency.

Toss all the salad ingredients in a large bowl, then drizzle on the dressing and toss again. Season with salt and pepper to taste.

BLACK COD WITH MISO AND SAKE

(SERVES 6)

Black cod (also known as sablefish) is a white-fleshed fish from the icy waters off the Pacific Northwest, and is renowned for its velvety texture and rich, buttery flavor (hence its other name, butterfish).

This style of preparing black cod was first popularized by the famous Japanese chef, Nobu Matsuhisa, who marinates his fish for three days before cooking. But I've found that one or two days in the marinade is plenty to impart its full flavor to the black cod.

I like to serve this dish with the traditional Japanese garnishes of pickled ginger (*gari*) and wasabi, and accompany it with sides of steamed rice and roasted bok choy drizzled with soy sauce and sesame oil. But the fish would also pair well with more Western sides such as mashed potatoes and a leafy green salad.

(Note: If you can't find mirin—a sweet rice wine—you can substitute dry sherry, white wine, or even rice vinegar. Just add an extra tablespoon of sugar to the marinade.)

Ingredients

¼ cup mirin
¼ cup sake

¼ cup white or yellow miso paste
3 tablespoons sugar
6 black cod fillets, about 6 oz. each
vegetable oil for oiling baking sheet and searing fish

Directions

Combine the mirin and sake in a small saucepan and bring to a boil. Turn heat to low, add the miso and sugar, and continue to cook, whisking until they have dissolved. Allow to cool, then transfer marinade to a large glass baking dish. Add the fish and turn to coat. Cover and refrigerate between 24 and 48 hours. Let fish come up to room temperature before cooking.

Preheat oven to 400°F and oil a rimmed baking sheet large enough for all the fillets (or you can line it with oiled aluminum foil for easy cleanup).

Scrape marinade from fillets and set them on a platter or baking dish.

Heat a large, heavy skillet over high heat, then add enough oil to create a thin layer on the bottom of the pan. (Use two skillets if necessary, or cook in batches, so as to not crowd the fish.) As soon as the oil starts to smoke, add the fillets, skin side down if they have skin.

Fry until browned, about 2 minutes. Then flip fillets onto the oiled baking sheet, browned side up, and bake until opaque and flaky—5 to 10 minutes, depending on the thickness of the fish.

TAGLIARINI WITH BROWN BUTTER, SAGE, AND PORCINI MUSHROOMS (SOLARI'S)

(SERVES 4-6)

Tagliarini is an egg pasta from Northern Italy, similar to its wider and more famous cousin, tagliatelle (the name comes from the verb *tagliare*, to cut). These thin, flat ribbons are often served with butter and truffles, but Mario prefers the earthy notes supplied by the porcini mushrooms and sage. If you can't find tagliarini, feel free to substitute tagliatelle or fettuccine.

Note that unlike many other pastas, tagliarini cooks extremely quickly—in three or four minutes for dried, one or two minutes for fresh.

Porcini means "little pigs" in Italian and is their name for the sumptuous mushroom known as the "king bolete" in the U.S. and as *cèpes* in France. You can substitute dried porcini for this recipe (soak them in boiling water for twenty minutes before using), or use crimini—those small, brown button mushrooms—if you can't find porcini.

Ingredients

¼ *pound (1 stick) butter*
2 tablespoons olive oil

1 pound porcini mushrooms, sliced
½ cup sage leaves, coarsely chopped if large (plus
extra for garnish)
1 pound tagliarini pasta
1 tablespoon salt
1 cup grated Parmesan or Pecorino cheese
freshly ground black pepper to taste

Directions

Melt the butter in a thick-bottomed pan over low heat. Continue cooking, stirring frequently to prevent burning, until the foam subsides and the butter begins to turn brown—about five minutes. (Watch carefully, as it can burn quickly.) Add the sage leaves and stir, and continue to cook another five minutes or so. Once the butter starts to release a nutty aroma and the sage becomes crisp, the sauce is done. Take the pan off the heat and set aside.

In a separate large frying pan, heat half the olive oil over medium heat and, when shimmering, add half the mushrooms. Spread them out in one layer and let sit without stirring until they turn a golden brown. Then stir and cook another minute or two, till cooked through. Remove with a slotted spoon to a bowl and repeat with the rest of the oil and mushrooms. Return the cooked mushrooms to the pan and set aside. (The brown butter/sage and the mushrooms can be prepared up to several hours in advance.)

Bring a large (at least 4 quart) pot of water to a boil.

Add the tagliarini and salt to the boiling water, and cook over high heat until *al dente* (still slightly firm in the center, 3–4 minutes if dried), stirring occasionally to prevent sticking. (If using dried fettuccine, it will take 10–12 minutes to cook.)

While the pasta is cooking, reheat the brown butter/sage and the mushrooms over medium heat.

Drain pasta and dump into a large serving bowl (without rinsing). Add the brown butter/sage and toss, then add mushrooms and half the cheese and toss again. Add salt to taste.

Serve garnished with the rest of the grated cheese, a few fresh sage leaves, and freshly ground black pepper.

DUCK À LA LILIKOI (GAUGUIN)

(SERVES 6)

Lilikoi is the Hawaiian word for passion fruit, the juice of which can often be found in the frozen food section of Latin American grocery stores (called *maracuyá*). If you use fresh fruits, four should yield about ⅓ cup. Cut them in half, scoop out the pulp, juice, and seeds, and press through a strainer. If you can't find passion fruit, feel free to substitute orange juice—but be sure to cut down (or omit entirely) the sugar in this recipe.

The sauce can be made while the duck is cooking, but at Gauguin we make it in advance and reheat as much as needed for each order immediately before service. I recommend doing this, as it's easier not to have to worry about it while you're frying the duck (and making whatever sides you're serving with the dish).

Ingredients

4 tablespoons butter (half stick)
¼ cup brandy
⅓ cup passion fruit juice (frozen, bottled, or fresh)
5 teaspoons sugar
6 duck breasts
salt and pepper

Directions

For the Sauce:
Melt the butter in a sauté pan over low to moderate heat and, once melted, let it simmer for one to two minutes, stirring frequently so it doesn't burn. Carefully pour in the brandy and cook another minute.

Add the passion fruit juice and the sugar and continue cooking, stirring frequently, for another minute or two, until the sauce thickens. Set aside.

For the Duck Breasts:
Slice through the fat on the breasts—but not into the meat—at half-inch intervals, then rotate breasts and score again (i.e., making a cross-hatch design). Season both sides of breasts with salt and pepper.

Using two large, heavy skillets (cast iron works great), place three breasts in each, skin side down, then turn on fire to low to medium heat. The idea is to slowly render the fat so you are left with crispy, golden-brown skin. The rendering process can take 10 to 15 minutes, and be sure to drain off any excess fat from the pan as necessary. (Save the luscious fat for later use—it's great for frying sliced potatoes!)

Once the skins are golden brown and crispy, turn the breasts over and continue to fry until they reach your desired doneness. Duck breast is traditionally served medium-rare (to an internal temperature of about 135° F), but feel free to cook longer if you prefer.

Remove breasts to a cutting board, cover, and let rest for five minutes. Reheat sauce while breasts are resting.

Cut breasts into half-inch slices, then fan out on serving plates and drizzle with sauce.

AUTHOR NOTE

As SALLY DOES with her painting, I have taken some liberties in this book and have rearranged the layout of the Santa Cruz Municipal Wharf to suit the needs of the story. Those familiar with the area may notice that I have added an additional boat launch, and have also moved the bocce court much closer to the old fishing vessel, the *Marcella*. And of course, since Solari's is a fictional restaurant, its invention throws off the locations of other real-life establishments on the wharf.

ACKNOWLEDGMENTS

I WOULD LIKE to thank Jane Lasswell Hoff, Nancy Lund-blad, and Robin McDuff, who took time to read and comment on the early manuscript of this book, and Shirley Tessler, for her assistance in editing the recipes. Moreover, I am grateful to those who let me pick their brains with regard to their various areas of expertise: Ian Cole of Ocean2Table and Dylan Buckingham (fishing in the Monterey Bay); Dan Jones (ocean currents); Jane Lasswell Hoff (forensics); Nancy Lundblad (medical issues); and Luci Zahray, aka "the Poison Lady" (toxicology). But please note that any factual mistakes that may exist herein are entirely mine.

In addition, I must acknowledge the helpfulness of the oral history titled *Malio J. Stagnaro: The Santa Cruz Genovese* (interviewed by Elizabeth Spedding Calciano, 1975), a part of the Regional History Project of UCSC. For anyone interested in the history and culture of the original Italian fishing families in Santa Cruz, this is an invaluable resource.

Enormous thanks are due, as well, to Jane Gregorius and Barbara Gunther, art teachers extraordinaire who helped me learn how to truly see.

Finally, as always, I am indebted to my terrific agent, Erin Niumata of Folio Literary Management, and to all the marvelous people at Crooked Lane Books, including Matt Martz, Sarah Poppe, Jenny Chen, Anne Brewer, and my amazing editor, Nike Power.